The Builder

Printed in the United Kingdom.

ISBN 978-1-910524-34-3

BIC-CLASSIFICATION
Fiction and related items (F)

EDITOR
Martin Locker

COVER DESIGN
Andreas Nilsson

LAYOUT
Tor Westman

ARKTOS MEDIA LTD.
www.arktos.com

Tito Perdue

THE BUILDER

William's House, Volume I

ARKTOS

LONDON 2015

ONE

That whole area is rich in deposits dating from earlier ages. Earlier still, warm seas had extended for a great distance all around, to Enterprise and Opp and continuing on to Georgia. *That* was when the world began, in the late August of that year when finally he lifted himself into a standing position and began to come forward, moving always nearer against the grain of the horizon. No one spoke, not in those days, and a great stillness covered almost everything.

Mountains formed and last of all came the sun, and still a very long time had to go by before he and the woman would come to grips with one another and marry in due course. And even the marriage itself lies a year or two in the future of these opening moments.

TWO

Later on, after these papers (receipts, etc., and bills of lading) had been added to the county archives, it became possible to see how things had stood in 1888 and the years following immediately hard upon. Reading those documents with attention, a person could now look back in their imagination and envision the status of the crops, of trains running across the landscape, and mules parked all day about the courthouse square. It was *not* of course the historical period that one would have chosen for himself, and instead of farming it was easy to understand why a man might prefer to go straight to paradise, avoiding the hard work that awaited in the Alabama of that day.

Instead, dressed in shirts and trousers, he soon abandoned the sand fields of the extreme south and, traveling mostly by starlight, began to make sudden appearances in the towns along his way, a source of surprise to those who might catch sight of him during his brief stays. Finding himself by October in the city of Luverne, he spent three days carrying out deliveries for the man who owned the lumber yard. But on the fourth day he was put to work on the lumber itself and after two months of it found that he and some dozen other men had set up a fine new house with five rooms in it. He liked to step into the half-finished parlor and, drawn by the scent of new-sawn wood, hypothesize that the building was his own and the wife as well, and that now had come the time to select his furnishings and other things. It might be an Age of Mules indeed, but that needn't prohibit him from having a clock on the mantle piece, together with other instruments of high quality with which to keep watch on changes taking place in the outside world both when he was awake and sleeping. As to the bed, it would be big enough for the both of them (himself and a wife), assuming that ever he could flush her from her hiding place. Wife, stove (he had stepped from the parlor to the kitchen), clock and other instruments, these might well serve as a kind of consolation for the ordeals that lay in wait for him.

He learned to build houses. It was said that he worked more quickly than the ordinary run of men and that the nails he drove fell immediately into place, as if wishing to reduce to the minimum the number of blows they must suffer at his hand. And then, too, he and the Negroes used to contend with each other in their carpentry skills, an undeclared competition in which William urged himself forward continually, remembering how his people had always been able to hold on to their dignity in the past and even to increase it when they could. And once he saw a man fall off a ladder and die, and bending over him saw the hideousness in his eyes as hell opened up and drew him down inside.

He did so good a job with loading the lumber, carrying it to various places and turning it into houses that soon he knew as much about the county as the man who owned the newspaper.

"Where you been, William?" the man would ask.

"Slocum's Corner."

"Ah. Other side of the levee, right? There used to be a lot of funny business going on over there."

"Yes, sir."

He much preferred to be organizing merchandise than hearing about the funny business. He could not, for example, imagine how screws were manufactured, all of them so exactly alike and so beautifully arranged in little white cardboard boxes bearing scientific labels. Seeds — he liked to plunge his hand deep into the bag and then, bringing up a sample for inspection, liked to estimate the quality of the crops that might accrue to the man who invested in them. And, of course, he liked tools, the most essential of all things. One had only to look at them to know what they were for.

He did especially well with lady customers, who esteemed him for his responsible ways and his well-known contempt for cigarettes and drink. Oftentimes he was seen in church even on week days — unless a house was going up or he was needed at the store. He had a suit, a pocket knife, and a pair of shoes with four or five months of wear left in them still. As to his sleeping place, that was in the warehouse itself where he kept a bright eye open for pilferers and vagabonds. He was not a large man and yet in his whole life no one had ever wished to irritate him beyond a certain point.

One day in late September he got into his suit and left town, traveling by horse in the direction of his parents' house. It was a clear day, the sun bright, and once or twice he could detect the sound of insects detouring around him at high speed. Two miles out a dog came up behind and began to bark, his face revealing how delighted he was to have been given some provocation at last. William paid no heed to him, not until the thing took hold of the heel of his best shoe and tried to remove it. There happened to be a farmer in the field at that moment, a sad-looking figure who left off hoeing long enough to observe William's method, the most effective in the world, for dealing with dogs of that kind.

The trail narrowed but then opened up again as William approached a river glinting bluely among the pines. Near to shore a persimmon tree still bore its quondam fruit, a shriveled stuff no longer eligible for consumption. The river however was sweet and he drank his fill of it, intrigued by how the matter lost its color when he ladled it up in his hand. Except for the little bit of weight that he held in his palm, a person wouldn't have known anything was there. Suddenly he stopped what he was doing and glanced to the woods.

He was being watched by hundreds of eyes. Discomfited by that, he strolled some hundred rods downstream until he found a kudzu chamber where he could undress in privacy and then slip noiselessly into the stream. The overhanging trees were hung with beards of Spanish Moss, spilling from the branches and halting just short of the water. Here in midstream they dawdled, the mare and he, neither in a great hurry to reach the other coast. He drifted through a congestion of water insects, a frenetic crowd, possibly insane, their transparent wings invested with a network of tiny black veins. Two ducks passed overhead, slowed, and then continued on disappointedly when they saw the river was pre-empted.

Leaving the water, man and horse climbed out into a field of brittle corn that ought rightly to have been harvested a month ago. Otherwise it was a memorable day, full of good weather and a fleet of clouds that looked like galleons searching for harbors in the sky. Behind them they could hear a wagon approaching slowly, whereupon both man and horse hurriedly abandoned the road and entered a clump of trees, an action that perturbed some half-dozen crows and sent them flying off into the east. He did not wish, William, to be offered a specimen of routine conversation and given no alternative but to ignore it.

His people lived on seventy acres of rented land. Shielding his eyes, William could see three men seated on the porch, another in the field, and a woman at the well. Soon he would be within hailing distance and soon thereafter could expect to be recognized by one or another of them. He rode forward calmly therefore, the sun glinting off his forehead. Already one of the girls had perceived him and was running down the lane. He had brought no gifts, not today.

"Willie! Willie! Mary Belle had kittens!"

He nodded but said nothing. She was the youngest of them and always had been more excitable than the boys. And then, too, she kept glancing to his saddle bags.

"Four of 'em!"

"Y'all need rain, looks like to me."

"And I get to keep the white one!"

They continued two abreast. The old man had come to his feet and then, seeing who it was, returned to his chair. William now stopped and waved to the whole group, doing it in dignified fashion. He had come to them in his best clothes, having managed to bring them over the river in good condition. He went first to his mother, a sorrowful woman, much smaller than the usual individual.

"I thought you might come," she said. "'Course, I been thinking that for a long time."

"Yes, ma'am. Well I got a position now, don't you see, and they keep me real busy." And then: "I was going to bring some presents, too, but..."

"Well, that's all right I reckon."

He turned to shake with the old man who as always on Sundays was wearing his gingham shirt. The man appeared to be pleased even if his thoughts seemed still engaged in the conversation he had just been having. William did not much like the looks of the other man, who had two tiny eyes set much too close together on either side of a nose that was far too thin. He shook with him nevertheless. The third man remained standing. Some moments now went by while no one spoke. The day was beautiful but time was passing quickly and nothing of importance was being done.

They gathered at the table and after prayers began to pass around the ham and biscuits. William was not the oldest of the sons but was allowed on these occasions to sit at the head of the table next to his father. The old man had forever been fond of sweet things and was continually encouraging those nearest him to share in the jams and jellies that sat before them in a pink glass dish with three compartments. The visitors had gone, leaving the family to enjoy a meal that brought to mind the old days, when all William's brothers had still been living. Now, twenty minutes into the supper, the old man began to speak:

"'*Position*,' you claim. Shoot boy, in my day we had *jobs*, we didn't have no positions. You want a position, boy, you got to go into *town*, 'cause that's where you find 'em." He lay aside his fork and looked at his son severely. "And I'm not talking any little old ord'nary town neither; I'm talking *Montgomery*."

"What kind of position is it, Billy?" his mother asked worriedly. "It sounds real nice."

"Aw, he sits up there behind the counter at Peddie's store — that's all in the world it is. Sells things."

Her eyes lit up, the girl with the kitten in her lap. "Things!"

"Well, we got lots to do around here, too. You could always come back, son, anytime. No, that's just the way we operate — anytime any son of mine gets into trouble, he can always come home. 'Course now you ain't going to find any *positions* here."

"No, sir."

"Just plain work. We're plain people. I got thirty acres in peas right now."

William acknowledged it. The peas might fail, lest rain soon came. His gaze went to the corner of the room where a poorly-constructed cobweb cast a shadow in the light of the paraffin lamp. No such webs had been allowed when his mother was younger and in good health. He looked for, and found, the framed painting of a bowl of green and yellow fruit, noting at the same time that it was turning brown about the edges. On the mantle piece the clock had continued to function though the sound of it now seemed weaker to him than of beforetimes, and further away. And then, too, there was that jar of preserves that twenty years ago had been opened, sampled, sealed up again, and then given the blue ribbon for that year.

It was a heavy meal featuring hog jowls and cornbread supported by buttermilk, collards, and black-eyed peas. Delighted by his presence, the youngest of the girls continued to look up at him admiringly while William strove to put on his best manners and maintain a somber face. Good was the food and the buttermilk full of tasty curds that dawdled all too briefly on the tongue before fleeing away quickly down the throat. He tried to retain the stuff as long as he could — until he grew aware that the kitten in Sue Ellen's lap understood what he was doing.

"William don't care for the peas, I reckon," his mother said sadly.

He served himself at once to further peas even though he had had 300 of them already. The gravy however was thin and tenuous and tended to run off the knife.

"Shoot boy, them's *good* peas."

He served himself to more. Through the open door he could see the sun going rapidly through its inventory of late-afternoon colors, coming ever nearer to that moment when it must recuse itself for a certain duration. Saw, too, the rooster, who had taken advantage to step *inside the house* and glance around in perfect amazement at everything.

The crops that year promised to be mediocre. Not so the crickets, who had proliferated to such an extent that they damaged a person's hearing with their songs. Moving out onto the unsteady porch, the family repositioned their chairs until they were facing into the music rather than allowing it to strike directly at the ear. That was when the noise came to an abrupt halt so that a nearby owl might insert an outburst of its own.

"Minds me of when we went down to —— County," the old man said, interspersing his words among the night sounds.

"What, daddy? What reminds you of that?"

"Didn't have no mules to speak of. Had to walk, most of us."

"*You* had to walk. Didn't you, daddy?"

"Didn't have no money, no flour. Well, Uncle Billy might have had a few dollars, but that's all."

"Yes, and he kept it all for himself! Didn't he, daddy?"

"I just wisht those durned crickets would shut up. And that tree frog, too."

"I reckon they have as much right as you do, Sue Ellen."

"They do not neither!"

One of the brothers, the largest of them, rose and stretched and went away. It left seven individuals facing off approximately in a north northwesterly direction where the blades of a windmill could be seen turning slowly in the moon. The night was cool and pleasant and yet the hens al-

ready were lining up in front of their unpainted house and one by one dis-
appearing inside.

"Didn't have no salt."

The bed that used to be his had been taken by one of the girls, wherefore William had to go to the attic and bring down an old cotton mattress
and then find a place for it in the kitchen. In this solitude he was free to
think of his own problems, a thirty-minute procedure during which he lay
perfectly still, oblivious to the sound of insects and family members rising from time to time and moving about the cabin. Twice the dog came to
check on him, surprised to find him still awake. Finally, toward one in the
morning, he took the notepad from his coat and wrote a reminder to himself about something that needed to be done. Still in an unsettled frame of
mind, he rose and went to the door.

The crickets fell silent the instant he stepped outside. In the eastern sky
a half dozen crows had run into some kind of difficulty apparently and now
were winging homeward in high indignation. William moved forward,
squeezing between the creamery and the barn and then setting foot in the
field itself. He had nothing to say of the work his father had done, even if
he himself would have given this field one more plowing at least. He would
have wanted better mules, too, and if that were not enough would have
harnessed the three sons his father still kept at home. Things were not perfect here and the house itself needed work — it began to stir up in him an
incipient anger that he managed however to set aside.

He went back, hushing all the insects within a certain radius. The
rooster, confused by this bright moon, had scaled much too early to the top
of the gable and was getting into position to wake the county before then
realizing his mistake and sadly climbing back down again. Pushing his way
into the carpentry shop, William noted how the tools, many of them, had
been removed from the chest and then put down at random with no regard
to anything. In the barn a ruddy-colored cow — William recognized her

and remembered her name — was suffering from an udder that no one had bothered to drain.

He was never able to understand why the world and its things were not any better than they were. He wanted *progress*, not just maintenance, and every human effort, he believed, should make some contribution toward the improvements that God craved. Going to the well, he sought about for the bucket which, of course, was lacking. Far down below the fluid itself sparkled darkly, like a fund of ink. Meanwhile, a granulated cloud had run behind the moon and he had to bend deeply over the well to identify his personal reflection breaking into several large and small fragments, riding on the swells.

THREE

In time, he came to know the district so well that he could make his deliveries by night. It was a problem when, in daylight, two wagons encountered each other on the narrow highway and he considered it an advantage that he almost never met anyone once the sun was down. Yes, he might see them on their porches, whole families sitting in silence as he navigated past. Some of these people owned their land outright and had sons and wives, level fields and barns full of cattle and the like. Of course he also knew about places that were an embarrassment to the county and proved that the people who lived there either were unable or unwilling to do what God wanted done. To think that he might also end up like one of those — nothing worried him more.

Arriving at his assigned destination, he would unload the wagon by starlight, a strenuous project in which it was sometimes necessary to take down one plank at a time and then drag it to the site through trees and undergrowth. On one occasion he dropped a keg of nails and had to spend an impatient time on hands and knees gathering up the contents. He could imagine the picture he presented to anyone looking down from the sky — a stooped figure on hands and knees gathering up the things as best he could in the little bit of light vouchsafed him. It was a punishment of course, as was indeed all of life, and not until after death could he expect to be told what the punishment was for.

Or, he might use the afternoons to help put up a house. He was more serious than other people even if his social skills were not always as advanced as theirs. He knew how to cipher and read and his spelling was adequate, but he could *not* (not yet) decode a blueprint. The world was a crowded place and had many people in it, but if there lived anywhere a man to take him in hand and educate him about blueprints... He no longer expected any such piece of good fortune.

He owned a watch, a knife, three outfits of clothing and a small collection of common tools that he carried in the wagon. Twice his youngest brother had appeared at the store bringing gifts of food from his mother. But far more important than any of these was his *reputation*, which had advanced from a more or less undecided position to the point at which it stood today. And instead of forsaking his church when the pastor retired and a lesser man took his place, William began attending services in two different places.

Of all the temptations — drink, cards, idleness — none endangered him more than a married woman who used to come three times a week to the store and experience great trouble in deciding what she wanted. Her waist was small, one of the smallest he had seen, but not for a moment did William forget about her husband, the most sullen and unpredictable of men. He had never known a woman, William had not, who possessed so many different hats.

"You're very kind, Bill, to put up with me. I'm just *terrible*, I know I am, but I just can't help it I guess."

William spoke but did it so softly that neither of them could hear. She wore two little black leather shoes with latches and heels.

In June that year he set out with four mules on a three-day journey that would carry him around the levee, across the river, and into the next county. His wagon was heavy-laden and bore all manner of shingling and fasteners and fretwork along with a great many heavy pieces of lumber cut to specification. He was pleased to be out and abroad and delivered from having to deal with people. Spring was finished and summer just arriving in full force, a transitional moment that entailed the death of certain flowers and the coming of other less colorful kinds. He regretted the honeysuckle most of all, his favorite of the vines; hardly had he become aware of them than the blooms began to drop off and the divine odor to dissipate and finally disappear altogether. He found consolation in *magnolia* flowers, where sometimes he was wont to park his wagon and even intrude upon a person's lawn in order to indulge his nose. He also approved of cows, hundreds of them grown lethargic and fat owing to this year's grass. They moved delicately, one step at a time amongst the hills while taking care not to agitate their cargoes of precious milk.

He moved on, waving to the people who waved at him. Twenty miles out the number of such people began to fall away quickly and he found himself before nightfall in unknown parts where the cotton was suffering from an infestation of some kind.

He carried a .32 caliber revolver but did not expect to need it. And when night came and the stars proved too faint to steer by, he drew off into the edge of the forest and made up a pallet beneath the wagon. Not that he expected to sleep, not immediately anyway, not after a day of so many sights and experiences.

He waited in vain for almost an hour and then left his place and walked along the edge of the woods for a distance of about a quarter of a mile before coming back and exploring a few hundred rods in the other direction. Finally he entered the trees and stepped to a clearing where at one time a house had stood. Nothing remained of that building save for the cornerstones and some fifteen feet of a chimney (its top part missing) made of clay and bricks. Ghosts, thick as bees, hovered about the household; pushing through them, he went to the back yard and wasted a minute seeking for the well before he recognized that a creek ran through the property. The moon was down, the stars feeble, and he could not be certain the water he was drinking was cloudy or clear. An owl saw what he doing and reported it to the woods at large.

He was on the point of turning back when he came to the top of a ridge and descried a village down below in the valley. Even at that hour a few lamps were burning tentatively, each lamp signifying where someone was awake and thinking. This was the time he cherished most, when people were asleep or at any rate silent, and darkness covered the imperfections of the land and forest.

He resumed his journey in the morning. He had developed a good opinion of his front left-side mule and a poor one of his right, and if he had started out by putting this animal on short rations, now was it time to use the whip. (He simply could *not* allow the understanding that existed between men and mules to fall apart, nor allow a creature like that to go about imagining that he was shrewder than a human being.) Finally, with the day half done, he stopped, unhitched the beast, and led it to where two trees stood near together.

His first blow landed on the pastern and left a crease along the fur. Too astonished at first to appreciate what was happening, the mule merely turned and looked back with a puzzled expression. This had the effect of angering the man yet further, who came down harder with the lash. The mule now kicked with both hind legs at once but missed by such a distance that William was almost tempted to laugh. And then, too, there was a woman with a pail coming down the highway who appeared to be disturbed by what was happening. William spoke politely to her and took off his hat, but opted not to explain himself to a person who knew nothing of the history that lay behind his action.

It was late afternoon when he came up over a rising and discerned a settlement in the distance. The maps that brought him here — they had been useful certainly but were by no means perfect. He spent a few minutes penciling corrections in the margin and then, after parking the wagon and locking the wheels, took his suitcase and went far enough into the woods to change over into his suit and new shoes without being viewed from the highway. Far away someone was burning stumps, creating a column of smoke that rose up half a mile into the sky before the breeze took it and forced it toward the south. He counted five houses in the hamlet (together with outbuildings) and some half-dozen Negro shacks where children were running and playing. A windmill was being put up behind the chicken house but hadn't yet been fitted with blades. He judged it a favorable place for human habitation, even if the ground looked somewhat thin to him and mixed with sand.

He drew up in front of the largest of the houses, parked, and went to the porch where a grey-headed man sat in a rocking chair. They looked at each other evenly; the older man trying to match the younger's gaze.

"Raining, they say, over in Dale County."

"You could use some rain here, looks like to me."

"We could, we could."

A dog came up, looked William in the face and then began to sniff his glossy shoes. The old man had taken his knife meantime and was trimming at his nails. A scent of biscuits came from the kitchen where William could hear two women talking. It was a well-built home, generally speaking, although William saw one or two features that could have been done differently.

"We didn't hardly expect you till tomorrow," the older man said.

"No, sir. Well I can wait till tomorrow to unload."

"Be dark soon." He looked at William's apparel, lingering upon his hat and crimson vest. "Our people can do the unloading."

It was a courtesy and William acknowledged it with a nod. He said nothing about the dog that by now had licked all the polish off one shoe and was starting on the other. He heard just then his first cricket of the evening, an impatient individual who could wait no longer for the sun to go away. Never in his life had William been so far from home.

They gathered that night around a long and narrow table built to the same proportions as the room. The man had three daughters who at once excused themselves before coming back a few minutes later in finer clothes.

William, who had always been able to stare down any man he met, dared not glance too closely at the girl across from him lest he find himself unable to look away. He knew this much, namely that her hair, which was exceedingly black, formed loops and curls that ran from her forehead to her neck — he could ascertain that much without actually looking at her. Her brothers, meanwhile, looked all alike and had apparently come into the world in quick succession, until their mother had switched over to producing girls. These men had *not* put on *their* best clothing, and when they spoke, they spoke to each other and not to the guest.

William had not had a decent meal in days, nor an excellent one in weeks. He divined that these girls had had an important share in preparing this one and that they were waiting with growing excitement as he sampled each dish. He started by taking up his biscuit and testing it slowly and with concentration.

"I always thought my mother made good biscuits," he said. "But these, whew!"

"Put some preserves in that biscuit, Mr. Pefley, if you please. We make our own, right here on the premises."

(The preserves were fine, but still had too many seeds in it.)

"It's a sin, food like this. I just can't tell you, ma'am, I just can't."

The mother blushed, the girls giggled. William went for the chicken and the pork, but took only modest portions. The tea was a pleasure and had been sweetened to just the right degree. There were beans, too, and squash and corn and no way on earth for him to know which dish had been prepared by whom. Suddenly he looked up at the girl across from him and made his first error of the evening.

"My aunt, they say she used to be real pretty, too. Lot of curls, you know."

There was a discernible silence in the room, especially from the brothers. Right away he followed it up with his second mistake.

"I doubt I'll ever get married. 'Cause no woman would have me."

Had he come to this place to talk about marriage and curls? The sisters were watching coolly to see what might happen next. Meantime the girl across from him, who seemed to be wearing rouge, was sitting "side saddle," as it were, as she sipped tentatively at her tea. Never had he encountered so delicate a person. He marveled at her, especially when they brought out the ice cream and she took only so much of it as could be brought to her mouth in one of the tiniest little spoons he had ever seen.

Soon came the time to retire to the parlor, a small room full of upholstered furniture trimmed in velvet, a piano (it took up a great part of the space), and two cabinets of fancy glassware that had been handed down, William assumed, from one century to the next. It was not until he had seated himself and had coughed politely once or twice that he saw that the brothers, who were not allowed in this part of the house, had gone out toward the barn, had mounted horses and had driven away.

"Yes," the old man said in a tired voice, as if his daughters had exhausted him with their fine meal, "she plays pretty well on that thing. The piano, I mean. Don't you Mary?"

"No, I don't." She looked at William. "I don't."

"Show him."

"Daddy!"

"And Deborah here — cooks just like her mother."

William looked to the mother, who seemed fully engaged in her knitting. She, too, was delicate, and not much larger than a child; right away he saw the resemblance between her and the five massive portraits on the wall in gilded frames. The opposite wall (and he had to turn to see it), bore the painting of a cornucopia with all sorts of fruit spilling out. He searched for something to say, finding nothing. That was when the mother spoke out:

"I'm surprised at you, Mr. Pefley, driving a wagon for somebody else. Psssht! Now if *I* was a strong young man... You should have your own wagon, that's what I think. And your own place."

She was right. "I *am* thinking about a sawmill," he admitted. "We need a sawmill, where I come from."

"Yes!"

"I'm going to the front porch," the father said suddenly, rising and stretching.

"It *is* cooler out there."

William would have preferred to remain in the parlor with its luxuries; nevertheless he rose with the others and held the door for the girls. There was no doubt in his mind but that the pretty one was wearing a perfume of some kind; it came to him as if from a garden far away. Halfway through the opening she turned and smiled at him brightly.

"Thank you!"

"He's a gentleman," the younger girl said. "And look how serious he is!"

"Oh Mary. Ignore her, Mr. Pefley, that's what we do."

The night was black and dense and full of crickets crying out in protest against it. Nearer at hand a whippoorwill was singing in the scuppernong vine. Some time now went by with no one talking. The girl's profile lay on the floor but yielded up very little detail about the girl herself. It was a strange thing, how the members of this family seemed in communication with each other without needing to speak. It was the old man who finally broke the silence:

"Real peaceful out here." And then after another long silence: "That Pefley fellow gone to bed already? I don't know, he just doesn't seem... *friendly* somehow."

"No daddy, he's sitting right over there by Mary."

"He is? Good, good. No, I think that would be a real good thing — sawmill business."

"And a brick mill, too. But it's going to take some time before I can..."

"Well of course. That's to be expected — time. You're still young. Shoot, if I was young I'd do *all kinds of things.*"

"You already did do things!" the younger girl said. And then, turning to William: "Him and General Longstreet — they were together, you see."

William looked at the man, or at his shadow rather, with new respect. The family dog had returned meanwhile and was finishing William's other shoe with his spoon-shaped tongue. The stars were highly visible and looked like broken glass; he saw how they were exchanging places with one another as they jittered off and on. Suddenly a large yellow moth came down out of the sky and began to thresh against the window pane.

"Another couple weeks, we would of won that war."

"Anybody want more ice cream?"

"Look at those stars!"

"The stars are all right but the moon looks kind of peakéd to me. Look at it."

"I got to get me an early start tomorrow. Lots to do!"

The grandmother came out, the first time William had seen her. She went from person to person, identifying each of them until she came to him. No one spoke when a raccoon or an opossum perhaps stepped out of the shadows, checked in both directions, and then went racing forward across the lawn.

The younger girl lighted him to his room.

"I thank you," he said. "Well, I suppose you and Deborah have to share a room, I guess."

"We used to. But now we don't."

"Shoot, I reckon she's already sleep by now."

"No, she's probably combing her hair, that's what I think."

"Oh. Combs it every night, I reckon."

"Yes, and she has a whole set of combs. Daddy gave 'em to her. Well goodnight."

He was left alone to think about it further. The bed was high and had a little set of steps leading up to it while on the mantelpiece some dozen books stood upright between two conch shells of unusual size. The mattress itself was good and deep and yet he was getting less sleep from it than if he were still bedding down on the cold hard ground. Finally, just after midnight, he went to the door and tried to puzzle out where a bathroom might be. It was his good fortune that he had been put on the ground floor where he could go out by the window and then come back in again.

He woke early the next morning and after putting the bed into the same condition in which he had found it, waited just outside the door until he could hear voices in another part of the house. He had a wagon to unload, mules to be fed, etc., instead, he came and stood in the entryway to the dining room where he made his third mistake.

"Well. Goodbye, I guess."

"What? No, no, come have some breakfast. We're not going to let you get away from here without some breakfast, for goodness sakes!"

Would he, or not, be seated across from the girl? He waited in dignity, flattered, pleased, and embarrassed when she took it upon herself to serve him coffee, a project that she carried out slowly while wearing a faint smile that comported perfectly with today's bright sun and her own white dress. To be served continuously by such a one as her — he could not imagine anything better suited to get a person through the hard work and ordeals that must be overcome in the course of years to come. And then, too, her silence sounded like wisdom to him, especially when he glanced (very hurriedly) into her face. Unfortunately he could attribute no such wisdom to the younger girl, who kept looking back and forth between William and her sister as she waited with growing impatience for his next mistake.

"Well now, you can't complain about the weather *today*, Mr. Pefley. I expect you'll be home by Friday, yes?"

He put down his fork, blotted his lips, and then got into his most serious expression. "Yes ma'am, God willing. Provided that..."

"Provided that nothing untoward happens?"

That was it exactly. He nodded gratefully to the woman, who seemed to understand about things. He had made no mistakes in several minutes although the two girls continued to wait for them. That was when he discerned a little pot of honey half-hidden behind a vase of flowers, the first time he had seen that particular condiment offered at breakfast time.

"Want some?" the younger sister asked. "It's just honey."

"Hush. More coffee, Mr. Pefley?"

He looked to his coffee which indeed was mostly gone, and then to the girl across from him who lifted up her thimble cup and sipped from it. The other hand she kept in her lap at all times.

He drove away slowly, never looking back until it was safe to do so. Two miles out he came to a juncture and delayed there for a long time trying to recollect the proper route. In fact he was confused and had gotten almost no sleep the night before. Far away he could see a purple lake that kept dodging in and out of view as he drove toward it, a specimen of the sea itself, as he liked to think. The notion came over him just then that he would like to possess this whole entire landscape, as far as he could encompass with his eyes.

FOUR

The walls of Luverne were visible from a distance of about two miles and soon thereafter he was able to make out the town's six scarlet pennants furling gaily in the breeze. The eastern gate had been thrown open to the world and never had he seen so many people in the square. He was wrong to have believed that he knew most of the farmers in the vicinity and he had difficulty distinguishing between the people of this and other counties. Women, too, he saw, most of them carrying shopping baskets and accompanied by children. The peddlers meantime had set up along a stretch of the highway where they were showing off their wares. A blind man was playing on a clarinet while just next to him a beggar had brought along a pail full of green and yellow snakes. William was tempted to donate a coin to this last person, until he came closer and saw who it was. All this activity was having a bad effect upon his mules. That was when he saw that a platform had been put up behind the courthouse and that the condemned man, wearing a straw hat with a wide brim, was sitting on a little stool while he chatted with members of the crowd.

William wanted nothing to do with any of this and instead went direct to the lumber yard, which had been closed for the afternoon. It seemed to him that the organization of things had deteriorated in his absence and that the new shipment of four-by-fours had not always been cut as squarely as it should. The stable itself was open and unattended and the horses and mules readily available to whomever might wish to steal one. He worked quickly, freeing his own mules of harness and yoke and then giving them the oats and water they had earned. He had come back with sixty dollars in his pocket, although most of it was owing to the man who owned the business. In addition he had a pocket knife, handkerchief, mixed coins, and a brass watch that weighed two-thirds of a pound.

He strode back quickly to the square, expecting to pass through the audience before the hanging could get under way. One of the farmers had come to town with two pigs, a great one and a small one attached to the same leash. Next to the platform William saw a crowd of women in odd-looking hats conversing with each other. He managed to avoid the insurance salesman, a nervous individual in cracked spectacles who called to him twice and took several steps in his direction before changing his mind and going after someone else. Another minute and William would have been on the leeward side of the courthouse and well out of view of this day's proceedings. And that, of course, was when the condemned man called to him, urgently, and summoned him to come.

Let it be any other person in the world and William could have refused; instead, he halted, debated, and turned back.

"I *thought* I seen you over there," the man said, bending forward on his stool and sheltering his eyes against the noonday sun. "What you been doing Bill?"

"Well, I..."

"Deliv'ring stuff! All over this whole county, deliv'ring and deliv'ring and deliv'ring!"

William admitted it. According to the courthouse clock, the man had seven minutes to live.

"Well now what about *me*, how come you don't deliver me? Shoot boy, I won't give you no trouble. I'll go anywhere you want." He made a sweeping motion from east to west, indicating all the places he'd be willing to go.

"Well I'd better..."

"You ain't got nowhere to go! Me, I'm the one that's going."

William looked off. He thought he saw a possibility that this conversation might devolve over onto a third person, who had just now come up and was shaking the dead man's hand. He left.

He had devised a desk out of sawhorses and planks and had a keg for a chair; now, taking out the little etui (not much bigger than a cigar) that held his nibs, he began to map out a letter to the girl. Five years and three months of schooling had taught him something of calligraphy and he was able to vary the thickness of his line by skewing the pen in one direction or another until the script took on the uncanny look of European penmanship in the age of kings. Trimming the lamp and installing his best nib, he wrote:

MISS DEBRA NAFTILE

DEAR FRIEND:

Doubtless you will be surprised to receive this. I venture to ask you for a correspondence. Though I am a very poor one my self. I believe I have met with you two times at breakfast and supper. Comparatively you are a stranger to me though you have never seemed as one to me. Some times I fear I have made too free with you if I have please for give me. My meeting with you has been very short. You may rest ashured it has been very agreably on my part. I am indebted to you of having a nice time the night when I was there. I dont think I ever enjoyed any thing better than that. I spent most of June in Loundes County near Sandy ridge. As I do not know wheather it is agreable or not for me to write I will not write any more until I hear from you.

I am very respectfuly your Friend.

WILLIAM PEFLEY

And having written, got into bed and turned out the light. It was a dangerous thing, as well he knew, to be mailing letters of *this* character to a woman of *her* character, and especially so in light of her brothers, who had looked to him like the sort of people who knew how to avenge an insult. Accordingly he rose again, broke open the letter and read it through, but then decided after all to leave it as it was.

He no longer expected to sleep extremely well, not since he had passed thirty years of age. And if when he was young he used to dream too much, now those dreams came both more seldom and for longer periods of time. For example: he had built a house with insufficient supports but was able to come awake and run outside before it collapsed and crushed him. Or, he dreamt that it was much later along in history than was generally known, and that the end would come either within his own lifetime or that of his sons at the latest. Or, he envisioned an immense cloud bulging with Christ and the Prophets appearing overhead just when people least expected it. Waking and sleeping, this was his dominant concern, together with his fear of the judgment that might fall upon *him*. Suddenly he awoke, dismayed to see that he had been sleeping.

Sitting on the edge of the bunk and thinking of his transgressions, he admitted that whereas he needed to be punished certainly, he hoped it wouldn't go on forever. Even a thousand years could seem like a long time, although he believed that he could stand up to that. Far across town he heard the four o'clock train running along the levee, its cars full of condemned cows. Yes, he could appreciate the utility of such vehicles, although it still seemed to him like a form of cheating. Transportation ought to come from the exertion of men and animals instead of simply falling into humanity's lap as a random consequence of mere ingenuity. And yet he, too, did oftentimes avail himself of goods and products hauled by trains.

He went outside and stood for a time listening to an owl blaring from the woods. The moon was in good color tonight but had come to rest in a matrix of clouds that looked like a hornet's nest. Themselves, the stars were jubilant, each of them darting back and forth wildly within a certain terrain. Even at this distance he could see the hanged man who had drawn his knees up under his chin and appeared to be sleeping in mid-air.

He went back, took up his ink and pen and, after composing the first part of it in his mind, began to lay out his next letter, which he intended to post before too many more days had gone by.

FIVE

Two weeks, and if the man hadn't written within that time... Well! she would know then what she needed to know and could begin to go about her business. But when just five days had gone by and the letters began to arrive, that was when the three daughters came together to consult about it.

"I told you. Told you he'd write. He did."

"Yes, but see how funny it looks!"

"No, no, that's just the way he does it. It's hard, making it look like that."

"Says he wants a *correspondence*. Oh God, what if daddy finds out?"

(There were three letters by this time, each more apologetic than the other. Each girl held one letter.)

"Aren't you going to answer him, Deb?"

Deb said nothing.

"Maybe she's already answered. Have you, Deb?"

"Me, I'd answer 'em, if it was me."

"Well sure *you'd* answer. You'd do just about anything, I reckon."

"Oh, I would not, not *anything*. Just *some* things."

The older girl gasped.

"I *might* answer," said Deborah at last, folding the letter and putting it away in her drawer whence the younger girl right away drew it out again. "Or, I might not."

"Well if you don't answer, then I *will*. It's *mean*, letting him suffer like that. Besides, I think he's *nice*."

"He's a Christian. That's what daddy says."

"He won't talk."

"He talks as much as you do! Land's sakes, you just sat there like an old stick or something. He must of thought you were *terrible*."

"Yeah, that's why he keeps writing all these letters."

They took them up again, the three letters, and passed them around to each other one by one. It seemed to the youngest of them that with each letter the script was getting fancier and fancier, until the day must come at last when no one would be able to read them.

SIX

He had assisted in the building of two houses and had sent off four letters before enough interest had accrued in the girl for her to write him back. He was to remember the excitement — a small square envelope of cerulean blue that might well be empty, judging by the weight. He was to remember the postmaster, too, an abdominal man with white hair who handed it over sadly, saying:

"This came in. Want it? It's addressed to you."

William took it. Twenty feet away a small group of men was watching shrewdly while at the same time sucking the last of the juice from their plugs of tobacco. He started to join them but then changed his mind and instead went to the far corner where a small boy was jotting down information from the posters of wanted men. Changing his mind again, he left the post office and hurried back to his quarters in the warehouse.

The lamp was fitful and almost out of fuel but finally he had it giving off a sufficient light. As to the envelope itself, he cut it open neatly with the smaller (and sharpest) of the two blades of his pocket knife. The message was short and the penmanship appeared to have been written down without any great attention as to how it would look upon the actual page. He knew, of course, that she was indifferent to him at this stage and that he had no right to expect anything beyond the courtesies inherent to a person in her position. She had written this:

MR. PEFLEY:

    I was somewhat surprised to receive a letter from you, although we do often receive letters from people that have visited us here. Yesterday we had a visit from Reverend Hodgkins and although I was unwell with the chills and unable to greet him, I know that we were pleased that he could stop by. He has been in the county only a few months but everyone thinks highly of him.

    You have mentioned that you were at Church on Sunday and also wednesday. I encourage you to persist with this laudable mode of life and also the habit you say you have of saving your wages in sofaras you can do it. I have no doubt that someday your dreams will come true and you will own a sawmill and perhaps a brick manufacturing establishment as well. This is a laudable ambition for a young man and I encourage you to persist.

Your friend,

DEBORAH NAFTEL

Six times he read it through from start to finish, until at last he was able to master his emotion and accept the compliments in a more or less serene frame of mind. Whether or not Reverend Hodgkins was a *young* man, he had no way of knowing. His impulse just now was to get him down to the river and go fishing for an hour or two in perfect solitude, an action that he would certainly have carried out had not some dozen men been expecting him back at the building site.

SEVEN

The letters continued to arrive, but she no longer allowed her sisters to read them. They were too young, one of them, and the other too spoiled; under these conditions, she preferred to go out to the barn and consult with Jesse, who had been toiling these past weeks in preparation for the Agricultural and Industrial Exposition to be held at Vandiver Park in late July.

"Gracious," she said, amazed at the products he had brought together. "And look at all those seeds!"

Jesse said nothing. He was dressed in an apron of some kind and was wearing a pair of wire frame glasses (she had never seen them before) that made him look older. The barn also had five mules and two horses in it, all of them seemingly entranced as they peered over their stalls. Deborah went now to the honey and, holding each jar up to the light, confirmed that the contents were evenly-colored and contained no little bits of stray comb drifting back and forth at hazard.

"My. I'll say this, Jess, that when this is all over, you'll have more prizes than anyone. I got another letter."

They went together and stood in the doorway where the light was better. There were far too many of these letters, but except for that Jess had not yet found anything of real substance to criticize.

"Look here, he's apologizing again. Always apologizing. That fellow ain't got but *one thing* to apologize for."

She waited for it.

"He apologizes too dang much."

"He wants to come for a visit."

"Does? You invite him?'

She admitted that she had not.

"Papa invite him?"

"No."

"Well then! he ain't been invited. Can't come."

"He wants to bring me a baby kitten."

"Oh well now, that's different. We need some kittens, we don't have enough. Need 'em real bad. Why, if we had another fifteen or twenty of 'em, why we could..."

She hit him.

"Tell him not to come. You ought to be helping me, is what you ought to be doing."

"I *am* helping."

"Are?"

"I'm making preserves!"

That was true. He put on a face that was designed to acknowledge it and then went back and began sorting through the hundred ears of corn collected from various parts of the county. He was a scrupulous man, famous alike for his bottled products and the appealing little labels on them that bore a picture of the sun.

EIGHT

Thunder in the east — he awoke to the sound of it and lay listening to the storm's footsteps as it stalked nearer and nearer before then veering off at the last moment toward the grist mill, two miles outside of town. For almost a full hour he harkened to it conscientiously before then leaping up out of bed and preparing for church.

Sixteen buggies were drawn up in a circle in front of where the Methodists met — one might almost believe that the mules and horses had come at their own discretion in order to confer about the week's developments. William entered by the side door and made his way to the vestibule where the people and their children were standing about in tiny groups. A woman in a pink bonnet — he could not remember having seen her before — smiled and waved coyly, as if she were tapping with her gloved hand at a pane of invisible glass. He saw the grocer, a religious man who kept yawing back and forth, impatient for the service to get under way. He had been wrong, had William, to imagine the storm had gone for good; he could hear it beating at the gates and filling all the lower part of town with rain.

He had expected to hear the Reverend Sikes today and was disappointed when he perceived the man substituting for him, a weak type, too thin by much, and whose faith, if he had any, was not apparent in any part of him. Even so, William was willing to stay until it should become clear whether the sermon had been composed for women and servants, or whether adult men. William therefore allowed the man to go on with it for about twenty minutes and then rose up politely, left the building, and sprinted across to

32

the Baptist Church where someone who had seen him approach was holding open the door. This building had the tallest spire in town, a golden shaft that acuminated to a very sharp point amidst thunder and the clouds. He shook hands with the usher and then, seeing that the place was almost full, climbed toward the balcony before then turning and quickly coming back down when he realized this area had been set aside for major contributors and council members.

The minister was a belligerent and disheveled-looking person who stood silently for long periods while turning his gaze back and forth, letting it rest on various members of the congregation. No one knew as much as he about the fate that lay in store for these individuals, and no one felt worse about it. Now, suddenly, he turned and stared down at a bald man sitting in the foremost pew.

Twenty years previous to this, William by error had taken in hand a horseshoe that had lain for a long time in hot coals. He had endured that experience and if necessary could endure it again. He might even have been able to go for weeks in that condition. But to go *forever*, forever and ever without hope or intermission, the pain never ceasing — it was too much, more than he could bear, worse than people realized. Better never to have been born than to live under the threat of what awaited so many millions and might probably be awaiting *him*.

Truth was, no one knew the practices he had indulged at various moments in the course of his life, just as no one knew what things transpired daily in his head, and never mind how he strove to ward them off. Yes, it was his *mind* that particularly deserved to go to hell, while the rest of him, the part that did the work, was pulling him toward paradise — this was the nub of his religion and it was this that he wished to hear in the mouth of any minister of his.

An hour and a half the sermon went on, although the gravamen had already come and gone before the sermon was one-quarter finished. Nor was he so sure, William was not, that the people fully understood what was being told to them. And, of course, there were always those for whom it was already too late.

He stood when the service was over and moved quickly down the aisle, emerging in time to see that the Presbyterians had finished already and were dispersing to their homes.

In the afternoon he made his way to the river and strolled down the shore to his usual place. He had set up three poles at about equal distance from each other and was in process of changing one of his lines when he perceived that a black family was watching silently from the opposite shore. William nodded to them but had to wait a long time before the man put up his hand and signaled back.

"Any luck?" William asked.

"No, suh; not much." And then, after another long wait: "Got a purch, my boy did."

William waited for the perch, which the boy seemed reluctant to expose. He was a serious youth who kept his eyes fixed all times upon the small territory of water just in front of him. The fish itself proved quite small, not at all the sort of thing a white man would opt to keep. William now took out three copper hooks of different sizes and attached them to his lines, a piece of behavior that caused the crows that had been yelling at him for the past few minutes to come in closer and take a better look. He was half-finished with it, William was, when a photograph of the sun, three times true size, came washing past on the surface of the river as it ran toward the sea.

William tended to each of his lines in turn, but then began to fall into a daze from following too intently the dozens of little black beetles skating about insanely on narrow feet that tended to leave imprints in the river. That was when the black man, Joe Butler so-named, called across to him:

"Yasuh. You been *travelin'*, Mr. Pefley? Thought I seen you last week driving in that big ole wagon."

William acknowledged that he had.

"*Big* ole wagon, yasuh! You sho knows how to handle them mules, ya-suh; umm um."

William said nothing. A small bird, erratic and mustard-colored, had gotten entangled in a clot of Spanish moss and was casting down filaments of the stuff.

"Yasuh. Mr. William, you ever take any of that lumber over to *Elba*, Alabama? Jus askin."

He acknowledged that he had. There were scarce forty yards twixt himself and the Negro whose voice, he believed, might drive the fish away.

"*Elba, Alabama* — yasuh. 'Course now, they don't have no *saw* mills in Elba. Why you has to take all them long trips over yonder. Spec so."

"Mr. Rettling operates the mill in Elba, Joe."

"Yasuh." He stayed silent for about a minute. "'Course now, Mister Rettlin', he always *drunk*, tell me. Me, I wouldn't know."

William said nothing. A drunk man, if that was what he was, had no business with machinery of that kind.

"And that's why *you* has to do it — travlin', travlin', travlin'. Travlin' every day!"

"Luverne's a good place to live, Joe."

"Sho nuff! Real good, yasuh. 'Course now, Luverne's already got a mill. Got *three* mills. And none of them is *drunk* neither."

William looked at him across the river. The boy had meantime come to his feet, had taken off his bait, had twined the line around his pole and gone away. The woman herself lay resting among the family's dogs and a jug of sweet tea.

"I don't know, Joe. I got lots of friends here in Luverne."

"Well sho you do, yasuh." He held up his hand to count them off but then, after a time had gone by, gave up on it and returned the hand to his pocket. "You got *me*, you got..."

"Lots of money, Joe, takes lots of money to buy equipment like that."

"'Spec so, yasuh." And then after another long pause: "I wouldn't know about things like that. 'Less you wanted to *borrow* it, I reckon."

He slept poorly that night. The storm had returned and was beating so powerfully on the roof that William feared it might actually buckle beneath the force of it. This warehouse had been put together in haste with inferior materials and was designed to be just adequate and nothing more. He despised this attitude, did William, for whom perfection itself was not perfect enough. Finally, unable to sleep, he rolled out of bed, ignited the lantern and then, holding it high, confirmed that the joists were too far apart and out of parallel.

He understood, of course, why carpenters so often behaved as badly as they did and why the world was not any better than it was. The punishments for bad behavior were too weak and too "far apart," and not dreadful enough to point people in the right direction — these were his thoughts as he again rolled out and put himself into an abject position at the foot of the bed. He never dared to pray while lying in comfort, or with his face directed toward God's own.

NINE

The letters continued to arrive at the rate of about three a week. Finally, after some months had gone by and her brother no longer bothered to tease her about it, she began to send off as many as two letters each week of her own. He (William) used to stop each day at the Post Office and from there hurry on to his quarters in order to read what progress he was making. *She*, on the other hand, was as likely to go about all day with an unopened letter hidden on her person, preferring to wait for night before opening it. Or, she might go to the barn, or climb into the loft, or retreat to her boudoir. She would have said that it was his honesty (William's honesty) that she liked most of all, and his willingness to write things that would have embarrassed them all had she continued to share the letters with her sisters (she did not). And then, too, there were those schemes of his for the future — the large house, the brick mill, the sons he would have had, had only he been the sort of person a woman might be willing to marry (he wasn't). This was the problem she addressed in her next letter:

Nov 25th 1888

Mr. Pefley:

I have received yours of the 17th instant and write to thank you for your kind wishes for my family. Jesse has worked so hard and I hope and believe he will receive the reward that he has so conspicuously merited. You say that you do not suppose there is any woman in the world who would contemplate embarking upon the voyage of marriage with you. Of course I can speak only for myself as I do not know the qualities that other women may seek

in a husband. However I feel sure there is probably a woman somewhere
that you could marry, although you must be patient and look for her until
you find her. Mr. Weaver was a visitor here yesterday, but could not stay for
supper. He is a laudable young man and we are always pleased when he can
visit. Mother bids me to send her greetings and best wishes, which I enclose
along with mine.

Your friend,

DEBORAH N.

He understood this to mean that the girl's mother was not his enemy, but
that Weaver was. Accordingly he used his mid-day hour to get back to his
quarters and to write in such a way as to demonstrate greater patience than
he had been able to manage herebefore:

DECEM. 2

DEAR MISS DEBBIE:

I was pleased to have your letter that arrived here today, but could not write
back at ten oclock because a man was buying lumber and staid for a long
time and talked. I red your letter three times, and this is what I am going to
do. I shall be patient because I can certainly understand why it is the wise
thing to do. I am glad Mr Weaver was visiting you at your home, and that is
what I would do to if your father and mother invited me to. I know that Jesse
will win a lot of prizes at the Fair. I know that you are helping him to. Well
Miss Debbie I had better close for now as I have nothing to add that you
dont know. I was taking some feed over to Mr. Oliver's place when my horse
took scared and Oh! the next thing I knew I was on the ground. We didn't
find her til next day. She got her harness caught in a limb but otherwise no
one got hurt. Well dear friend I will write again when I can do so and hoping
you will do the same.

Your friend,

W. PEFLEY

Satisfied with it, he went back to the six-acre plot where one of Mr. Oliver's
brothers-in-law was building the largest, the costliest, and the best-engi-
neered home this side of the river. He took pleasure in it, William did, until

at about two in the afternoon when a wagon full of inferior lumber was brought forward and the men began at once to use it for the flooring. It was too thin and yielding, the sort of material that would give under even an ordinary person's weight.

"Can't use this," he said, speaking quietly.

The foreman looked at him. "Can't?"

With the claw of his hammer William began to loosen the two or three boards that had been installed.

"Now just what in the hell do you think... Hey!"

"Have to send it back. Cut wrong. Quarter-inch too thin."

"Well I'll be dagburned. Now just who in the devil do you think is boss of this here operation, hm? That's what I want to know."

William put down his hammer but then gathered it up again and tucked it beneath his belt. The foreman was a blasphemous man who carried a knife and had two little deposits of congealed tobacco juice in the corners of his mouth. He waited until William had collected a half-dozen of the planks and returned them to the wagon.

"Well I'll be Goddamn. See what's he's doing there? I told you once boy, I ain't telling you again: just put them planks right back where they was!"

"Too thin."

The men were watching. William had no fear himself, nor had he ever been able to understand why anyone could fear a human. Turning to the Negroes, he commanded them to load the wood and carry it back to whence it had come.

"Goddamn A'mighty! No, when it comes to this, I guess you're just about the worst I've ever seen!"

"Too thin."

In the afternoon they turned to bricks, the part that William preferred above all others; no one did better work than he nor did it more slowly. He liked to lay them straight and tamp them down and tie them all together by filling the sills to overflowing with yet further mortar. The foreman mean-time had drawn apart and was watching sullenly from a distance of about twenty yards. The Negroes were singing as they worked, but apart from that no one spoke until late afternoon when by ones and twos the men began to come, not to the foreman, but to William for their instructions.

TEN

Three days went by, until the bricks ran out. He spent the fourth day, did William, with the man who operated the city's premier sawmill, an irritable sort of person who detested anyone who wished to tell him what to do.

"Heavier," said William, "and thicker. I want 'em heavy enough so that when a person walks across that floor..."

"So that's what you want then."

"I do."

"But you see we aren't real interested in what *you* want. We're only interested in what *we* want."

William turned and looked around the premises, trying to find who the "we" might be. Finally he said this: "We got fourteen men out yonder" — he pointed in the direction — "just waiting for these boards."

"That right? Well I tell you this Bill — when I want to have me a house built, I'm going to get you to build it. But in the meantime I don't give one goddamn little ..."

"'They shall suffer hell fire.'"

"What?"

"Hell fire." He spoke calmly but sadly. "Thousands of years, Mr. Grambling, and it just never stops. Never, never, never. Here on earth it might last for a minute or two and then it's over."

"And that's another thing about you. You can't be so all-fired sure about everything all the time. Why you ain't nothing in this world but a goddamn little...!"

"I'll pray for you. I'm not saying it'll do any good of course."

The man would need two hours to cut the boards, wherefore William decided to use the interval to stop by the Post Office. He had hoped to have a letter from Deborah and was both disappointed and amazed to find that she had neglected him today and that her mother had written instead. He took the letter quickly into his own hands and, saying nothing to the postmaster, went outside and strode for a distance of about a hundred and fifty rods until he came to the oak and willow grove that stood between the stationer's and the tinsmith's shop.

DEC. 4, '88

MY DEAR MR. PEFLEY:

I had not written to express Mr. Naftel's satisfaction with the supplys and molding you delivered to us here in September, but I am sending this letter today by the post to say that we were glad to receive them. We consider it an honor that you could stay for supper too and I know that Jesse and the other children enjoyed your acquaintance. We would be glad for you to come back when you are able to do so and to see the exhibits which Jesse is entering in the state Fair on the 16th and 17th and 18th instants of next month which is of the new year. He already won a great many prizes last year and it is a tradition in our family to win them when fortune smiles upon us. Hoping to here from you by the next mail I remain

MRS. AGNES ROON NAFTEL

Twice he read it through and then turned it over in hopes some mention of Deborah might be there. He was pleased, pleased beyond measure to have an invitation of this kind, but worried, too, that they had ignored his friendship for the girl and had applied it wrongly to the boy.

ELEVEN

He set out in the second week of January, traveling on a borrowed horse. His saddlebags had good gifts in them, including a bottle of plum wine — (he wanted nothing to do with it himself) — for the old man. The weather, to be sure, was colder than he liked, but otherwise normal for this part of year. He liked to see fog coming from the horse's nostrils, a testimony that the animal was putting forth the best efforts available to her. He passed a farm house built alongside the road (its windows filled with curious faces) and a windmill turning slowly in the breeze. He never envied anyone, William did not, and yet the barn was red and high and spilling over with some of the richest-looking hay that he had seen that year. He appreciated the hens as well and had respect for the discipline that kept them within in-visible boundaries between the barnyard and the road. But mostly he was affected by the parcels of loaf-shaped smoke lifting from the chimney and tumbling ever so slowly to infinity — it told of the self-respecting family happily gathered about the fireplace for winter's duration. It was too much and when he came to the top of a knoll and saw down below a valley with just the number of habitations — not too many and not too few — just the number that he himself would have chosen, and the cheerful cows, and saw a lone traveler wending down the high road (coming home after all these years), and the fine blue sky with forms of life in it... Well! It appeased and tempted him, and made him wonder whether such things as these might not after all justify life's ordeal.

But no, he had not gone much further before he happened upon a tavern with horses parked out front, and then soon thereafter a half-starved hog that had lost its mind and was walking in circles within a pen that was poorly constructed. He should have known better — that men are bad, that things fall apart, and that even the landscape was full of imperfections and signs of sloth. He could feel a headache coming on together with a developing sense of anger that made him reach for the whip. To his left a barn had gone to ruin even though it might just as easily have been saved with but a modicum of human effort. Ten thousand years must go by, longer, before humanity would have done its duty and repaired the earth and made it congruent with paradise — *this* was his philosophy and it was this that kept him grim and silent almost all the time.

He came within sight of Elba in the late afternoon and rode slowly past the outlying farms. It was a prosperous place full of orchards and as he pushed into the heart of the city he found that it boasted some dozen homes of advanced design. Here he paused, trying to divine the floor plan of the noblest of them, a vast structure set in the midst of a scattering of Negro shacks with rocking chairs and burnt-out hounds on every porch.

He drove past the sawmill and gave it a quick inspection before then proceeding on to the owner's home. The yard had considerable amounts of rubbish in it, including parts of a churn, a rotted harness, a box of empty jars. The man himself was also decayed and appeared unwilling to come out onto the porch.

"I stopped by your... operation," William said. "The blade's missing."

"I know it. Got tore all apart. Some son-of-a-bitch drove a spike into that old larch and it's going to cost me plenty. *Plenty*!"

"Aren't no larches, not in these parts."

"Well. It got torn up anyway." He turned and began to retreat into the building.

"I'm thinking of setting up business here myself."

The man came back. "Saw business?"

"Yes, sir; that's what I'm thinking."

"Wouldn't hardly be enough cutting for the two of us."

"Expect not."

"You the fellow…?"

"I am."

"… hauling stuff from Luverne?"

"I've seen forests here, fine-looking trees growing in the sand. I don't drink neither."

"Well. You could buy me out, I reckon."

"No, sir. I expect to have a whole lot better equipment from what I saw at your place."

"I been here forty years, near about."

"I'm thirty-one myself."

"Well. My boy's been asking me to come to Ohio. He lives there don't you see. Wife. Kids."

They shook, the man reaching out through the opening and looking off into the distance where night was coming in.

He rode forward, informed by starlight and the utterances of owls. The trees seemed prematurely old, owing no doubt to the clots of Spanish moss that burdened them so. And then, too, there was always the river that wended in and out of his route, a serious obstruction that several times sent him out of his way in search of a bridge or ford.

Toward two in the morning he pulled off and after victualing the horse rolled himself up tightly in his tarpaulin and managed to grab off perhaps an hour's worth of medium grade sleep. Cold weather it was and when he awoke the clarified atmosphere revealed a great many more details than were ordinarily visible in the sky. A crowd of stars paled suddenly but then turned bright again, as if a tissue of some kind had drifted between the world and them. The moon, meantime, was afflicted with bad places, a vision that brought him to his feet so he could inspect them at closer range.

The sun did finally arrive and after delaying for a long time in one position, came to rest in the limbs of an antique oak behind the house where
Deborah lived. It was possible that the girl herself might emerge and stroll
to the barn or to the well or chicken house, but when after some minutes
had gone by and she remained indoors, William retreated deeper into the
woods and got into his best clothes. He had wanted to arrive in dignity, a
project made more difficult by the two dogs who had uncovered his hiding
place and now stood by muttering darkly at him.

Having at last gotten into his suit and tie and cuff links, he turned and
walked slowly toward the door, ignoring the half-dozen hens stunned by
his temerity. He considered it a friendly sign that the door came open before he reached it to reveal the girl's father waiting for him with a smile. He
removed his hat, William did, and was about to hand his gift off to the man
instead of reserving it for the girl.

"Well, well, well, you seem to have made out all right, coming all this
way. Good." (They shook.) "He's here!"

"Yes, sir. I would of got here sooner, but I had to stop by..."

"Yes indeed! We're glad to see you, boy! Jess, especially. 'When is Billy
coming, when is Billy coming?' That's all he talks about."

It was an untruth, the first such untruth he had heard from this family.
William always tended to fall silent when in the presence of lies.

"And the girls! I know they'll be delighted."

The wife emerged wearing an apron with flour on it. He waited as she
wiped off her hands and then used them to take his coat and hat. She *did*
seem pleased. Or satisfied, rather, that something that could have been expected had in fact come to pass.

The parlor was as he remembered, save that one of the old-time portraits had been taken away and a new one of Deborah set up in its place.
He looked at it with appreciation and then, to be fair, spent some time
with the other framed and colored photographs hung about the room. A
large Bible lay open on a polished stand. Again he looked at the painting of

Deborah, surprised with himself that he had not completely remembered how beautiful she was.

The three people sat at equal distance from one another on high-backed chairs. A minute having gone by, the old man took out his pocket knife and began whittling at his nails.

"Cold, last night!"

William agreed.

"And again tonight, looks like."

"Yes, sir."

"She'll be down pretty soon. Well tell me, my boy, how are things over in Crenshaw County?"

He thought seriously about it for the space of several moments. "Not too good. Cotton is just six cents and some people are getting out completely."

"Oh?"

"Yes, sir. I stopped over to Elba, you see, and it looks to me like..."

Just then the youngest girl came running in, causing William to rise to his feet.

"Morning," she said in her song-like way, smiling and holding out a hand that had two rings on it. It would not be proper to kiss it and yet, given the distance, he was also unable to shake it.

"Mr. Pefley says he's leaving Luverne."

"Well I don't wonder! They don't appreciate him over there, not really."

"Moving to *Elba*. Start a business."

"Elba! She'll like that."

"Well I think that's just wonderful," the mother said, holding up her hand to forestall everyone. "The world *will always need lumber*, Mr. Pefley. Isn't that so?"

"First I got to borrow the money, and then..."

"Lumber *and* bricks. No, you can do both, Mr. Pefley, if you've got the ambition. And I think you *do*."

From where he sat William could see the staircase whence he expected the girl soon to descend; instead, that moment, Jesse came and stood grinning in the doorway. William divined that he had never been allowed actually to pass over into the parlor itself and that he had no aspiration to do so now.

"Isn't that remarkable, Jesse, that Bill would come all this way?"

"I reckon."

"Just so he can help you out! I hope you appreciate what a friend you have."

The boy grinned and nodded and then looked down at his left hand in which he carried three screwdrivers of various girths and lengths. "Looks like he brung a present for Debbie," he said, pointing to the package.

"Will you take tea, Mr. Pefley? We generally like to have ours at about this time."

He agreed to it. It was well past ten in the morning and yet, so far as he could see, there was no activity of any kind taking part in house or yard or in the razed field that extended from the highway to a ridge of limestone outcroppings where the cultivation came to a stop. Further still he could see a crow that had ventured too high and now was falling ever so slowly across the face of the sun. It was time to speak although William had nothing to say; all the more grateful was he therefore when Deborah and the remaining sister came and began to portion out the tea.

He noticed two things at once — first that she was hardly aware of his presence and then, secondly, that she was even more tastefully dressed than on the first occasion. She wore a shawl over her shoulders and had lace at her wrists and waist. He glanced away, focusing rather on the portrait than on the girl herself.

"This is our eldest daughter, Mr. Pefley."

"Oh, mother!"

"Oh that's right, you've already met haven't you?"

"Shoot yeah," Jesse said. "They been writing *letters* to each other, and what-all."

The tea was sweet and William stood in need of it after his long ride. But when a dish of little frosted cakes was passed around, he refused to partake of any even though he stood in need of those as well.

"Jesse has a great many things," the mother said. "Wonderful things, but I just don't know that he can get them into order in time."

"Order, that's important," the old man said.

"You have experience, don't you Mr. Pefley? I'm sure you have to keep things in *very good order all the time*. Because you work in a lumber yard, I mean."

William blushed. There was no man on earth could stand up to him in this particular field — of creating order out of nothingness. "Yes, m'am." And then, after a moment's pause: "You have to make things do what *you* want 'em to do, instead of just letting 'em do what *they* want."

"I see! And you're good at that?"

"Yes, m'am," he said, looking at her evenly.

"And people? Do they have to do what you want?"

"No, m'am, not unless they want to." He looked to Deborah, who was watching him closely. "Of course now, most people never will do right unless somebody makes 'em."

"I see!"

"We used to do right," the old man said sadly in a voice that seemed to come from far away. "And William here — he must of gone a half mile into them trees before he'd even *think* about changing clothes."

"Well I've tried to make my children do the right thing, Lord knows I've tried. But after they get to be big... I don't know." She nodded in the direction of Jesse who, however, had disappeared, and then toward the younger girl who was wearing a languorous expression together with what appeared to be an application of lipstick.

They all went out to the barn, Jesse and his sisters and the visitor from Luverne. He was astounded, William was, when he saw the objects that had been brought together and set out on display on several bales of hay being used as tables. Here twenty cobs of corn lay side by side, including an abnormal species with red and black kernels that appeared almost to have been painted to look that way. William gazed upon it.

"And he grew it himself, all these things!" Deborah said. She was proud, proud of her brother. Turning from the corn, William now turned and gazed at *her.*

"Yup, got 52 varieties," Jesse said. "Last year, the fellow what won, he had him *twenty* varieties. Shoot, maybe not that many."

"Not nearly that many."

Some of the corn had been stripped off the cob and the kernels used to fill a mason jar. William took one of the containers, held it up and viewed it from all sides. He could see why the horses were as plump as they were, if they were fed on this.

"Honey!" said the youngest girl, running to retrieve a bottle that held a quart or more of the stuff. "See?"

He took the honey and held it to the light. The fluid was light in color — a good sign — and had facets in it that sparkled as it turned. One of the bees, unfortunately, had floated to the bottom and drowned.

"My grandfather tended bees," William said slowly, remembering it.

"Yes, but this is *clover* honey. Those judges, they're going to be surprised."

William counted seventeen bottles and then, going to the next table, six more crammed full with bits and pieces of the original comb. Other jars were filled with purified wax. Seeing all this, William could feel a certain respect for the boy taking root inside him after all. He said:

"Not going to be easy, getting all this stuff to Montgomery. However, I reckon it can be done."

He went back to the house with the younger girl and Deborah. There was a desk in the hallway, an old piece of furniture with a few lapsed newspapers on it and not much else. Appropriating it for himself, William sent the younger girl off for scissors and writing materials and the like. The only person now remaining in that room was Deborah, who stood by quietly waiting for instructions. Somehow she had prepared her hair in such a way as that the number of curls that fell over her forehead was even greater than before. In all his life he had not spent more than 45 seconds actually looking into that face, wherefore he could not be absolutely certain that it remained always the same from moment to moment.

"We have paste."

He nodded. Her parents were now sitting quietly in the adjacent room where he could see one or another of them looking around the corner from time to time. The long journey to Montgomery, it would need seven hours at least, and all in all, considering the work that still had to be done, he didn't see how any of them could get any sleep that night.

Those scientific names! Many times they had to start anew, splitting the words so that the letters didn't run off the labels. Meantime Jesse could be heard whistling softly in the barn as he packed his specimens in feed bags and loaded them into the wagon. William waited till the last moment before calling to the mother:

"Time for the preserves, I guess."

She jumped to it, although the jars themselves had been brought together half an hour ago and stood waiting on the kitchen table. He had finished the labels, most of them, but now was doing some of them again. It was a strange thing with him, that the closer he came to perfection the more exasperated he grew.

"They're good," said Deborah. "*Very* good."

"They're not perfect though."

They looked at each other. He had not been wrong about her face — it was unchanged.

"Well, nothing is perfect."

"Should be," he said. (He realized of course that she was not *perfectly* perfect, and that she had a gesture or two that were not as graceful as the rest of her, that her face was better at certain angles than at others, and that her penmanship worsened the longer she stayed at it whileas his own continually improved. On the other hand, she seemed to expect to be told what to do.)

"Am I coming to Montgomery, too," she asked suddenly.

He thought about it. "Yes. But your folks should stay here I think."

"Why?"

"It's just better that way."

"Oh." She went to tell them.

They set out in late afternoon, moving into the sun. It gave him pleasure, it did to William, that Deborah was coming with them. The mules, on the other hand, were not as obedient as they should have been and William was close to disciplining them, which is to say until he remembered that the girls might not wish to witness it and that the mules were not his own. Finally, about two miles outside of town, he took the reins from Jesse, whose thoughts were drifting far afield.

It was the best sort of highway and soon they found a set of tracks that corresponded perfectly to the axle-span of the wagon. They passed a child in a tree, a man setting up fence posts, and then a community of Negroes sitting silently in the heat. The sky was disturbed and rain was threatening. William turned and looked at Deborah for only the fourth or fifth time in their relationship and found that she was dressed in a green wrap of some kind and what looked like a sailor's cap. Meantime behind them, the youngest girl went on singing loudly as she sat in the back of the wagon with her legs dangling out. William clucked to the mules, urging them forward. Clouds were moving in.

They entered and then passed through the village of Peluria. He could detect a lamp glowing behind the curtain and a child in one of the windows upstairs. A dog came out to warn them away but then changed his mind and, returning to his tiny home, leapt inside it. The town was famous for unmarried women and the number of boys who had served in the war. William saluted an elderly man (he did not wave back) leading a calf by a string. As dim as it was, with great clouds seething overhead, a person would not necessarily know whether this were daylight changing over into night or the other way around.

They went on for a little distance further and then pulled off and got beneath the wagon as it began to rain. Huddled together here, they could hear bells tolling forlornly from a town or village just over the horizon. All of Jesse's works, his dozens of exhibits and the jars and boxes that held them were protected solely by the canvas tarpaulin that the girls had thought to bring along.

"Raining," Jesse said. "It's going to be raining all night and we wont get there anyways so we might just as well turn around and go back home. I knew it would."

"Oh gosh, he's doing it again. It's *not* going to rain all night, and we *are* going to get there. Those clouds are real thin up there."

"Well how do you know they're real thin if you can't even see 'em — that's what I want to know."

William held up his hand to stop them. "We'll get there, if it was meant for us to get there."

A minute went by as they reflected upon his words. Debra had meantime taken the food basket and was dealing out the slaw and fried chicken, large pieces that still retained some of the cooked-in warmth. There were also six jars of buttermilk, as if the old woman had imagined that she and her husband were coming as well.

"Raining harder," Jesse said, looking out at it pessimistically. "Mules getting wet."

"They like it."

"Oh they do not. Gollee, you'll say anything wont you?"

William held up his hand. "They have a job to do." And then: "Dudn't matter whether they like it or they don't like it."

The rain slackened and then intensified, but then soon tapered off into a desultory sort of drizzle that might remain with them all the way to Montgomery. He was worried about the time, William was, and about the girl sitting just next to him. They had come to the point in their affair where they could speak more or less freely to each other, but still remained far from being able to look one another in the face.

"I think Deborah should put one of those blankets around her shoulders," William mooted to Mary. "She's liable to get sick."

"He says you should put one of those blankets..."

"No, I'm fine."

"It'll sneak up on her, and she'll get the chills."

"I won *four* ribbons last year," Jesse said. "Not going to win any this year, that's for sure."

"Well go on home then! *We're* going to Montgomery, us."

The rain had resumed, forcing them to the side of the wagon that fronted on the woods. It didn't usually endure for long, a storm as strong as this.

"I'm getting wet!" the youngest girl said.

William snorted at her. "If He wanted to, He could make it rain like this all the time, every day. He used to."

A wagon was coming on slowly toward them, the driver a bare-headed man who held the reins in one hand and in the other a stick with a lantern dangling from the end. No one spoke as the man drew up to them, halted, and then extended the lantern tremulously in among the four people. Jesse, who had given up all hopes of everything, allowed the light to play upon his face for a time, until at last the driver drew it back, waited, and then again probed with it, almost touching the boy upon the nose.

"Montgomery," William yelled out to him. "Going to Montgomery."

Came now the light to shine on William's face.

"How come?"

"Because we're going to the fair!" Mary said. "The *Alabama* fair." (The man couldn't hear her.) "And that's my *brother* you're bothering with that..."

"What?"

"Good luck to you," William yelled.

He nodded, the man did, and then whipped up his mule and went away.

The rain relented and stopped, soon to be replaced by clouds tenuous enough for the moon to shine through. The two girls climbed back aboard the wagon and reviewed the cargo while William went to check on the mules. Of all God's creatures, he admired these most of all, who gave a good example of how men and women the world over ought to behave. They weren't surprised to have been left out in the rain, nor did they expect anything better. He spoke to them softly and adjusted the harness lest the moisture had caused the leather to shrink.

The trail had very nearly been washed away, but William soon found other (and deeper) tracks to follow. Suddenly he turned to see whether Jesse had come with them. The younger girl had not entirely finished with her meal and wore a penumbra of buttermilk about her mouth. Finally, saving her for last, he checked on the girl sitting next to him. No doubt about it, she was an uncomplaining sort of person, always wide-awake and always looking forward eagerly to see what might happen next.

"Your brother..." William started to say (and it was the first time his words had been addressed to her alone), "your brother is looking kind of peakéd back there."

"No, that's just the way he is. He can do some things real good."

William drew out his watch, glanced at it, and then brought it closer to his eye. It was strange, how the clouds had taken on the appearance of grand insects inspecting each other with evil intent. In front a bridge came up that looked to be sturdy; even so, William had the mules step out onto it for a few inches and test it with their weight. This journey of theirs, it was his way of locating a wife and he could think of nothing worse at this time than to spill her into the river and see her carried away.

The sun, when it came, came up so stealthily that William had to verify it with his watch. Meantime the girl Mary had snuggled up between the dog and a half-empty feed sack and seemed to be having dreams. William was surprised at the improvements that had grown up this side of the river, including especially two sturdy-looking gristmills facing off against each other across the road. By now the mules were tired but still determined and neither was willing to cause the other to do more than his own proper share. They would live in Paradise someday — William was sure of it. Suddenly he drew out his watch and looked at it.

The girls came awake at just before six and were clutching at the gunnels as they drove into town. William nodded to one of the pedestrians, a man in a suit who had stopped to stare at them. A train was in process either of entering or leaving town, and if William were not already confused enough, he was assailed just then by the smells of bacon, pastry and manure coming from various places. A file of Negroes, six in number, was marching off with shovels over their shoulders. It was too early, it seemed to him, that such a quantity of people should be outside at this time and going about their day. He turned to speak to Jesse but then changed his mind when he saw how pale the boy was and how oppressed by the tumult going on about them.

They halted at the intersection and waited as a buggy with a woman in it crossed in front of them. The buildings here, sitting shoulder-to-shoulder with no space between them, attained heights of four and five stories and more. Of the shops themselves, some had windows taller than a man.

At the corner they came close to brushing up against a second wagon that had converged upon them from the contiguous road. William lifted his hat to them but then quickly put it down again when he realized the people were carrying the same manner of objects that they themselves had brought. Mary saw it too.

"Hey! They're going to get there before we do!"

William slapped with the reins, pulling ahead of the other wagon and by taking up the better part of the lane, blocking anyone else from getting ahead of him. They passed a smithy with a man in an apron standing out front with folded arms. Came next a three-story hotel built over a saloon that was full of people at 6:45 in the morning. William glanced once or twice in that direction, enough to notify him of the debased expressions on these people's faces.

They moved slowly now, saying nothing as they passed the Confederate Capitol and the house where Davis used to dwell. A hundred years must go by, longer, before these buildings would be restored to their proper use. *He'd* never see it. And his children? Someday maybe.

The pavilion was attached to a building with six purple pennants furling gaily in the breeze. Moving slowly and with dignity, William brought the wagon to the back of the structure where he parked and tethered the animals. It was a place where a person could have use of a toilet and sink, have a cup of coffee and put him- or herself into order once again. Deborah disappeared inside at once, followed by Mary.

"Well!" said William. "We're here I reckon."

"It don't matter whether we're here or not," Jesse said. "Those folks over yonder" — he pointed to them — "*they're* going to get all the prizes. We won't get nothing."

He made no response, William.

"We ought just as well turn around and go back home. These people don't care about us."

The man at the table was tall and thin and had a pile of papers in front of him together with a depleted plug of tobacco in a little porcelain dish that was larger than a twenty-five cent piece but smaller than a pie plate. It held, that dish, some other material as well. William saw right away that this was a sarcastic human being, the sort who had to strain to keep from saying things.

"We're from —— County." (William gave the name.)

"Is that right? Well I'll be jiggered. I used to know a fellow, good friend of mine."

"From —— County?"

"Oh hell no, he wouldn't be caught dead in a place like that." He grinned. The girls had emerged from the place to which they had gone and looked much improved as a result of it. He took note of this, William did.

"My name," said William, enunciating plainly, "is *William J. Pefley*, and these people are with *me*."

"I figured."

"And we're here to sign up."

There was a short pause as the man went rifling hurriedly through his inventory of sarcasms. He seemed to have found one, too, but for some reason decided not to use it after all. He was not a large man, William was not, but had a certain demeanor to him. Next, taking up the pen, he signed for all four of them and paid with two single-dollar bills that vanished at first into the man's spatulate hand, and then his clothen purse. The pavilion extended down almost to the river, a distance of perhaps seventy-five yards in that direction. Already Jesse had taken some of his exhibits to a certain booth where he stood talking, or disputing rather, with a blond-headed fellow wearing a paisley vest. William went to them.

"He won't leave," Jesse said.

"No, sir; I got here first and it's mine."

William looked around at the innumerable cubicles, most of them unoccupied, that either of them could have taken.

"That's right," Mary said. "This here is *our* booth. No, it's always been that way."

William looked to Deborah, who confirmed it.

"There's lots of other places."

"Yes, sir; and so why don't y'all take one of 'em?"

"Why don't *you*!"

"No ma'm; I was here first."

William drew back to think about it. If there was any distinction among the booths, he couldn't see it.

"You'll have to leave," he said finally.

Jesse came forward. The quarrel had brought him out of his snit, so much so that he had begun fuddling wildly with his collar and buttons to keep them from trembling in plain open view. "How about you and me going outside?" he asked the boy. "Want to? I'll shoot you dead, sure will!"

"*Shoot* me?"

(The sarcastic man was enjoying this.)

"There's four of us!"

It was true that the fellow had already set out most of his items on display, commonplace artifacts, inferior by far to Jesse's. Next to a magnifying glass, a few dead insects lay on a pad of cotton in a tiny white box.

"You're going to shoot a fellow just so you can cheat him?"

"He will, too!" Mary said. "I know him better than you do."

The boy shook his head sadly, very disappointed that the world could have produced such people.

They had emptied the wagon and by seven-fifteen had set out the majority of the display. Rain, unfortunately, had gotten into the cotton samples and it was by no means possible to squeeze it dry without depreciating the appearance. More important to Jesse were the *seeds*, hundreds of them categorized by scientific name. He worked with them while the horses were being judged, fine-looking animals romping in a circle down by the river. Twice he exchanged glances with the blond-headed boy, who had completed his preparations and was glaring back sullenly from across the pavilion. The girls meantime had gone into the corner of the booth and were laying out the sorghum specimens on four sheets of glass. That was when the sarcastic man climbed on stage and after calling for silence, led the group in prayer.

The judges were four, middle-aged men and a woman dressed in black. Jesse, standing in the center of his booth with his arms behind his back, refused even to look at them. Better never to have come, but having come, better if the judging were finished already, the meeting dissolved, and himself at liberty to return his things to the wagon and for the family to be on its way. Indeed, he would have preferred to be passed over entirely and for the awards, all of them, to be given even to the pale boy who continued to stare back from across the floor.

To his left, a group of farmers stood whispering and grinning and passing around a bottle that tended to leak. Not one person had taken a serious look at Jesse's collections, a favorable sign suggesting that he would soon be able to leave the place without having brought down any attention upon himself. Deborah, it is true, continued to watch him worriedly, while as for the stolid fellow who had driven them here, he seemed to have no facial expression at all.

A certain length of time now went past. Outside, he could hear the sound of snarling and woe, evidence of the dog trials going on. The impulse came to him that perhaps he ought to witness that event and then when it was over, go directly home. Instead, he drew from his pocket a tiny tin box of *Rawleigh's Cathartic Pills* and swallowed one of the things before putting it away and then again taking it out again and removing yet another. He was sick, no question about it — too much rain, not enough sleep, and far too many strangers. And then, too, he could see that the judges had already arrived at the next booth and were wearing severe expressions.

He kept his eyes fixed on a far-away place. Even if the judges were to insult him out loud, still he'd make no move nor say anything. Still gazing off into the extreme distance, he took out his tobacco pouch and rolled a cigarette in a swatch of newsprint. The first man to his booth was a studious-looking sort of person, a banker or surveyor dressed in glasses with two very unalike lenses in them. Jesse could not divine what he was thinking and, of course, didn't greatly care. The second judge was a city woman of some kind continually writing at high speed in the disorganized notebook — William looked at it — that she carried. Mary was next — she had come up pretending to be a stranger and was gasping at the wonderful things on display. He did not like the fourth person, Jesse did not, who kept probing with his finger in the little boxes of bird eggs, as if to prove whether they were real. Jesse supposed that ten, perhaps fifteen minutes had gone by before the woman stopped writing suddenly and put away her pen.

"You must have had some help," she said.

It was true that he had had *some* help, most of it from William. "Yes m'am. He shore does know how to handle mules."

"Mules?" She waited for the explanation.

"Why these other people don't have *anything*," Mary said, indicating around at the pavilion. "Compared to *him*, I mean. Really, they shouldn't even be here."

Across the floor the sullen boy had gotten on tiptoes to see what was transpiring with the judges. Not so far away a yodeling contest was under way, a competition between auctioneers.

"You seem to have a lot of different species of cotton," the banker said when at last the noise abated. "That's good."

"Yes, but see how wet it is!"

"And all sorts of corn. Where in the world did you get holt of all that corn, boy?"

Jesse stepped forward, looked at the stuff, and then cleared his throat to speak. "It don't matter if corn gets wet," he said. "It don't hurt it none."

The judges nodded and looked at each other. The boy had also brought along a sizable collection of shotgun shells of various gauges, although these had nothing to do with the subject under review, narrowly speaking. The man who looked like a banker chuckled once or twice and then suddenly broke out into unrestrained laughter.

"Never seen so much stuff in all my life! Good God A'mighty boy, I'm just surprised you didn't bring a bunch of *manure* while you were at it. Comes in all sizes you know."

Mary made haste to open one of the honey jars. She had brought three little silver spoons and was disconcerted when one of the men instead dipped into the fluid with the same finger he had used to disorganize the hummingbird eggs.

"I don't mind having me a little dab of honey once in a while," he said, dipping twice more and cleaning it up with his tongue.

"Oh gosh. I brought these spoons on purpose, but he won't even use 'em!"

Already the chief judge, chuckling still, had begun to edge toward the following booth. He hadn't tried the honey. Indeed there were many things he had not inspected, nor had he written anything down.

"There they go," Jesse said. "I just hope we get home before dark." He gathered up two of the larger cartons and began to move off toward where the wagon was parked.

"You did good!" Mary said. "And she liked it a lot, that lady did."

"Nope."

William, who had been standing to one side, went to fetch the wagon. Clouds he saw, clouds as big as earth, though not of the rain-bearing type. Glad to be away from the crowd, he conversed briefly with the mules and then continued on toward the bright blue river that wended in and out of view. The girl had followed him for a certain distance and stood uncertain whether to continue or return to the fair. Seeing her there, William turned and went back to her.

"We ought to leave pretty soon."

She nodded.

"But first we need to put everything back in the wagon."

She agreed. He had seen her before of course, but never had he looked specifically into her *eyes*, as it were. It was easy to imagine a world in which she did not exist; he supposed therefore that she had been set down at this time and place for purposes that perhaps were hidden from them both. As if to verify it, he took out his watch and looked at it, never suspecting it marked the beginning of a thousand generations.

"Want to see the swans?"

There was a place where the current formed into a pool and where a family of black people was fishing seriously with bamboo poles that reached a good distance. Here, not far from shore, two swans had been circling each other all morning until at last they had gotten their necks grievously entwined. Now, slowly and slowly, they disengaged and got free again. They knew each other well.

William allowed the girl to go on watching for a short while and then ushered her downstream where the water was shallow and it could be seen that the floor was littered with red and yellow pebbles of various size. Standing just behind her, he could see that a wisp of hair had tumbled from her arrangement and was tapping at her cheek. Her profile was noble and calm, and he himself in a state of despair.

"It won't be long," he said, "and I'll be living in Elba, I reckon. It's like I said in my letter — I just can't afford *not* to go."

"Oh, I think you should."

"You do?"

"Why yes. You have to think about the future."

"I do, I think about it all the time."

"That's good. You're young and ambitious — everybody knows that. I think it's laudable."

"I could build a whole house, if I had the time. And lumber."

"See? How many other young men can say that?"

He thought about it. "I know one. But he won't never do it because he's too lazy."

"See? That's what I mean."

"'Course now, there's not much sense in building a fine new house if I don't never get married."

"No."

"And I can't get married if no one will marry me — that's the problem."

"Yes but you have to be patient. I'm sure *someone* would marry you."

"No, I was talking to a fellow last week. He doesn't think anyone would marry me either."

"Anyway, I know lots of people who never got married."

"*You'll* get married of course. Easy! All those visitors, and whatnot."

"Oh! If I wanted to marry *them*, why I'd just go ahead and get married. But I don't."

"How many people have asked you to marry 'em, I wonder? Dozens, I expect."

She said nothing. The anger that was rising in him was unjustified — he admitted it. "Is it dozens?"

"Oh look, that little boy caught a fish!"

"Your father, I bet he's real particular about people. He wouldn't let you marry just anyoldbody."

"No. I wouldn't let me either."

"And there's not a chance in the world that he would let you marry *me*, of course. No, he wants you to marry a *minister* or a newspaper man, or something."

"Ruth married a minister."

"Ruth?"

"She's my cousin."

He wanted to weep. He cared nothing for Ruth and only very slightly for Mary, Jesse, their parents, and the entire Agricultural Fair. The one person he did care about had just now gathered up a sweet gum ball of unusual size and was marveling at it. Suddenly he said this:

"Those fellows that want to marry you, you ever let 'em *kiss* you, I wonder?" It was his fourth social mistake, he blushed deeply. She looked back at him as if she had not understood the question.

"You'll like Elba," she said.

After the mules were fed and watered and the pavilion pulled down and folded away, William looked at his watch. They would not arrive home before dark, not even if they left at once, nor did he look forward to another night on the open road. There were hotels to be sure, and Montgomery was full of those.

"We could stay in a hotel," Mary said. (The four of them had come together and were conferring among the noise of people and animals and overburdened wagons setting out on long journeys to some of the furthermost parts of the state. William lifted his hat to a numerous family that had come all the way from Huntsville and now were going home again. Drawn by two white oxen, they could expect a slow but steady voyage.) "... hotel," Mary was saying.

"No," William replied slowly. "Your parents expect you home today."

"What?"

Impossible to converse in this place. They walked together to the middle of the field and began again to review their situation.

"It don't matter if we get there or don't get there," Jesse said, taking out a vial of calomel and sipping at it. "Besides, it's going to rain for sure and we'll just have to get all wet again anyway. I'm already sick."

"Listen, if we can get *here*, we can get *back*," Debbie said.

"...hotel."

William held up his hand to stop them. "We're leaving right now."

They jumped to it. Jesse had made up a litter for himself in the back of the wagon but was experiencing some difficulty with his too-long legs. William could *not* understand it, how that a girl who had been kissed as many times as Debbie would nevertheless choose to sit next to *him*. But instead of remarking about it, he climbed down, took the lead mule by its cheek strap and brought the wagon around to a better position for starting out. He just then saw that a thin man in a dark suit was running toward them across the field.

"I didn't know if it was you or not," the man said, struggling for breath. "My stars, you've won all the prizes, most of 'em, and you're *leaving*?"

Jesse sat up.

"Well shoot yeah. You came out *way* ahead — all that stuff and everything. They didn't even have to take a vote."

Embarrassed by it, Jesse lay back down again. As if he imagined that *she* had done the work, the man now came around to Deborah, who in turn pointed him to her brother.

"What's the matter with him?" the man asked.

"It's just the way he is."

"What, dudn't he want his medals? He won 'em fair and square."

It was a black velvet sachet they were being offered, about a foot in length and two inches thick. Mary peeped into the contents, but then quickly handed it off to Jesse who let it rest in his lap. He had seen these awards before, indeed had brought more than a few of them home with him in previous years.

"Look at that. Aren't you even going to open it!"

Slowly he got up onto his elbow and tried, uselessly, to pry open the box with one hand only. Mary had to help him. The container, also lined with velvet, held five great medals made seemingly of gold. He took one out, Jesse did, but then shortly returned it to its recess where it fell adroitly into place. The box had been designed for seven medals, and two were gone.

"Well my heavens alive, you can't expect to win *all* of 'em!" the man said. "That one there was for *bee keeping*, for Christ's sakes. They give it to Jim Lee."

"I keep bees."

"Well my heavens." He turned to William. "Never seen anything like it! Nobody wins five of these things, nobody. But *this* fellow, he just... I don't know."

"He's sick!" Mary said, adding then: "OK, he's not sick. But he *is* shy though."

"Shy."

"Yes."

"Your ordinary person would be jumping up and down right now. But not him."

William shook with the man and thanked him and then, in preparation for leaving, began speaking in undervoice to the mules. Mary continued to weigh one of the medals in her hand. Knowing as little as she did about gold, it was the foreign inscription that primarily entranced her. It was clear weather in the south and indeterminate in the east, and for the moment it seemed not to be raining anywhere. Itself the fair was nine-tenths empty now, with only two or three families still picnicing on the grounds.

They drove hurriedly through the enormous city, coming out in safety on the other side. Jesse had taken his prize and hidden it and he and Mary were sitting in the back with their four legs hanging out. William quickly tired of the songs they were singing but chose not to say anything at this time. He had come to think that the girl next to him was perhaps older than he had realized, owing to all the things that she had done. And yet when he turned to look at her, she looked about the same as in October. To stay in good standing with her parents he needed to get these people back to their own home and soon, before the worst of the darkness filled the road.

They passed a rider who had pulled off to one side and gone to sleep in the saddle. He too was sleepy, William was, but preferred to pay no attention to it. Never did he smile and never complained, and if need be, he was prepared to go on forever without any sleep at all. Up ahead a community now came into view, a place of seven or eight well-made homes with lattice work around the porches and new-painted fences running up and down the contours of the somewhat hilly land. William slowed. Here things were as they should be, save where one of the palings was out of square. Calm, rational, full of right angles, it was a place in which a man could get a good night's sleep and never be disturbed by dreams. He hated to leave it, especially when he espied a Negro settlement looming up just ahead.

This next place comprised, not homes, but satires of them set up, as he had to suppose, for comical effect. No one could have counted the number of repairs that needed to be carried out here, but instead of repairs, the one individual that he could actually see was slumbering on his porch. The next house — and he could see clear through it, from the front door to the back — the next house had twenty people in it, all of them screaming out loud and jumping up and down. A broken-down cart lay in the roadway and twenty yards further the remains of a hog.

He drove past quickly, refusing to let his indignation overwhelm this pretty day. He estimated the time and then took out his watch to see how accurately he had guessed. These clouds, that sun, such clouds and sun and the coming of late afternoon accompanied by an Alabama wife — these ought to be enough to get him through the required ordeals of a longer than average life.

"My granddaddy had *two* wives," he said suddenly without obvious reason.

"Well that happens sometimes," the girl said. "Just as long as he didn't have them at the same time."

He turned and looked and, finding that she was grinning wickedly in his direction, tried to make a laughing noise of his own

"No," he said slowly. "The first one died."

"Oh."

"And then the other one died, too."

"Gracious."

"And then he married Ramona."

"Ramona. But you said he had *two* wives."

"Why, yes." And then, slowly: "I didn't say that was *all* he had."

She was now laughing out loud at him, the first time he had seen her doing so while in that particular blouse. He felt a sudden onset of desire which however he put aside after a short struggle. She had some deviltry in her, no question about it, and yet he believed that a certain amount of that might be excusable, provided the rest of her was good. And then, too, the declining sun was touching down upon her hair, which sparkled now and again in gleeds of gold and brown.

Two miles further William slowed, turned into a populous cemetery that paralleled the highway for a distance of about 200 yards, and then drove to the tomb of his uncle, assassinated in 1864. He wanted no one to come with him as he climbed down and then strode to a clump of trees where the man lay buried among four or five other soldiers of his Division. Down below in the ground his uncle had turned to bones, a spine perhaps and a few ribs that must remain where they were until he was made whole again. This whole area was busy with the spirits of people, some of them hovering overhead, some resting in the earth, and some just visiting on wings of thought. So far as he knew he had never done anything that was seriously wrong and he was content to stand here now in full view of the dead and be judged by them.

"I'm here, uncle," he said, talking half-aloud. (It was why he had wanted no one to come with him.) "Yes, sir, been to Montgomery but now I'm going home. Be dark pretty soon. I'm thinking I might get me a wife, too, like you did." Suddenly he put up his hand to stop the man. "No, sir, I'm not saying *this* girl will marry me, and I'm not saying I'd ask her to, neither. Not saying I would, and not saying I wouldn't." And then: "I know you can't see her; she's right over there." Himself, he could see her very well, and saw it when she turned to peer in his direction through the gathering night. As pretty as she was, she would never be this pretty again, and it was easy for him to foresee the deterioration that must follow hard upon until she, too, grew old and full of dust and also lay in the ground.

Darkness had settled down over Alabama. No sound of tree frogs came to them, not in winter, nor crickets or any other thing except for a single owl who continued to hoot at them from the protection of the woods. It was a pale moon tonight, somewhat shriveled and smaller than ordinary. Meantime Mary, by far the best person among them for sleeping, was lying atop a pile of quilts with her mouth opened to the stars. He could not see Jesse, William could not, but assumed that he was with them still.

"He's not feeling well," Deborah told him.

"Well, you won't have any trouble — just keep along this road and you'll be home pretty soon."

"Yes I know, but..."

"I have to be at the store in the morning." He pointed to where the road branched off in the moonlight. He could move much faster by night, he believed, and do it in greater safety when the population was mostly at home and in bed.

"What are you thinking! You can't *walk* all that way, my gracious!"

"Not but seventeen miles."

"There he goes," Jesse said, "leaving. Look Mary, he's leaving."

Mary was asleep.

"Just keep along this road."

"Yes, but...!"

"You've got your brother. He won't let nothing happen."

"Oh! You don't know him the way we do."

William pulled out his watch and compared the time against the position of the moon. Jesse meantime had drawn himself up and was staring palely into the woods. William shook with him and then went around to Deborah.

"You'll be all right," he said.

"But what if something happens to *you*?"

William snorted. "No, people like that are already in bed by now. Anyhow, I know how to walk real quiet."

He shook with her, the first time he had done so. It was true that her hand was thin and rather like a glove, but was not so small that she couldn't hold the reins. Now, taking the more intelligent of the two mules by the harness, he led the animal forward a few paces and sent the wagon on its way.

TWELVE

Three weeks more went by before he transferred over to the town called Elba in southeastern Alabama. Land was cheap there and he was immediately able to acquire nine acres that lay over against the river on one side and marched for a distance of about eight hundred rods along the city boundary. The place had some good pines on it, but few deciduous trees of any real importance. At night, walking out into the middle of his new property, he marveled at the height of those pines, like manifest people reaching eagerly skyward with very long arms.

He had paid absolute cash for the place, leaving him with just thirty-four dollars in bills, five in script, and a pound and half, approximately speaking, of large and small metal coins. With these resources he went around to the house where dwelt the sawmill owner:

"I can pay thirty dollars right now," William said. "Or, if you'll wait a year, I'll make it forty."

"What?"

"For the boiler."

The man came out onto the porch. "What time is it?"

"It's in pretty poor shape, that thing, and I'm going to need a full-time man just to get it up and running."

"Shape? Wait a minute." He withdrew. There were two women in that room and William was able to see them more and more distinctly as his eyes adjusted to the dark. He lifted his hat and nodded to them courteously. One was smoking a cigarette, the other was dressed in a robe, and both had their hair up in curlers. The house was *not* well-made and William sensed that the underlying joists were suffering beneath the combined weight of the furniture and people. That was when the man came back and, holding up his finger as if to test the breeze, said:

"Wait a minute. Are you the same fellow what..."

"Yes."

"... about a month ago?"

"Be better for me if I could wait a year. That way I'd have my brick mill all set up and I could pay a lot more than just thirty dollars."

"Jesus. You come around here. Today's Sunday, I guess you know."

William reeled. He had lost account of the days, the first time he had done so. And then, too, he knew that he was scarcely presentable, owing to the nights he had spent sleeping out-of-doors on his property. It was too late to get to church, nor did he know precisely which church would finally be his. Again he took off his hat.

"All right, I'll make it thirty-two. But that's about as far as I can go."

One of the women, the older of the two, came to the screen and stood looking out at him. "He's offering you *money* for that old thing. Take it. It ain't no good anyway."

"Well don't tell *him* that for Christ sakes! Ain't no good, she says."

William drew out his watch and looked at it. A small sputtering dog had been striving for the last half-minute to force his way out into the open air; suddenly, noticing William for the first time, he screamed out loud and retreated into the depths of the house. He was able, William was, to reach his thirty-two dollars through the opening and into the hands of the woman.

Having fouled this Sabbath day, William drove to the levee and crossed over it. Here large numbers of Negroes were living together in a community of some ten or eleven shacks, fragile structures coated out of the same can of bright yellow paint, now seriously flaking. He rode slowly, passing a woman transporting a jar on her head and then, next, a full albino hastening to get out from under the sun. The man William sought would have to be strong and middle-aged, god-fearing and humble to the core.

"Looking for a man," he said to the woman who had come out to sweep her porch with a broom of sage grass bound together in string.

"Yas, suh. Him's at church."

"Church?" (He had found his man.)

"Yas, suh."

"Y'all got any mules?"

"Yas, suh."

"Got any sons?"

"Yas, suh. Got two."

"Which church?"

He drove straight to it, a ramshackle building leaning perilously to one side. Even now it might be saved, provided only someone were there to save it. Waiting before the church in bright light he began to grow impatient with the speed of time (always too slow for him), and the tedious persistence of the passing of minutes. The music, at least, was good, nor had he ever impugned the singing of Negroes. Again he drew out his watch and looked at it.

The sons turned out too small and the man, who was slow to understand, proved balky. His voice had a sorrowful sound. "Don't got no mules," he said.

"Yes you do. Bring 'em both. And bring your wagon, too."

"Yas, suh."

Dismounting, William hoisted the younger of the sons onto the horse and then climbed back into the saddle. He had three hours and some minutes and not a moment more. Church was mostly over and by now he could identify all sorts of Negroes loitering on their porches or trundling down the crest of the levee, some of them more capable-looking than the person he had actually chosen. He called to one in particular who, however, ignored him. He had just three hours and sixteen minutes of light along with perhaps thirty years more of life, barely time enough to accomplish something before he must perish and go to judgment.

He rode back in haste to the drunkard's house and took from him the key that he should have taken earlier.

"I don't know what I'm going to do with myself," the man said, "without my boiler. I gave it away too cheap."

"Yes. I was surprised you'd let it go for that."

"You have to have a license."

"No, sir. My place is just over the line."

"Oh. Right now I'm wondering how come you got Marcus sitting up there in that big old saddle?"

The woman came out. "I'm a *real* good cook," she said. "After you get your business all up and running I mean."

William thanked her and took off his hat. He had just three hours and two minutes and the sun, always unenthusiastic this time of year, was deteriorating only too quickly as it fell.

He came to the shed and unlocked the door. The apparatus was smaller than he remembered and lacked one of the hinges needed to hold the door. And yet it looked to him as if the thing might still be capable of work, to judge by the heap of smooth-cut lumber waiting to be collected. But would it win him a wife, this thing, as also a house and business and a position in the village, or had he made a mistake?

He had hoped for adult men; instead the wagon, when at last it arrived, was loaded down with further children. William went to the father and looked into his face from about three inches away.

"It's a fact," he said, "that I haven't lived here very long. But I can always tell when somebody is trying to get out of doing work."

The man looked down.

"I was going to pay you, too."

"Yas, suh. I been feeling kind of poorly."

"No you haven't. Now bring that wagon closer. This way you won't have to tote it so far."

The mules, too, were balky, nor was William so certain that the vehicle would bear up beneath the weight. Better to have one full-grown man than all these children, who were too fascinated by the project to be of any help.

"You lift that side Horace," (he didn't know the man's real name), "and I'll pick it up over here."

"Yas, suh."

The instrument itself weighed three hundred pounds, but owing to William's great luck on this day the thing was positioned almost precisely on a level with the cart. Together the two men shoved it forward until it settled in the bay. The Negro expressed surprise; William, however, was more concerned about the falling sun.

"We need to hurry Charlie, if we're going to get there before dark."

"Yas, suh. No, suh, it's too late now."

"Hurry."

He did know how to rouse his mules, the Negro did. William watched with the first admiration he had experienced that whole day. Meantime the sun was getting smaller and its warmth, such as it was, was about as weak as he had ever seen it.

They moved in stately fashion, the white man and Negroes, the mules, instrument, and children. After two blocks of it William began to feel his exasperation climbing, but managed to push it down again. Never would he understand it, how that some people yearned to accomplish something with their lives and others didn't. In addition, one of the mules had picked up a limp and might not be able to proceed all the way to William's acres. They could have moved so much faster, had only the children agreed to travel under their own power. And meantime the sun, the sun.

It proved impossible to take the machine down from the wagon without first breaking it into parts, another tedious and lengthy process that required a heavier wrench than any of William's. The children meantime had

begun one by one to drift away, either because they had grown bored with
it or because night was coming in. This was the short season and another
three months must still go by before William could have the sort of days
that he needed for his projects.

"Be dark soon," he said.

"Yas, suh. Dark *now*. And me, I aint et nothing since mawning!"

William, who disbelieved in the practice of eating every day, made
no remark. One single child remained to them, who had crawled into the
boiler. It might rain, it might not; in any case, it was clear to William that
he'd cut no wood till tomorrow at the soonest. Accordingly, he took out his
purse and paid the man (who seemed displeased with it), a good deal more
than he had merited. It was the usual way — to appear disappointed with
no matter what one was actually given.

"Need to get started early tomorrow," William said. "You can leave
your tools here."

"No, suh! I got to work for Mr. Wade 'morrow."

William stopped and looked at him evenly.

"No, suh! He be mad at me!"

"Eight o'clock, you hear?"

He managed to get the instrument back together in one piece again
before the incoming gloom turned to outright night. His horse meantime,
who had fed on nothing all that day, was alternating between fits of apathy
and sleep. His lantern, too, was low and beginning to flutter; taking it with
him, William retreated into the shack, secured the door, and lay on the
blanket for a short time to give his mind a chance to clear.

His saddle bags held two meals, a remaining blanket, a .32 revolver,
and some dozen letters, more or less, inscribed on lavender paper. He especially prized the message the girl had sent to him in December, a three-page
document in which she had come near to expressing herself freely, as it almost seemed, before then changing her mind at the last minute. He liked to
spread it flat upon the table and try to guess at the emotion that had caused

the handwriting to vary like that when she broached some of the subjects that they had spoken of before. But how many other such letters had she not already written to how many others like him?

He was reduced to writing with a pencil on brown paper, he who in times to come would possess all the ink and as many pens and sheets of stationery as anyone in town. But first he jotted down a short note to Joe Butler in which he enclosed a drawing of his property, an advance payment of seven dollars, and a summons for the man to come and join him. Too late he realized that he had used his last stamp on Joe and had saved nothing for the girl. Nevertheless he wrote her anyway, using the opportunity to compose a more detailed picture of his land and contraption and the home he intended to build. Finding that he had some knack for it (drawing), he sketched the horse as well and enclosed it along with a joke or two about his present threadbare condition. Truth was, he wanted to describe his poverty from the start, expecting to reap all that much more credit for his achievements later on. "The children will want their own bedroom," he wrote before he realized fully what he had said. Having erased that, he said: "I've haven't never built a house all by myself before. But I can."

THIRTEEN

They arrived home in safety from the fair, just as William had guaranteed. Three miles from town, Jesse sat up suddenly and began to glance around. It always gave him the most extreme pleasure to arrive late at night and find the curtains pulled back, the dogs waiting, and a carbide lamp glimmering greenly behind the glass. The world was large and full of cities, but as for him he never felt right about things until he were in *this* county and *this* land, which is to say either the sixty acres that lay across the highway or the eighty that ran down to the lake and back.

She had done well in bringing them home, his sister had, and he was content to let her feed and put the mules to bed while he set about removing his products from the wagon. He worked quietly, intending that his younger sister might go on sleeping all night in the open wagon (he grinned) if she would. No. The old man had come to the back door and was waiting impatiently for their report.

They gathered in the parlor.

"Late, you're late," the father said. "Very late. Mr. Pefley, he *promised* me that…"

"No, daddy, he did good. He took us and he brought us back, and nothing happened."

"Brought you back? Don't look to me like he brought you back."

"No, daddy, he came with us all the way to Maudry's Corner."

"That is a *considerable* distance from here, that corner is."

"No, daddy."

"I'm tired," Deborah said, yawning.

"Now if we'd of gone with you, your mother and me, why then everything would have been fine. But oh no."

"Well I think it was right generous of him," his wife said, "to go all that way. Not every young man, you know, would... Did he say anything?"

"Well sure. We were there all day."

"Yes, you were there all day. And *I* was in the kitchen."

"I still don't see why that fellow couldn't of...."

"Did he say anything about the *future* — that's what I'm asking I guess."

"Yup," said Jesse, "he did."

The whole room turned to look at Jesse who, however, had finished speaking. The younger girl spoke up:

"Now I have been sitting here all this time and nobody has even asked if Jesse won anything. Not one single person."

"Did he say when he's coming back for a visit?"

"We could write and ask him," Jesse proposed.

"No, that's just the way it is in this family. Go to Montgomery, come home, nobody cares."

Deborah rose and was about to go to bed when her mother caught her. Jesse, meantime, was speaking to himself in tones of dark amazement: "Seventeen miles. It's dark out there and he's walking real quiet. Walking right now."

He retired to his room and was preparing for bed when he chanced to catch sight of himself in the looking glass. He was a pale sort of person, Jesse, rather thin, and although he did not usually think of himself in these terms, his hair also was pale and thin. Soon he was hopelessly bogged down in the mirror, appalled to find that he had eyes that were watching themselves watching. That clock on the table — had it also been sent forth into the world, not merely to count the time, but to count the counting? He sincerely hoped not.

He climbed into bed, lay there briefly, and then rose and checked on the five recumbent medals preening in their box. Given the silence inside the house and the absence of crickets without, he could be confident of getting no sleep that night. A dog was barking on someone else's farm while further still he could hear a train probing deep into the countryside before then turning and running back out again.

He went downstairs and stepped to the barn where in spite of his precautions he touched off a disturbance among the hens. The larger animals were silent and in any case were accustomed by now to these interruptions of his. The night was not so cold, he said to himself, that he shouldn't be able to sleep in this place, provided only that he borrow a blanket or two from the horses and then go up into the loft where...

He slept until five the next morning. There would be no peace for him however until he clambered down from the loft and fed the hogs. But hardly had he finished before the sun came up and began to infiltrate the barn with narrow rays. It assisted him in the feeding of the chickens at the end of which time he walked to the door and flung it open with great aplomb. It *was* the sun outside, it *had* climbed high. Studying it more narrowly, it looked to him like a bladder sagging with molten gold. Here, too, were the buildings that he knew so well, all of them still in their places after the long black night. He greeted the birds, especially a little yellow specimen who stood just overhead grasping the branch in its fingers as it strove to form English-language words with a beak that did not lend itself to that. The moon, meantime, had gone away, leaving behind a stain that would persist for another hour or two at least.

He strolled to the end of the land and, after hesitating briefly, stepped out onto his neighbor's field and began to work his way through the cattle that only begrudgingly gave way to him. This place had numerous roosters, all of them now yelling off in all directions from several rooftops at once. He waved to a farmer who stopped what he was doing and waved back in return. In front a creek came up, the sort of creek he had been able effortlessly to leap when he was young. This time he stepped across on a rock. It meant that he had trespassed over onto Jacob Hardy's land, a thin stretch of territory with nothing on it but thistles, a collapsed windmill, and the remains of a burnt-down house. He crossed quickly and then went down into the edge of the woods where he could travel without being seen. A moment later he had come to a place among loblollies and cedar trees where he kept a supply of matches and cigarettes along with a mason jar with molasses in it. Seated in his usual place, he could see far, but especially the hundred and some twenty-odd acres that belonged to the Sunquist family. Wait here long enough and he'd see the cows exiting his neighbor's barn in single file for a long day's excursion among the haystacks. Wait further and he'd see the girl.

He had to wait even further than that. An hour went by as he watched, first, two squirrels and then, next, a thin stalk of smoke rising from some distant field. He knew nothing about impatience and would have been pleased to go on waiting forever, had it come to that. He chuckled at the sun, which took on different shapes and sizes as it climbed the sky. His thoughts turned to William, who had been walking quietly homeward all this time. And then his mind turned to the girl coming toward him. He waited until she drew near.

"I didn't know if you was coming."

"I couldn't get away," she said.

It seemed to him there was nothing left to say. She *was* here now, and so was he. Moreover she was wearing a red jacket that he particularly liked, and a scarf that had been a gift from him. Came then the old feeling that one day would finally drive him insane — that she was but an aspect of the earth and pasture and had come forth into the light for a few minutes that he might look upon her before she disappeared.

"Did you win any prizes Jesse? In Montgomery I mean?"

He laughed bitterly. "Oh for God's sakes. They aren't about to give me any prizes!"

"They gave you one last year."

"Not if you're me. No, ma'am, not if you're from *this* county, oh no, no, no. You have to be from *their* county if you expect to win anything in Montgomery."

"I just knew you were going to win *something*."

"Ha! Anyhow I don't care. I just do it to make people happy."

"Did you show 'em those little bugs and everything?"

He waved it away. He did not wish to talk about bugs when he had but minutes with the girl. "I'm fixing to take you into these woods. So's I can *kiss* you."

"Yes, I figured you'd say something like that sooner or later. You are *the most awful...*"

She went with him however. Thanks to the evergreens, he did not have far to go to bring her out of sight of the world. He gave thanks, too, that she was not very pretty, and so could be for him. They kissed.

"What do you imagine your father would say, if he could see us doing this?"

She thought about it. "Well, I guess he'd be furious."

"Sure he would! Your mama, too."

"I suppose."

"'Goddang that boy!' — *that's* what they'd say."

"They probably would."

"And all these people" — he swept the whole countryside with a wave of his arm — "*all* of 'em. Shoot, they'd be so shocked and surprised they wouldn't believe it."

"They'd faint. I know ole Miss Casey would."

"Yeah, and Charlie Freed."

(They shivered with the danger of it and kissed.)

"I'm thinking you ought to take that jacket off."

"Oh sure, and then what? It's a good thing it's winter or else you'd be... I don't know what all you've got in your mind but I can tell you this much, that..."

They kissed and then went apart and sat in two different places to allow their nerves to settle. He let a minute go by before asking:

"Did you get some more of that medicine?"

"Yes."

"What did he say?"

"He said to take all of it, and if it don't work then I got to go to Atlanta."

"What!"

"They got a doctor there."

He groaned. Once in Atlanta, she might stay. Or come back a different person.

"*I'll* take you there."

"No, we're going on the train."

He did not like to think of her among persons from other counties. "I'll come with you."

"No. Besides, I'm coming straight back."

"*Now* you're talking. And we'll get married next year."

She nodded vaguely. "When you're twenty?"

"No, when you're eighteen."

"But I won't be eighteen for two years! You know it's true."

He groaned. "OK, we'll get married when *Mary* is eighteen."

"Mary? Golly, that ain't going to do *us* any good. I just don't know about you; you're getting crazier and crazier all the time."

"OK, we'll get married in spring. Then you won't have no excuse about taking your jacket off. And everything else, too."

Horrified, they kissed.

He did not wish to be seen on his homeward trip; accordingly, he ran around to where the woods petered out on the northern side and then cut across to McBurney's field. The sky was white and the clouds, which had not moved in several days, looked like curds and whey. One single beam, about twenty-four inches in circumference, touched down harmlessly at a point well off to Jesse's right. He thought he perceived a bone sticking up out of the ground but continued on for another thirty yards before stopping and coming back for it. He knew of course that Indians had dwelt here once and he had been hoping that he might come across one of them someday; instead, the bone belonged to a cow.

It was the worst time of day, the world flooded with a granulated sort of light that had pushed through the cloud-filter overhead. It had been like this in the time of the first man, a pathetic creature all covered with hair who had spent his entire life looking uselessly for another like himself. "Must of have figured he was the *last* man instead of the *first*," said Jesse to himself, snorting out loud at the thought of it.

The creek ran more deeply here and made a noise as it washed over the pebbles. A crawfish had put himself beneath a rock where Jesse could see one of its whiskers sticking out. But even more interesting were the smaller things, germs and whatnot tumbling head over heels in the current. He simply could not imagine the sort of experience it was to be like one of these. For some time he watched carefully while trying to decipher the pattern, if they had one, of their lives.

He never liked to go for more than three or four hours without some measure of sleep; accordingly, he got down now and after stretching out each limb and spreading it flat, lay looking up at the white sun. A few minutes of this and he began to make out the hills and seas of iridescent glass that ran across the surface of that planet.

FOURTEEN

William rose up early the next morning and after putting himself into order walked hurriedly to the center of town. No one knew him, not yet, and when he entered the bank and took off his hat, he could not immediately identify which man was in charge, whether the bald one at the desk or the worried-looking person standing at the window with his hands behind his back.

"Pefley's the name," he said, going to this latter individual. (They shook.) "Should I talk to *you*, or *him*?"

"Well sir, I guess that depends upon what you want to talk about. If you want to talk *savings*, why then you talk to me. But if you want..." William brushed it away. "Need to borrow five hundred dollars."

"Do?"

"Yes, and after two years is up, I'll bring you a thousand dollars. Now if I don't have a thousand dollars at that time — I expect to have it — then you can take my saw."

"Old man's McClary's saw?"

"No, sir. Mine."

"Ah. And so you've gone and set it up over there, have you, in the middle of that swamp?"

William looked back at him evenly. It was not all swamp, not altogether, his land was not. His eyes took on a metallic look.

"Well, you might be right," the banker went on. "The town *could* grow in that direction and, who knows, maybe someday — it's possible. Now this five hundred dollars, that's a right smart of money. And by the time it falls due, why your saw is liable to be all worn out!"

"No, sir; I wouldn't allow that."

"Or even sooner. Now if it was me, but it isn't, hell I'd give you the money right now. But it isn't, and that's just the way it is. But I tell you what Mr. Pelfrey, let's go back here in my office."

William followed him back, the first time he had been in an office of this caliber. Apart from two or three photographs and a globe of the world of about the size of a cantaloupe, the man's desk had nothing on it. Suddenly the banker took out a pad and pencil and began doing some mathematics that ran over onto the next page.

"Five hundred, you say. Two years."

"Yes, sir."

"Well, that seems fair. But I wouldn't be able to take that old saw for collateral, Mr. Pelfrey, just couldn't. Boiler's no good. And I wouldn't want to be standing next to you when it blows up neither."

William looked back at him calmly. "I pay my debts. Always do. But if I don't, why then I wouldn't care to own any land."

"Wouldn't care to hold on to his land, he says. Well now, that seems reasonable. Yes." (They shook again. William noted this detail — that the man was wearing a heavy ring with a cobra on it with two tiny red diamonds for eyes.)

He took his money, signed some papers, and then went straightway across to the bank across the road where a much more elderly sort of person, more dignified and better dressed, was in charge. They shook slowly, each man looking for integrity in the other and believing that he had found it.

"I admire anyone," the old man started out, "who's got the gumption to do business..." (he made a tired gesture in the direction of the other bank) "... with *those* people."

"Need to take out a loan."

"We can see everything that goes on over there you understand. And he can see over here. Matter of fact, he's looking right now."

"Five hundred dollars is what I need."

"Five." He wrote it down slowly and then, taking out a key, wasted several minutes trying to get his drawer open. "Tell me you're fixing to set up a *brick-making business* here in town."

"I have collateral."

"Collateral? Oh, I don't know about that. It's got a bad boiler and anyway we don't generally operate that way. You expect to pay it back, don't you?"

"I'll go to hell if I don't."

"See? That's a whole lot better than collateral. He's still looking."

William went with him to a cabinet in the extreme rear of the building and waited as one by one the banker opened and went rifling through three or four over-full drawers. His eye caught sight of what he took to be a hoard of high-grade bonds, judging from the gilt and elaboration that ran around the edges. To possess those bonds, or even just a few of them — it was a more abstract and more advanced form of wealth than anything, certainly, that ever William had owned. Land and machinery and the rest of it were but first steps toward the ownership of bonds.

"Yes," said the man, "bonds. You're not ready for that yet, Mr. Pefley, and you might not be ready for a long time. After all! I was near about fifty before I... Here, take a look."

William took the topmost bond into his own hand and held it as if it were a saucer in danger of spilling over. He knew almost nothing about government matters; he did however know that these things had a way of increasing in value without the owner doing any work.

"Now this one here belongs to Mr. Jernigan. See there where he's got his name on it? And that number there, they got a record of that number up there in Washington D. C."

There was a dignity to these documents, printed as they were in shades of grey. And then, too, they were all of the same size exactly and tended to line up perfectly, one on top the other, where they lay. After this, the five hundred dollars failed to give the same satisfaction that he had experienced on the other side of the road.

He signed and put the money in his vest and after taking a short drink of whiskey with the banker — (he allowed himself this on some occasions) — came out onto the street at about 9:45 and headed to the Post Office. Inside, the sheriff was conversing with a crowd of men. All fell silent when William took out a hundred-dollar bill for the four stamps that he required.

"I can't make change for something like that!" said the clerk, an emaciated man whose face was also as thin as a stamp.

The sheriff came up. "Goddamn it Clarence, give the man his goddamn stamps. He'll pay you. Hell, he'll probably come back and pay you before the day's over."

William was nonplussed. He was a stranger here and yet the sheriff had come forward of his own volition and done a favor for him. He kept a list, did William — it wasn't long — of people who had dealt kindly with him over the years. On the other hand, the man had used the worst language possible.

"I'll pay you this afternoon," William said.

"See? You can't ask better than that. Now give him his goddamn mail, Clarence."

He received it quickly, a light blue envelope with something in it. He was not accustomed to giving thanks to people; nevertheless he turned now to the sheriff and made a signal that could have been interpreted as an expression of appreciation.

He walked two blocks, went into the dry goods store, strolled down the aisle and came out the other side. His knife had two blades in it, one of them an ideal tool for opening envelopes made of delicate paper. This time the ink was paler than usual and tended to vanish in the color of the stationery. It surprised him that the girl's mother had added a statement of her own, a four-page message in which she invited him for a visit and then went on to describe again the family's appreciation for what he had done. The girl herself had little to say, perhaps because her mother had been standing just next to her at the time. In addition to the messages there was an enclosed newspaper article bearing a portrait of a morose-looking Jesse in his black suit:

The exhibit was declared the most complete, the most artistic, and the most general of the entire exposition, it being upon these points that the judges decided the contest. Contained in the showing were seven different varieties of cotton, on the stalk, in the lint, and seed accompanying; also fifty-two varieties of corn on the ear and on stalk; four varieties of sugar cane, in the raw plant and made into syrup; a large number of pumpkins and kershaws, declared to have been the finest on exhibition; honey in the comb and extracted, as well as bees-wax; twenty-four varieties of hay, loose and in the bale;[1] seventeen varieties of peas, shelled and in the hull; grains of every description in the sheath and threshed; ribbon, green, and red syrups, wines and fruit juices, and all kinds of fruits and vegetables, including four varieties of Japanese persimmons, which attracted wide attention among other things shown. There were samples of conserved and canned fruits of every kind grown in Alabama, all in perfect condition, along with entomological specimens of considerable interest and importance. The exhibit attracted beyond a doubt, more attention than any other agricultural showing in the building at Vandiver Park. And while Mr. Greland Rees was a close competitor in several respects, the judges declared Mr. Naftel's exhibit as the most complete in every detail, and tendered to him accordingly a majority of five of the commemorations granted this year.

He read it through three times, William did, and then put it away in his wallet. He had not really expected a man of that type to come away with any awards at all, far less to have been given such attention in a newspaper.

---

1   They had brought no hay.

FIFTEEN

He separated some of his money and in the late winter of that year began to build his home. Given his abilities, he was able in advance to see what it would look like and could predict with fair accuracy the features that were most likely to appeal to a wife. It was for her use that he put in a closet, a long, narrow chamber with nearly as much area as the bedroom itself. It would need to be big enough, that closet, to hold her wardrobe and the children's toys, the jewels and family papers and anything else she might choose to bring. Thinking of it, he got to his feet and paced about nervously within his one-room shack. The Negro named Joe Butler had arrived four days earlier and already had a cabin made from the bark and branches of the pines they had felled — a more solid and rain-resistant structure than William's own. Throwing a blanket around himself — (it was March now) — he went out into the night, walked the short distance to Joe's place and then called to him through the canvas curtain that functioned as a door.

"That porch, it needs to go around the whole house," he said, pulling the man out into the night and using his finger to draw in the sand. "Now the joists, I want 'em twelve inches apart, Joe. Not eighteen. Twelve."

"Yas, suh."

"I wont have any two-by-fours in *my* house, no sir."

"No, suh! Lord no."

"Now the sooner you get started, the sooner we can get this business up and running and..." He stopped. The black man had closed his eyes and appeared to be about to go back to sleep again.

"... sooner we get started, why the sooner you can bring your family here. Look over there at those elms, Joe. That whole area could be yours. Four acres, five maybe."

The man came awake.

"You do the cutting" — (he pointed to the saw which sat in moonlight like a crouching animal) — "and I'll get the business. We're going to be rich, Joe, you and me. Well anyway I'll be rich, and when *I'm* rich, shoot, you're going to be the happiest nigger anywhere around here."

Joe grinned. The blueprint in the sand had taken on the same gables and fretwork seen in the original drawing, as also four bedrooms and the wrap-around porch. He was not a whimsical man, William was not, he didn't have time for it and yet, tonight, he added the picture of a cat sleeping on the porch.

"She loves that cat."

"Yas, suh."

"You do the work Joe, and I'll provide the money."

"Yas, suh. Don't be talking 'bout no *money*, Mr. William, cause you're liable to *lose* it if you ain't too careful."

"Don't you worry about that, Joe. I keep it in a good place."

Joe Butler looked off into the distance, muttering bitterly in a voice that seemed to be addressed to the night. "Says he keeps it in a *good* place. Lord, Lord." And then in louder voice: "Why that's the first place they're going to look, Mr. William!"

William said nothing. He was not accustomed to listening to the advice of others and was opposed to it on principle.

The land had good trees on it, although they tended to stand rather too far apart from one another, particularly in places that were damp. And then, too, they had only one lantern and a few candles between them, which even when added together gave but a feeble light. It was the most exhausting form of work ever devised, to fell a great tree with a gap-toothed cross-cut saw with missing teeth; each time William drew the blade to *his* side, the error

other man pulled it back. A half hour of this and it became a question as to which would be the first to quit. He was wearing gloves at least, William was, whereas the other man was not.

"Where're your gloves, Joe?" he asked, halting momentarily.

"Ain't got none."

The moon was running in and out of the clouds, sometimes giving aid to the lantern and candles. The men knew of course that they were being watched and that the animals of the forest, whom William now also considered his own personal possessions, had gathered around to see what they were doing. Deep was the night and rich with insects. A train could be heard yelling in the distance and nearer at hand the sound of a preliminary cricket that had come awake a little too early this year. Soon enough the woods would be full of them, yea, and tree frogs, too.

By 1:45 he had felled his first elm, had hitched the mules to it and pulled it to the saw. He didn't really expect the machine to work properly, not immediately anyway, and was taken aback when the fire blazed up brightly and the fuel began to turn to steam. At first he could count the rotations, until the disc began to spin at too high speed. Joe, who had backed off into the edge of the forest, came forward now and helped to leverage the log into the cradle.

Compared to human labor, this was a far better way to reduce a tree to boards and planks. He marveled at it, the efficiency, the speed, the way the slabs fell apart, almost as if they had been separated years ago and only kept together in the meantime by an envelope of bark. Joe, he saw, was grinning happily in the candlelight. As for William, who almost never grinned, he was thinking of the money, the boards and planks, his new home and everything that these portended.

They had toppled four large pines and were at work on a fifth when the first light of the sun wormed its way into the forest and began to ricochet among the trees. He wanted to drop to his knees in worship of it, but was constrained by the presence of another human man. He had predicted rain but began to change his mind when he saw the clouds had thinned out and taken on a paler color. There was no doubt but that they were on the verge of spring. He watched as two smiling crows climbed repeatedly to a level in the sky and then went jumping off again. William kept his eye upon them and the brightening woods, and then went and yelled through the noise into Joe Butler's ear:

"Just keep working."

The man nodded.

It was but a short stroll to town and when he got there William saw that the place was full of noise that came from his own property. The Post Office was closed and of the two banks only one was open. He saluted the sheriff, who seemed not to understand that daylight had blown away the shadows where he'd been lurking. A mule-drawn wagon passed slowly down the road driven by a confused-looking man wearing one of the town's six or seven pairs of glasses. He knew, William did, that he had been assigned to this era and that he had quite as good a chance of making large accomplishments here as if he had lived during his grandfather's day, or the time of the Prophets.

A church was going up on the southeastern corner of the courthouse square but William had a poor opinion of the lumber they were using. He walked all around the thing, finding deficiencies everywhere. It was true that the bricks had a mellow cast to them and were of good color, but when he lifted and smote two of them against each other they proved all too brittle and weak. A nail had been driven wrongly and he needed a full minute to pry it out with the blade of his knife. Hell lay waiting for the man who drove that spike. On the other hand the shops and stores were generally tidy and were in process just now of opening for the day.

He crossed to the Post Office, mailed his letter and, saying nothing, reimbursed the man for the cost of the four stamps. He did not understand people of this sort, who were content to sit on a stool so many hours each day.

"I wadn't worried," the man said. "Shoot, I knew you'd pay me."

William, who had already decided against this person, said nothing. Nor did he pay attention to the woman who had just entered with a market basket on her arm — they knew nothing of each other and she had no call to smile at him that way. It bothered him, too, that he could hear his new machine everywhere he went, and that the thing was wheezing in an unwholesome way, as it seemed to him.

The sun was high, white, and much more stable-looking than when it had started out two hours ago on its daily route. He stepped into the hardware and after exchanging a word with the man at the register, went to examine the guns and tools. The place was full of farmers, shy people who jumped back out of his way whenever he confronted them in the aisles. Nor did he find anything to criticize in the children, who had been trained to silence. Yes, and he had also been wrong about the women, a serious and thrifty people carrying out their husbands' behests with eyes cast down. He lifted his hat to them, a new behavior on his part.

He went to look in on the horses at the livery. The big mare that he had seen two days ago had been sold apparently and finding nothing else that appealed to him, he came out and was on his way to the grocer's when his attention was drawn to an empty lot bordered on one side by the barber and on the other by a bakery doing a fitful business in hot cross buns and gingerbread men. It was a narrow slice of land, worth very little it seemed to him, inasmuch as it ran back at an angle, growing thinner as it went. Testing with his foot, he walked out finally into the middle of the piece, counting as he went. Here, too, even here between the sheltering buildings he could hear the noise that came from just outside of town.

SIXTEEN

Jesse: he had taken the newspaper and cut out a clipping, had put it in a frame and hung it on the wall. A week and two days went by, at the end of which period he took down the frame, removed the clipping and threw it away. Why? Because it had come to his attention that some other party had taken the prize for blackberry wine.

The days grew longer. He would have instead preferred long nights featuring continuous warm weather, but never expected to see that combination again. Instead, he used to go out every day to the barn and comb the horses, or drain the cow, or snatch up half a dozen eggs and fetch them inside. His friend William had reached home in safety (he learned), after tiptoeing all night through several counties; thinking of that fellow, he snorted out loud in amazement at him. He no longer expected to become that kind of person himself, not since he had reached the age of twenty and had come at last to recognize what sort he really was. And then, too, he was spending more and more time in the hay loft where he had set up an apartment, as it were, with bedding and other equipment.

Now came Friday and with it a degree of excitement that would likely be his ruin. Already he had told six lies, lying to Mary and to his mother, lying even to Deborah at first, until he began to mix his lies with truth. His worries did leave him for a short period when at about two o'clock in the afternoon a new baby chick was born into the world with an extra finger on its foot. He marveled and spoke to it, and then decided to preserve the specimen forever in a bottle of clarified molasses.

He set out at just after three, traveling in the shadow of the levee. The town of Opp was so-named, he believed, owing to all the operas that had visited there over the years, and although he had not himself attended any of them, nevertheless he considered it the best sort of entertainment for the person who had agreed to meet him there. His excitement increased. Up until this point he had done nothing to be ashamed of and yet when he met another rider on the trail, a friend of his who wanted to stop and speak, Jess brushed past him quickly and continued on.

The clouds had lifted during the last half-hour, uncovering again the volcano fields that lay some one hundred and twenty miles to the north-northeast. He paid no attention to them, nor to the twisting string of smoke lifting ever so slowly from the largest and most famous of those hills. *His* eye was for the trail in front of him, for evidence of April and whip-poorwills and things waiting in ambush for him.

Toward four he came into a ruined village burnt down twenty-eight years ago by foreign soldiers. These were the scenes that made him wish for sons, strong boys, well trained and endowed with the taste for revenge; thinking of it, he broke out into a horrible grin that persisted until he had to leave the shelter of the levee and ride across a long and level field where he put on a more neutral expression.

It was night itself that lay in ambush for him. He came up slowly to it, felt along its surface and told the horse to go inside. Somewhat darker than he was prepared for, the place was thick with owls and full of noises that were endemic, he had to suppose, to the region. The moon also had broken into pieces — until he realized that those "pieces" were but an escort of nearby stars. And so thus the two of them, man and mare, hurried forward eagerly while scattering crickets from their path.

He approached from long distance, dismayed that the city walls had deteriorated down to such a state that mounted horsemen could have entered easily riding four and five abreast. Verifying that he was in the right place, he conducted his horse off into a side street where he parked and dismounted and bit off a chew of tobacco and tried to get his emotions into order. Already he had espied the girl, which gave him the advantage of being able to judge in secret her clothes and the rest of it as she stood waiting in front of the theater with her younger brother. This brother, both younger and smaller than Jesse had been led to believe, was an unsophisticated sort of person who had come to town in a straw hat, and very glad Jesse was that the boy would not be entering the theater with them. His own hat was of felt; he took it off now and folded it and put it away in the saddle bags. Suddenly he pulled out his watch and looked at it. He had three minutes, no more, if he wanted to adhere strictly to their appointment.

She was wearing a yellow gown of some kind that sorted with her complexion. Her gloves, too, were yellow, and came up to cover her left elbow while leaving the other exposed. Nervous, wary, excited, she put on a smile when she detected him marching toward her. Careful about the expression on his own face, he went and stood next to her for a time, waiting to see who would be the first to speak.

"Gosh, is *that* him?" her brother asked.

"Hush."

"Well," Jesse said. "Looked like rain this morning, but seems to have cleared up some now."

She looked to the sky. It was clear above but crowded in front of them with quantities of people moving up and down and coming in and out of restaurants and hotel lobbies. She was still holding the stub of a railroad ticket in her hand.

"Left my horse over yonder," said Jesse, "but your little brother here, he can tend her while we're inside."

The boy looked up at him with displeasure. Jesse went on:

"Boy howdy, I saw that yellow dress soon as I got to town. I mean!"

She blushed happily. He saw now for the first time that she had a flower, also yellow, affixed to her sleeve. Suddenly he grabbed for her hand and, pleased that the boy remained behind, drew her into the crowd.

It was a short stroll to the theater, a two-story structure freshly painted in purple and gold. He had been everywhere and seen all things, and yet it still surprised him how these city people dressed. In comparison with them, he grew increasingly pessimistic as to whether they'd actually be let inside. Instead, the woman smiled sweetly as he took the chits from his vest and passed them over to her. He hurried to locate the seats and make claim to them, puzzled that so many people had stayed behind in the lobby in order, apparently, to discourse with one another. The stage meantime was hidden by a dark blue curtain that, as he gazed upon it, trembled slightly in the torrents of the breeze.

"I knew you was going to win a lot of medals," the girl said, "but I never figured you'd win *that* many."

Sadness came down over him. "You must be confusing me with somebody else I guess. I didn't get the wine prize."

"No, but…"

"Some other fellow, *he* got it."

"Oh."

A woman had arrived and had parked just next to him where he could not fail to see that a percentage her bosoms — this done deliberately — was visible. He had a pretty good notion of the sort of man who would bring such a woman here, a judgment that confirmed itself when he turned and looked into the person's face.

"Yes?" the man said.

Disdaining to answer, Jesse now opened the brochure he had been given and read a few paragraphs. The girl also strove to read but was distracted by the people who at last were beginning to come in numbers and take their places. Yes, it was an important evening for someone like her, who had never been anywhere and seen almost nothing. Jesse, who had been to Birmingham and had seen Montgomery several times, put on an amused expression.

"That man," (she pointed tentatively at a certain individual but then quickly drew back her hand), "he's wearing a..."

(Cape.)

"I seen it," Jesse said.

"We ain't supposed to be here!"

Jesse snickered at her. He *was* worried that they could be asked to leave, provided there were not enough places for everyone.

"Listen, I *paid* for these tickets, fair and square."

It calmed her.

"Anyhow, they'd probably let us come back some other time." Suddenly they both reached to gather up the bouquet that had fallen to the floor, their two heads colliding with a hollow noise. She groaned. The haughty people next to them had arisen meantime, had worked their way to the aisle and could be seen moving up and down in search of other seats.

The lights went down and the performance got under way. He had expected the curtain to open in the middle; instead, it lifted quickly toward the ceiling to expose a Roman soldier standing in moonlight with a sword and shield and a melancholy expression on his face. He would soon be singing, to judge by the music and the way the fellow turned, as if by coincidence, to face the audience.

"He knows we're out here," Jesse said, whispering to the girl. And then, when she failed to respond: "He's fixing to sing." Suddenly his eye was caught by the bass fiddler, a tall man standing up to his neck in the pit. He had known people of this type — eyes seated too close together on opposite sides of a nose that was itself too thin. To get a view of the other musicians, he had to come half way to his feet and peer over the hat of the woman seated just in front of him. The man on stage had meantime begun to sing, and although Jesse listened as studiously as he could, he was able to make out no word of it.

"What did he say?" he asked the girl.

She made a gesture, as if it were too complicated to explain at this time.

"How can you see? What with that hat, I mean?" (He reached forward and touched the brim of the woman's hat with his index finger.)

"I can see a little bit."

"Little bit? Shoot, I didn't bring you here to see a *little* bit."

"It's all right."

"Is not neither." He bent forward and tapped the lady, very courteously, on her shoulder. It surprised him that she made no move at all but instead continued looking straight forward at the stage. But far more surprising than that was the behavior of her escort, who turned suddenly, glared at Jesse with a stricken expression and then pulled back his arm and slapped at him with main force. The blow, which was short, merely grazed Jesse and did no harm. The two men now sat staring at each other among the general disturbance they had created.

"I reckon I'm going to have to kill this fellow," he whispered to the girl. And then, speaking out loud: "I reckon I'm going to have to kill you."

"Outside. Now, right now!"

"Awright." He stood and began to work toward the aisle, oblivious to the girl who was trying to hold him back. Later on he would remember about the woman in the hat, and how she had continued to face the stage, never moving in the slightest.

It seemed to him that all this had happened before, a thousand years ago, and that everything was proceeding on schedule, just as he had always known that it would. He was quite calm; indeed, it was only this abnormal calmness of his that gave him grounds for concern.

The night was cool and full of stars. He waited politely just beside the door, nodding in a friendly fashion to the people, perhaps fifty in all, who had come streaming out of the building in order to watch. He thought he saw a woman from his own county, but changed his mind when he got a better look. The man himself, who was perhaps twenty years older than Jesse and about two inches taller, wore an expression of extreme anger that seemed out of all proportion to everything. They faced each other at the bottom of the steps.

"Son-of-a-bitch. How do you want it — knives or firearms?"

Jesse thought. People didn't ordinarily call them "firearms," not if they had a close familiarity with such things. "Firearms," he said. (The girl, still clutching her yellow flower, had come outside but then had turned and run back in again. She had now come out for the second time and could be seen at the back of the crowd wringing her hands.)

"Son-of-a-bitch. I'd just as soon cut your gizzard out."

"No," said Jesse. "Firearms."

"I'm not carrying," the man said, opening wide his vest.

"I got a revolver," someone offered.

A new person now stepped up and, after lifting his arms to call for silence, tried to bring some coherence to the process.

"Now just hold on here! All right, we've got a revolver. Now does anybody else got one?"

There was a short silence while an elderly man pushed his way forward with solemnity and then turned to confront the people. "I got one."

"Well all right, that makes two."

"But I have to go get it."

"Oh Lord. How long will *that* take I wonder?"

He scurried off, the old one, just as the music from inside had reached a high point. The first revolver had meantime been given over to the angry man, who was inspecting it carefully.

"You want this one? Or do you want to take your chances with whatever that old fellow comes up with?"

"I don't much care," Jesse said truthfully. "You're going to be dead in about five minutes anyway, and it don't matter to me if I use *this*" — he pointed to the revolver — "or *that*" — he pointed in the direction in which the old man had disappeared.

"I got a shotgun," someone said.

Jesse felt that he was in danger of getting bored. The girl had once more gone inside where, he presumed, she would finally be able to get a view of the opera. He looked for, and found, his mare peeping around the corner of the dry goods store. It was a nuisance, to be taken away from his first opera, especially in consideration of the tariff he had paid. He took out his tobacco and rolled a cigarette. That woman he had at first thought to be from his own county? She was. That was when the older man came running back holding out in front of him a big black pistol pointed at the ground.

Jesse took the weapon and aimed it at the moon. That it was fully competent to do the thing that needed to be done, he could have no slightest doubt of it, once he had cracked it open and taken one of the cartridges and weighed it in his palm. From inside he could hear a chorus of children singing sweetly whereupon there came to him the amazing realization that between the two of them, one at least would be dead before the song was ended. Thinking of it (he was gazing at the bullet nestled in his hand), he broke out into a rather peculiar smile that seemed to win the admiration of certain people standing about.

"Shit! He don't look like he's scared of *nothing!*"

"No. Most unusual."

"I'm betting on *him.*"

"Me, too," Jesse started to say, until forestalled by a small person at the back of the crowd who already had taken his money out. The angry man meantime was holding up his revolver and showing it around, demonstrating that of the six available chambers, only one actually was loaded. Jesse looked at it closely, not understanding at first that he was expected to do the same.

"O.K., boys" said the man coordinating the event, "now I want you" (he touched the angry man on his cuff), "to go off down yonder for a piece, that's right, and *you*" (he pointed to Jesse, who still had the remains of a smile on his face), "I want you to come over here. And when I say it's O.K., why then you can kill him. Or, he can kill you."

"That's fair," the small man said.

Jesse went to the place and stood there. These matters had happened long ago with the results that were known, if not to him, at least to the people contemporary with those times. And were those same people now looking down upon him from their position in the past and were they cheering for him still? He genuinely did not know. He did know that the angry man had lifted his weapon and was pointing it in his general direction. He could not, however, Jesse couldn't, judge very closely the quality of his aim. The chorus had ended but so far as he knew both he and the other man were still alive.

He received the bullet and heard the noise at the exact same time. "Ha!" he said. (It hadn't occurred to him that the thing might enter where it did, which is to say about a half-inch above the corner of his mouth. [Traveling at breakneck speed {no pun intended} the slug had moved quickly through his oral cavity and then, slowing somewhat as it came into contact with resistance, had glanced off his jaw and continued on in the most favorable direction possible under the circumstances, which is to say out into the open night where it had all the room in the world to exhaust itself in purposeless flight.] He touched the spot where it had entered and then, giving everyone plenty of time to understand what had happened, pointed to the exit wound.)

"It don't hurt," he said. "Well! maybe a little. But this ain't *near* as bad as a snake bite, shoot no. Shoot, I remember when... "

"My God man, you going to stand there talking or are you going to shoot that son-of-a-bitch? He was going to *kill* you!"

Jesse was not so sure but that perhaps he *had* been killed. He was brought to his senses by the two little streams of blood weaving down his chin, and a third such stream, smaller still, proceeding from just behind his ear.

"Maybe I ought to fire back at him," he said.

"Yes! You're supposed to. That's what you're supposed to do, for Christ's sake!"

He lifted the pistol, which was heavy, and at first aimed it at the wrong individual. He couldn't help but notice that the angry man had retreated somewhat and was giving evidence of wishing to mix with the crowd, a thing which the crowd itself seemed *not* to wish. He was still a good target, even at forty feet. Jesse trained upon his forehead but then changed his mind and aimed instead at the man's left eye. He never did anything with impatience, nor did he see any cause for hurry in a case like this. And then, too, the fellow appeared to have lost his anger quite completely and it was an altogether different sort of emotion that at present Jesse saw inscribed upon his face.

"Shoot!"

"All right."

"When?"

He shot. The bullet, rotating smoothly on its own axis, moved forward at high speed to crash into the man's *other* eye, the only one that Jesse had never actually targeted. "Ha!" he said, flabbergasted at the way things so often turn out. "He's dead, I reckon."

Five or six men immediately converged upon the corpse. The women, of course, were screaming, although they had needed a delay of several seconds to really get started on it. Now he knew, Jesse did, what had happened all those years ago. Working slowly, he returned two of the cartridges to the magazine and then handed off the remaining bullets and the pistol itself to the man who had fetched them. Someone was daubing at his neck with a handkerchief that had been dipped in an ether of some type.

"I'm a doctor," the man said.

Jesse tried to shake with him. "My uncle was a doctor. Dead now."

"Don't think I've ever seen anything like this. Goodness gracious, that bone is just as true and straight as the day he were born. And look here, that clean little hole!" And then: "You better get on home boy."

"Naw, he's alright," someone said. "That other fellow's from Massachushits. *Was* from Massachushits. Ain't nobody going to give him any trouble about that."

The girl in yellow took him by the arm. He could not remember having ever seen her in this aspect, with her hair in an uproar and her face so shriveled and pale. She had managed to turn him around and, although the opera was by no means finished, was guiding him step by step toward where her brother stood waiting in a stupor of admiration. If he could not view the opera, Jesse's next intention was to stay with the girl until her train arrived; instead she nudged and prodded him to the horse and then prized loose the reins from her brother's grasp.

He drove resolutely to the north-northwest but began to slow when the mare turned to look back at him resentfully one or two times. He wasn't sure what the doctor had done to him, save that it had failed to staunch the blood. He crossed the railway, arriving there in time to ride in parallel with the train that was coming for the girl. Mounted as he was, he could see clearly into the dining car, and had to laugh out loud when he perceived the expression on those who caught sight of him riding in the opposite direction. He grinned. Came next a ruined windmill bending to earth on splayed legs, its propeller half-buried in the sand. The moon was waning now and entire provinces of it had fallen into a dark phase likely to persist all night. He thought he saw, Jesse thought, an enormous bird sitting in the upper branches of a tree — until forced to admit that it was but a cluster of pine cones that looked the way that it did. The pain in his cheek and neck (and his tongue, too, which had taken some punishment), wasn't bad; he had experienced worse than this on three or four occasions even if he couldn't right away remember what those occasions were. Soon he would be in his own barn, far from the jurisdiction of people stopped by the county line.

It was past midnight when the fear assailed him at last. The panic, which at first hit him in the legs, spread quickly to other places and forced him to halt and leave the saddle lest he fall out onto the road. His eyes were full of bullets, all of them coming straight for him. It was the horror of it, the good possibility that he might have been killed and left to rot, that once he were rotted he would remain that way, that he was too young for this, that he could be hung for what he had done and his whole family along with him, that his appointment with the girl had been a failure and, finally, that he was bringing home two holes in his head, one of them quite small and the other much less so.

SEVENTEEN

With spring now coming in, the work grew harder. And if he were skilled in gardening, as Joe Butler certainly was, he did not for that reason prefer to produce a greater harvest of vegetables than two men were likely to consume in a normal year. He preferred just the right amount.

One day in April, after he had finished cutting and stacking 5,000 feet of cedar for old man Hollings, he went with his shovel to a flat place where the sun was neither too strong nor yet too weak and began to put in his garden. Working slowly, *too* slowly perhaps, he turned the earth (clay actually, bright red and running with blood) while at the same time conserving any worms who came to light. He had it in mind to plant corn, also tomatoes of course, a modicum of turnips, the ordinary beans and rutabaga and, as a concession to a long-standing whim of his, two rows of fancy gourds that, judging from the label, were liable to take on all sorts of sizes and configurations. He was humming, too, although the music was likely to fall silent in places where the soil was hard to break. Concerning gourds, he liked them pudgy and with long necks, liked also to paint them various colors and hang them up where birds would build their nests inside them. He planted scuppernongs, too, setting them in such a way as that in times to come the vines might engulf his shack after he had forsaken it.

He had found a filbert tree in the forest and had pounced upon it. Plums — the woods were full of these, so many indeed that he could afford to ignore all but the noblest of them, amber-colored beauties full of juice.

He had furthermore stumbled upon a persimmon tree growing by the river, but when he tested it, found to his dismay that it was evil.

Truth was, he had not been living in this place two full days before he stretched his first trot line across the river. Catfish were plentiful, he soon understood, though not as much so as the eels that came in two different varieties differing importantly from each other in several respects.

Apart from that he was doing well — spring was coming in, there were trees needing to be cut, and he had yet to meet in this town a single man who wished to interfere with a Negro known to be William's. He ascribed it to the sort of person this white man was. Suddenly, that moment, a dark silhouette moved up and threw itself over the garden patch. Bending nearer to it he was able to make out the broad-brimmed hat whose shadow was even darker than the rest of the man.

"Yas, suh," Joe Butler said, never having to see who it was.

"Mr. Hollings pick up his wood?"

"Yas, suh, he done come and got it long time ago. Say he pay you later."

"Are you planting greens, Joe?"

"Yas, suh. No, suh, we don't need no greens. I got *punkins,* I got *pease,* I got... I got near 'bout everthing, Mr. Bill."

"Greens are five cents the bunch now."

"Yas, suh."

"Now Joe, what did you put over here?" (He touched the area with his toe.)

"Got persnips, too. This here's *good* ground, Mr. Bill; shoot yeah."

"And what's this over here Joe?"

Joe's voice grew low. "Yas, suh. Put me some gourds over there, sure did. Just a few."

"Gourds." (He probed at it with the toe.) "We don't need that."

"No, suh."

"Don't like to see you waste your time like that Joe. Now if it was me, I believe I'd put collards here. Lots of 'em."

"Yas, suh." Using his little spade, he began to stir the soil. Already he had twenty worms; now suddenly he had two more. No one talked. He had guessed, correctly, that the man's shade would remain in position for a long time, but had *not* expected to find that the man himself had already turned and gone away.

EIGHTEEN

He went to bed late and woke early, *too* late and *too* early, and lay for a long time thinking about his circumstances. Through the window he could see nine stars of various strength, one of them sputtering badly and on the verge, it seemed to William, of shutting down. If truly he had the power of prediction, that star was on fate's agenda and would certainly die within the next ten, possibly fifteen seconds. And when in fact all things fell out as he had foreseen and the last sparks had faded into nothingness, he stood and got into his shoes and went outside and put a saddle on the horse.

"What you fixing to do, Mr. Bill?" asked Joe Butler, who had emerged from his hut in his underwear.

"Want you to finish up with those cedars Joe. Need to finish *today*. Lots to be done, Joe, lots."

Joe Butler went back inside. William could still hear him however, owing to his voice ricocheting among the walls:

"Going off! Yas, suh, going again! Don't know *where* he going, he jest going!" And then again putting his head outside the shed:

"Where you going Mr. Bill? We ain't got no fule [fuel]."

"And clean those bream."

"Damnation!" (He was back inside his home.) "Do this, do that. Lord, Lord, Lord!"

He traveled at a gallop. It was far before dawn and the town was quiet and empty save where two men were in process of delivering a keg of fresh oysters to the vender's stand. The highway, soft and cream-colored in moonlight, lay open before him and could have taken him all the way to Florida, had only he the time for it and the necessary rations for himself and horse. Pushing his mind forward, he asked if it might be in his fate to see the ocean someday, but once again received no answer. He had asked too much already and must content himself with the prophecy that had come to him during the night.

A few miles outside of town he stopped and dismounted and walked the horse to a small but well-maintained cemetery, his favorite in all the county. Swept clean every fifteen years or so (each time the river flooded), it was an immaculate piece of private property belonging to certain families, and although he foresaw no real possibility of being admitted to it himself he had made it his practice to visit whenever he could. Here in this grave lay a woman who had died young, the inscription proving more legible in moonlight than ever he had seen it by day. Enthralled by silence and knowledge, she slept below with folded hands. And yet it was not his way to be envious of people simply because they had preceded him in the course of time. He walked past the sculpture of an angel (her smile tolerant and bemused and endlessly patient), and then continued on to the earliest of all those inhumations — a sunken place marked by a oblong slab that had grayed so much over the years that this person's life and times had been lost to the historical account. Likely he had been a fine person in his day and likely, too, that someone had loved him once, even to distraction, yea. But not now, not in his current condition, no, nor she in hers. Love had blown away.

He stayed longer than he intended and the sun, when it came, set up a conflict between its beauty on the one hand and on the other his need to arise now and set about his life. Even so, he went on watching until at last the thing tore loose from the horizon and began to reveal its intentions for the day.

He met almost no traffic the next hours as he rode through the country-side. He harkened to a rooster atop a silo who called in all directions for the people to arise now and take advantage of the weather. Because today the sunrays fell slantwise on Alabama and the world looked as if on the first day when a man could travel for years seeing naught but well-kept farms and random flowers littering the fields. Behind him were hills, smoke coming off the summits, and in the far distance a band of peace-loving cows, mildest and most courteous of the known ungulates. All things worshipped the Lord of all things, as did William himself.

He watered the horse at just before noon and then, drawing off into a grove of sycamores, prepared a bed for himself out of bundled weeds and pine needles. By and large he was contemptuous of food and sleep, worthless preoccupations that bored him to tears. Didn't have time for them, not when he had so short a time in which to redeem the share of the world ascribed to him.

In the afternoon he came to where the river folded back upon itself and blocked his way. A ferry, such as it was, had been winched up on shore where the ferryman himself sat making a repair to one of his shoes. William drove up near to him and after waiting uselessly to be acknowledged said:

"What's the charge to take me across the river?"

The man looked up slowly, chewed, and then looked down again. "I'll take you acrost. No charge."

"That's very cordial of you."

"'Course now your horse, that's a whole different matter."

William waited for it.

"Cost you a dollar for the horse."

William looked back at him evenly. As always he was entirely calm. He touched the .32 caliber revolver that lay in its holster against the neck of the horse.

"I asked you a question," William said calmly. "Matter of fact, I'm one of the Pefley brothers."

"And I give you your answer, too!" the man said, looking up at him hotly. "Dollar for the critter, nothing for you."

"For a dollar I could buy a boat like that one. Better."

"Well go buy it then! This here is *my* boat by God, and..." He hushed as William climbed down and walked toward him. He was not a large man, William, but enjoyed the advantages that come to people who look forward to the end of all things. Suddenly, recollecting that he had left the revolver behind, he turned and went back for it. It was then that the man began to give small but compounding indications suggesting that he did have within him the capability of modifying his attitude. It was all the same to William whether he modified or not.

"I guess I'm used to being treated with respect," William said. "Anyway that's generally what I do when I'm dealing with people."

The man mumbled something or another — William couldn't hear it — and then put aside his shoe. "Well, maybe I could give you a *discount* in your case, seeing as how."

He went into his pocket, William did, and without waiting to hear the fare took out a dime and gave it over to the man who gathered it up with perfect courtesy.

By early afternoon he came into the devastated terrain that lay over against the town of *Acedia near Pleuron*. Everywhere ruined villages were going back to seed and nothing but rubble was left to show that they had been places of importance in the old days. Smoke still lingered on the horizon where union troops had passed, and further still, steam and fog could be seen lifting from the half-score of volcanoes perceptible in the distance. He saw a plowshare sticking up out of the ground where someone many years ago had run off and left it and then, next, a mule's skeleton turned to chalk through the combined action of heat and light persisting over long periods. The clouds in this region, though few and far apart, looked like household objects and farming equipment. He saw an ostensible churn floating upside-down in the sky.

Night came on very quickly. He had found a good sleeping place (he thought), until driven from it by mosquitoes and the canted ground. He would have preferred to move on through the night and would have done so, had not the trail already petered out fifteen miles ago. Nor could he make much sense of the stars, which seemed out of pattern tonight. Instead he walked for a distance, coming at last to a place that offered better viewing and the voices of the cicadas were in full ken.

With him, an hour's worth of sleep balanced twenty-three of activity, a proportion that applied as well to his horse. As for nourishment, he very seldom had any, regarding it as a capitulation to human sin. And when he mounted and rode out, his eyes shielded from starlight by a wide-brimmed hat, and noticed someone far away wading through the corn by lantern light, and witnessed a long and wavering file of crows yawing homeward toward the moon, and counted three places where the horizon was on fire, and bethought him of the dream wherein he had been promised many things but especially the girl... Well! He relented then and joined for a moment in song with the whippoorwill perched athwart his saddle horn.

He breached the line at about two in the morning and found himself in a place where the Alabamas began to diverge, broken apart by two important rivers that crossed in and out of each other's path continually. The settlement, when he came to it, looked like a recumbent animal of great size waiting sententiously for dawn before continuing on its way. Here William dismounted and got quickly into his new shoes and clothes, his two-pound watch and his golden chain.

It was not a recumbent animal that blocked his way but rather two dark houses and their associated outbuildings. He went on tiptoe to the largest of these homes and after reconsidering his purpose, knocked four times politely. Behind him he heard the door of the crib fall open with much noise and was surprised to see Jesse looking out at him from that direction. He had expected the dogs to make a tumult; instead they merely produced a few peevish sounds and then rose painfully and squeezed beneath the house.

He knocked again and counted slowly up to twenty-three. He was pretty sure that he could hear someone treading across the bare floor and then coming to a halt just on the other side of the door. William took off his hat. The door opened.

"Howdy," said William, striving to shake with him. "I know it's early, but I..."

"Oh God, what is it *this* time? You gone and got yourself all shot up again?"

"No, sir, this is William."

"William? Oh. Oh yes of course!"

He had expected, William had, to be invited into the house.

"I've come for Deborah."

"Come for her?"

"Yes, sir."

"How do you mean, 'come for her?'"

Saying nothing, William probed into his left pocket, took the little box that held the ring, but then had to wait while the man went to fetch his glasses. It was a considerable thing, that ring, for a man who hadn't achieved very much as yet. It sparkled almost as brightly in candle light as when William had at first tested it under the sun.

"She'll like that," the old man said finally. "Real purty."

"I've got me a sawmill business now you see."

"So I hear."

"And your daughter's going to have the biggest house in town — oh I'll see to that."

"Sounds real nice."

"Going to build it myself, Joe Butler and me."

"Really!"

"Little bit chilly out here, this time of morning."

"Look at that scoundrel peeping out of that barn. God, God, God."

"And that's not all. I'm going to have a brick-making business pretty soon, too."

"I told Deborah a long time ago that I'd see she got *a thousand dollars* on the day she got married. One thousand American green dollars. Yes, sir."

"Well I knew she had a generous father, I just didn't know how generous he was."

"And that furniture up in her room up there? I expect her to keep all of it, every bit, yes sir. Except the cedar chest of course. Belonged to my grandmama don't you see."

William waved it away. "I got a cedar chest already."

"She's so young. It'll do her good, being in a big town like Elba."

"She sure does love that old grey mule, too. Talks about it like it was hers!"

They looked at each other.

"All right. But I've only got the one harness."

William waved it away. The man still had the ring in his possession but William remained confident that he'd get it back again. Two women in bathrobes now were standing on the staircase, one of them carrying a little tray with a candle on it. William hastened to remove his hat, forgetting that he had already done so.

"Who is it, Hubert? Is something wrong?"

"No, no. You go on back to bed. It's just William, and he's fixing to leave."

"Well invite him in! Gracious. The children will be so happy to see him. I'm going to wake Mary right now!"

"It's not Mary, dear. He brought a ring."

"And I'll fix some chocolate."

William was left alone at the door. He saw a meteor pass over, saw it turn sharply and change directions in a way that he had never seen before. There were now at least five lanterns aglow inside the house, including in the room where Deborah lived. Several moments having gone by, he seated himself on the topmost stair and took out his pouch and formed a cigarette. His watch had ceased to function several weeks ago but still blended well, he thought, with this dark suit. That was when Mary came and, shielding her eyes, peered at him through the screen.

"I knew you'd come back."

"Getting colder out here I believe."

He was allowed inside where he got a sudden glimpse of Deborah running up the stairs in a dark blue robe of some kind. Going to his accustomed place in the parlor, he sat in dignity while waiting for his chocolate milk. Atop the piano sat a basket of roses that no doubt was responsible for the pollen that covered the keys. He had always had a good opinion of the house in general, but most of all he esteemed this room. Esteemed, too, the delicate little cups (designed for hummingbirds) in which the chocolate was poured and served. Testing the rim of his cup between his thumb and finger, he guessed it to be no thicker than a... In fact he could not begin to think of a comparison that was as thin as that.

"Why Mr. Pefley, what brings you to our part of the country? Are you traveling on business and just happened to be close by?"

"He wants the mule, too."

"You're going to injure yourself, Mr. Pefley, working so hard."

He waved it away. "Lots to do. Of course now if everybody was like me, we could get it done pretty quick."

"Let me get you some more chocolate. Oh Hubert, can't you read that old newspaper some other time?"

He waited for further chocolate, aware at the same time that he was being judged and tallied by Mary, who had always been interested in everything that had to do with the connection between Deborah and himself.

"How old are you Willy?" she asked, blushing suddenly. "No, just tell me when you were born, OK?"

He was not unwilling to answer and would have done so had not Jesse just then appeared in the door. The boy did not look particularly well, it seemed to William.

"Yes, that's him. But don't expect him to say anything. His jawbone is all ruint."

The boy pointed to the injury and after striving to speak, used his finger to trace the stitches that held it together.

"We tried, Mr. Pefley, we did try. But you know what they say — that if just one of your children turns out good, why then that's something you can be proud of."

"Yeah, and Deborah's the one they're proud of," Mary said. "They aren't proud of me."

"Oh, hush."

He was aware, was William, that Deborah had arrived at the top of the stairs and was beginning, very slowly to make her way down to the parlor. Her tunic was pink and composed, apparently, of chiffon. And if her hair still looked as if she had been sleeping in it, she now had ruffles at her sleeves and several strings of pearls. Her father, setting down his paper, motioned at her with the stem of his pipe:

"Not every woman would go to that much trouble at 3:30 in the morning." He cackled. "Good cook, I will say that."

"Why Deborah! It's so nice of you to greet our guest."

Her dress, which might almost have been made of tin, produced a noise like far-off thunder. Delicate she was, noble and thin, and after watching her move back and forth among the furniture, William's eye began to sparkle.

"And how is your family, Mr. Pefley?" she asked. "They're well, I hope?"

"We're starting next week," he said, "Joe Butler and me. I was thinking three bedrooms, but now I'm thinking four." Bending forward, he began to trace the blueprint in the rug. "You'll need a sewing room, and I want you to have one, too. The fireplace goes here." (He drew it.) "I use two-by-sixes, always do, and if other people want to use two-by-fours, well that's got nothing to do with me. Big garden. 'Course now if you want to use it for flowers, that'd be all right, too."

"I got some seeds," Jesse said.

"Gracious!" the older woman said. "You're taking my breath away with all these ambitious plans! Why you almost sound as if you were *betrothed*, Mr. Pefley."

Her husband turned, put down his paper and looked at her for a long time. "It's settled, Betsy. You were in the kitchen."

"I got almost enough hardwood to do the job right now," William went on. "I admit the boiler is thin." (He drew it.) "But I plan on getting some solder tomorrow in Enterprise."

They looked at him with expressions of admiration, confusion, and dismay. His little cup of chocolate had somehow ended up lying on its side and a few drops of the liquid had dropped off onto the milk-colored carpet where everyone pretended not to see them. Mary, meantime, continued to stare with fascination into his face, as if to learn once and for all what sort of people men were.

"Gosh," she said, "I bet they have so many babies they won't know where to put 'em all!"

"Put 'em in the barn!" offered Jesse, who laughed briefly and then blushed for a long time following. A thin rivulet of blood had run down onto his neck and dried there, though here, too, everyone pretended not to see it. Suddenly William slapped both knees, uttered, and then drew himself to his feet.

"You're not thinking of leaving? My God man, it's only three-forty-five in the morning!"

"Need to get that solder. Told Joe I'd be back. That sure was good chocolate milk. Well good-bye."

"Look at that. My God, the least you can do is stay awhile! Visit. We're going to cut a watermelon tomorrow."

William sank back down. Twice he had ventured to look in Deborah's direction, finding her calm, silent, and wise. The craving was still there and it did no good to pretend that it wasn't — to have her stand directly in front of him as he measured her waist with his own two hands alone. He was agitated by other cravings as well, but managed each time to wave them off.

"Why, yes," the girl's mother said. "And in the morning everything will seem so much clearer."

"Well shore," Jesse said. "The sun."

NINETEEN

They were supposed to rise at about seven the next morning and then go together to the spring where the melons were cooling. And might have done so, too, had not William perceived the old man's carbine resting on the mantle piece.

Instead of watermelons therefore, the men gathered unripe gourds from the garden, hung them up and shot them all apart. Finally, after twenty minutes of it, the old man went and retrieved his hammer and sunk a ten-penny nail about half-way up to its neck in the side of the barn. Standing back at a distance of about forty yards, he tried three times, unsuccessfully, to drive home the nail with leaden bullets.

"Ah me," he said, "I'm not as good as what I used to be. I shot me a yankee one time and he was a *lot* further away than that."

"Yeah. And his brains was hanging out, too, weren't they Pa? He didn't know he was about to get kilt."

"No, he never knew anything about it. Not till it was too late leastwise."

The three men glanced around at each other in satisfaction and joy.

"I wish to God they was standing over there right now, the whole stinking mess. All I ever wanted was to kill 'em all, *ever last blesséd one*!"

"Just have to be patient," William said. "The time will come."

"When, William, when will it come?"

"Got to be patient."

"If one of you boys could drive that nail all the way in, why the time might come a lot sooner."

There was reason in what he said. Taking up the rifle, William tested it for weight and balance and to get some sense of its personality. It might almost be better to aim for that blackbird circling in the sky, a thing no larger than the mote in Jacob's eye. And then, too, he felt that he was shooting for his bride, and all the things that she implied.

They marched to the river, arriving at just before eight. The watermelons, which were of various size and weight, had been cooling all night and now were drifting slowly in a circle with the majority of their volume riding below the surface. Squatting on shore, Jesse waited for the one he liked best and when it came, quickly pounced on it and took it up into his arms. He took another, too, and then walked some hundred rods downstream and set it up on the riverbank for the benefit of the half-dozen Negro children splashing in the surf. It was the best of places for swimming and watermelons, for wild quinces, horse apples, and Spanish moss. That far-away blackbird — (it was in fact a crow) — had meantime come down out of the sky and was watching sardonically from where two magnolias had fused into a single growth.

They turned and began the journey home, the two younger men passing the selected melon off to each other every quarter of a mile. It happened to be in William's possession when they passed through the gap in the levee and found Mary running toward them in a state of high excitement. They could not read her signals at that distance and had to wait until she came even with them.

"He's back! And he's been climbing in our trees, too!"

The old man paled. "I told him, told him *six times* to keep away from here!"

"And he's got a great big ole sack with him, too!"

"It figures." He turned to William and explained in quiet voice: "White trash. Stole a pig last week."

"Well I guess he wants to go to Hell then," William said. "And he's going to be real surprised when he gets there — that's all I have to say."

The old man threw a cartridge in the rifle and closed the bolt. "Mary, I want you to go up on the levee and point him out to us. We'll find him."

"Just keeps on burning and burning, forever and ever."

They departed in tandem, William, Jesse, and the dog in one direction and the girl in the other. The path was narrow and the briars tended to grab at William's tie and/or lift off the black broad-brimmed hat that he generally wore. Even so he was traveling at good speed (he thought), until he recognized that Jesse had managed to put himself at least thirty yards ahead of everyone else. He would have been satisfied, William, to leave the man to Hell, but had to recognize that the supervision of this property belonged not to him but to those who owned it. The dog (enjoying this), also belonged to who owned him, and the crows as well, all of them now grown hoarse from too much excitement too suddenly brought on.

Already Mary had climbed to the top of the levee and, taking a position there, was pointing silently with outstretched arm to Blephy Ford. In the distance she looked like a famous piece of sculpture that William had seen some years previous in downtown Birmingham. Following her signal, he crossed the brook and continued on toward the road where Jesse stood waiting with his rifle, his melon, and the man called Blephy Ford. No one spoke, not until the old man joined them and been given time to recover.

"Howdy, Blephy," he said. "We hadn't seen you in two, three days. Where you been?"

Blephy grinned. "Well I've been so busy you understand." He hummed. He had bald spots in scattered locations about his cannon ball head. "Believe we're going to get that rain after all."

"Looks to me like you're trespassing."

"Rained yesterday over to Green County. That's what they tell me."

"What you got in that sack, Blephy?"

"But it cleared up later on, 'round about three o'clock, and they had 'em a real nice day!"

"If that was a chicken in there, she'd be jumping around and what not. But she's not."

"Dead," said Jesse. "Probably."

"I'm going to shoot you, Blephy, if you've got a chicken in that sack."

"You'd shoot a man for that?"

"Well I wouldn't shoot him dead. But I might shoot him in the toe."

Blephy looked at the sack and then at his toes. His shoes were in appalling condition, as were indeed his teeth and most of the rest of him as well. William had seen Negroes appareled better than this.

"I didn't take no chickens," the man said at last.

"Stealing watermelons!" Mary said. "I wouldn't put it past him."

"No, sir; I don't even know where you keep 'em." And then: "Where *do* you keep 'em?"

"Can't be a snake in there. Is it a snake, Blephy?"

"Pecans, he's been stealing our pecans!"

"Pecans?" He had to laugh at that. "They ain't even ripe yet."

To seize the bag and look inside it would have been incourteous; instead, they stood about in a circle and continued to guess at the contents. Finally:

"Blephy, I'll give you *fifteen red cents*, if you let me look in that bag."

Blephy said: "It ain't a chicken and it ain't a melon; it ain't a pig and it *sure* ain't no snake."

"He never lies."

"Is it... ?" He thought hard, the old man did, but could come up with nothing else of his that was as poachable as that. That was when Mary, the only person there who, socially speaking, could do so, took one step forward and snatched the bag from out of his grasp. It held, in fact, a...

"'Possum!"

They gathered around, nudging at a thing that seemed to be asleep. William could have cited Negroes who disdained this particular dish.

"Dadburned 'possum! You just keep getting worse, Blephy, worse and worse and worse."

Blephy grinned.

They marched back together to the deep part of the woods, Mary leading the way. It was an unattended place, the trees superannuated and no longer productive. The girl went right away to the tallest of them and touched it.

"This is where he was, right here." (She pointed to the upper branches.) "Before ole Blephy came along."

"That's a pretty good-size tree," the old man said in a tone of wonder. "I need to get down here more often. Now Blephy, I want you to scoot right back up to the top there and put this 'possum back where you got him from."

Shielding his eyes, the thief ran his gaze slowly up the tree, until leaves and branches disappeared into the sun. "That's a mighty far piece," he said, "all the way up there. But I'd be happy to chop some firewood for you, Mr. Naftel, shoot yeah."

Saying nothing, Jesse gingerly placed the melon in the grass. It was an old-fashioned sort of rifle, his father's, with bullets that were large and blunt and made, seemingly, of brass. Working slowly, he withdrew the existing shell and after allowing Blephy to gaze upon it, replaced it with another.

"Now let's just hold on here a minute! You wouldn't shoot a man over a 'possum, would you?"

He climbed steadily, arriving at a level about thirty feet above the forest floor before he stalled. Down below the dog and four people waited patiently, some of them giving suggestions as to the route he ought to take. The day was clear and bright, the tree so tall and the sun so brilliant that Blephy seemed tempted to leap off into the flux and run back home again; instead, he turned and called down to them:

"This here is where he was."

"He was not neither!"

"Blephy?"

"Sir?"

"You want me to give the gun to her?"

He climbed further. The branches grew more tenuous and further apart the higher he went and meantime the people had abandoned the space beneath him in the event he fell. From the house there came the smell of cakes and loaves, and the sound of Debbie and her mother conversing cheerfully among the pots and pans. He had a pretty good idea of what to expect today in the way of a meal, did William, based upon these women and their skills; running his mind forward, he could predict which dishes would be prepared by which cook. But now he had to run his mind back to present times in order to account for the activity taking place in front of him. The old man was talking:

"Blephy, I want you take that pore little creature and I want you to apologize, and then I want you to take that little tail of his and I want you to *wrap it around that limb just like it used to be.* You hear?"

"Yes, sir; I'm doing it right now. See? One, two, three..."

"And apologize."

"He won't fall now."

"And apologize."

"One, two, three — that old tail, it's wrapped real good now."

"And apologize."

"I can't do that, Mr. Naftel. Why if I *did* apologize, why pretty soon everybody in the county will know about it."

"No they won't. We're not going to tell anybody, are we Mary?"

"Certainly *I* won't tell," Jesse said.

"Yeah, but what about him?"

"Him? That's Mr. Pefley, and he never tells anybody anything."

"Well that's sure enough the truth," Jesse said. "We don't even know where he comes from."

Finally the miscreant did apologize, doing it quietly but at length into the ear of the animal still pretending to be asleep. Everyone was shocked when Blephy suddenly produced another and much smaller animal from his bag and hung it up as well.

"Goddamn you Blephy!"

But in William's view, the use of that language was worse than anything of Blephy's. He said nothing however.

They gathered on the lee side of the house, out of danger from the sun. The watermelon, an egg-shaped affair of about nineteen pounds in weight, had been handled roughly since pulled from the river and there was some fear that the contents had been rattled. Jesse thumped at it twice, testing for ripeness, and then stood back as the old man came forward with a length of twine and used it to saw the thing into two almost equal parts. The heart itself was red and filled the cavity to overflowing — a sigh of relief went up from everyone.

"People in Enterprise and Opp," the old man said, holding up his hand for silence, "they take their melon *after* supper. We take it like this."

It was true. Debra had brought dishes meantime and although these were not strictly necessary they gave a touch of dignity to the feast. William took note of her wise and silent smile, and how it was that she took pleasure in the pleasure of others.

"Aren't you going to have some?" he asked, looking at her evenly.

"I might." She smiled. He took further note of her cheeks, that were as red and merry as the interior of the melon. He would remember this. Now again the old man held up his hand for silence.

"This melon," he said, "it means that William" (he pointed to him), "and our own little Deborah" (he pointed to her), "are getting married."

His wife gasped. "Why Mr. Pefley! No, this is too much. You children should have said something!"

Mary did say something that however could not be heard owing to the wedge of melon jammed in her mouth. She was without shoes, (she usually was), and had some twenty or more little black seeds adhering to her feet.

"And the next time we gather here will be when *Mary* gets married."

"Ha," she said. "Oh ha, ha, ha. Nobody will ever marry me, never, never, never."

"I reckon not," said Jesse sadly. "Hey, I was fixing to have me another piece of that good melon but now it's all gone, most of it."

They went inside and conversed of small matters until 5:45, when Jasmine rang the bell. The table itself was long and narrow and they approached it from widely unalike angles, William having chosen to come at it from the door that led outside. He would have preferred to take a seat at the far end of the bench just under the historical engraving of the death of Wolfe at Quebec; instead, Debbie's mother pointed him to a place next to the old man. From this location the stove was visible in the next room as were also the two steaming pots of vegetables leaning up against each other in the warming closet. In front of him were goblets of water or wine, fried okra pods, squash and green tomatoes. He further descried black beans with new potatoes, crowder peas, asparagus and cauliflower stewed in milk, corn both on the cob and off, biscuits and quince jelly, a cask of white butter, watermelon rind pickles, goat's cheese and green onions, a gilded dish holding three kinds of preserves, sliced cucumbers, walnuts and haws, filberts, muscadines and possum grapes, persimmons, ground cherries, sweet tea and buttermilk (still cool from the milk hole), dumplings and duck, partridges and shrimp, pork roast, honey and ham, venison in aspic, pot roast and catfish, gingerbread and sauce, peaches and strawberries with ice cream and farkleberry pie. Turning from the food to the silverware, William attested that they had brought out an even heavier and better grade service than on the occasion of his first visit there. And, of course, the napkins and cloth were richly embroidered — Deborah's doing, to judge by the fineness of the work and the way in which the pattern was replicated in the collar she was wearing.

In fact she was dressed in blue and her hair, pinned high, caught up the light in flecks of violet and gold. There was no doubt but that she had a nobility to her and that it was owing to her wisdom that she seldom had need to talk. William nodded to her politely, receiving in return a smile designed for him alone. She smiled, too, at the Negress who stood at head of table warding off the flies with a crabapple wand.

"I have to apologize for this meal," her mother said. "Molly just hasn't been her usual self." (She indicated toward the black woman in the kitchen, a resentful-looking quantity who wore two several aprons, fore and aft.) "But we forgive you dear," she called out loudly.

Jesse had been too quick to transfer one of the biscuits over onto his own plate and now, instead of consuming it, had taken out his pocket knife and was cleaning under his nails. The old man had a newspaper. Returned now Mary, who had gone upstairs to put on shoes and eyeliner.

"Mr. Pefley? Will you say grace?"

He thought rapidly. He understood that his theology might differ in some respect from theirs, and that it was incumbent upon him to work around such differences if he could. Finally, looking toward the ceiling, or through it rather, he began: "Oh Lord Jesus and Christ, help us to do right and help Deborah to be a good wife. We know that sin is everywhere, right here amongst us, and that we shall all go to hell someday. God, help us to do what *you* want us to do and not what *we* want us to do, and help us to make the world the way it used to be. Please let it rain *regular*, about once or twice a week, instead of like last year."

"Biscuits getting cold."

"Look after Jesse and help him, and for God's sakes help Mary, too. It was *your* desire that Coffee County have a sawmill and behold, it has one. But do I have the strength Lord, and the wisdom to bring about your other desires as well? No one knows."

The old man had left the table, but then shortly had come back again and was sugaring his tea.

"We know that life is long and hard, and that it is only because of our suffering that You and the prophets have any pleasure at all." Here he paused, still trying to draw upon memories of some of the phrases he had heard. It flattered him that the women at least had kept their eyes shut throughout the prayer and were keeping them that way still. It was a procedural point that might later on come up between his bride and he. On the other hand, he admired the way she kept her two palms pressed together, forming a little steeple of her two white hands.

"And Lord, we know that you are looking down upon this food and these good things to eat, and we commend them to you for Jesus' sakes amen."

"Well!" said Deborah's mother. "That was real nice. And now Mr. Pefley, would you care to start the sweet potatoes?"

He did. The potatoes, which lay side by side in an enamel platter that bore a tiny painting of a bouquet of yellow and green flowers, had a crust of sugar on them. He took one only and then passed the plate along to Blephy who took three. Because both men were saving themselves (as they soon made visible) for the meats.

They drew apart from one another for the afternoon respite. William went first for the hammock but found it taken already. Next he climbed to the hayloft and would have settled there had not Jesse sat up suddenly and hissed at him. Finally he made his way to the arbor and climbed up into the manifold and interlocking scuppernong vines that formed a cradle, as it were.

The warmth of the South had not really begun, and William had to content himself with a two o'clock temperature of some ninety degrees of mercury or even less. The women, meantime, had retreated into the house itself and from his position William could plainly see where the curtain in Debbie's room was wafting back and forth in a calm and moderate fashion that seemed to represent the girl herself. She would be lying on her bed, unless he missed his guess, and her skirt would be spread out around her, as in one of those paintings showing girls like her sleeping in the forest. Or, perhaps she was sitting at her bureau while combing out her long black hair in graceful strokes. In that case she would be gazing at herself in the mirror and her expression, which would be entirely serene, would show neither haughtiness nor discontent. Moving mentally into the room itself, he thought he saw a stuffed animal on the dress of drawers, and in one of the drawers itself, a compilation of his own letters held together in a pastel ribbon.

Jesse had gone straight for the barn and had precipitated himself onto a bedstead composed of nine bales of straw and, for pillows, two of hay. He had a horse blanket in lieu of a spread, but in warmth like this he saw no need to crawl beneath it. He was a thin man and the pumpkin pie had been too much for him, so much too much indeed that he had caused himself to vomit three times before climbing back to his roost beneath the eves. Now, reflecting back upon that meal, he felt that he was being called upon to return and finish off the little bit of pie that still remained. And that, of course, was when the William fellow came and put his head through the hatch and stood waiting for his eyes to adjust. In the meantime Blephy had gone away and Jesse believed that he could identify the sound of his whistling as it faded away across the field that led to where the Negroes lived.

She had tarried for a certain time while the table was cleared, the dishes put away, and the chairs returned to their usual positions in the house. She could not go and lie upon her bed, not yet, not until the iceman had come and gone and been paid. And when finally she did go and did lie down, soon she sprang up again and began to do what needed to be done with her hair.

She fell into a trance. The warmth of summer had only just begun, life was slow and she was calm. From below she could hear the chimes of two o'clock, a reminder and a suggestion of all the years still to come. The warmth of summer had only just begun. And this: the sound of someone whistling merrily down along the meadow far away.

The old people — (they were not so old) — lay next to each other on the carved bed that had comprised an appreciable part of the woman's bridal equipment. The warmth of summer had only just begun. And if the husband had a pretty good idea of where the men were resting, where was Mary? That was when the chimes struck the hour of two o'clock. It wasn't so easy, falling off to sleep, not when he had someone next to him slapping every few moments at the summer's flies that had only just returned.

"July, I reckon," he said.

"Pshaw, they won't wait till no July. You saw how he was looking at her."

"Yes I did. But what was he seeing?"

"That's not for us to judge."

"Six cousins, every one of 'em better looking than her."

"Quiet. It's in the *beholder* — you know that."

"And that mule business — I didn't think he'd do that."

"Ssssh. He's going to go far and do us proud. And so just hush up about it."

He nodded slowly. "Yes, he probably *will* go far, he has so far to go. Now if you'd of asked me in advance, I would of said that he'd of taken off that big hat of his at dinner time. But oh no."

"Well what do you want Hubert? Want her to sit up there in that room for the next fifty years? They're going to do just fine. And I'll say this: by the time that boy is *your* age, he'll have six times more than what we've got."

He grumbled.

"Mary's the one that worries me."

"I wouldn't say that. You saw how Blephy was looking at her."

"Oh God!"

etc.

Some of them slept and some did not and when it came to be four o'clock William climbed down from his place and went to look in on his mare. He was surprised to find that Mary and Deborah had arrived there before him and had been talking to the animal and combing her until she had grown so prissy and vain that she now refused even to look at him.

"She's ruint now," he said. (He knew how to bring her under control however.)

"You haven't combed her in years!" Mary said.

"Never have and never will," he said, looking at her evenly.

Deborah had not spoken although he was aware of her standing just to his side. The two girls had been working so diligently that both were breathing heavily, a circumstance that affected William. And then, too, the elder of them had two or three little curls that had come down upon her forehead where she had four, possibly five, beads of sweat. Never had he seen her in this state — breathing, sweating, her hair disarranged. Perhaps now the younger girl would go away.

"And you ought to feed her better, too!"

A raven flew into the barn and then, seeing the people, ran back out again. Far away they could hear the sound of thunder or, mayhap, the earth itself breaking up. They continued to look back evenly at the younger girl. Finally:

"Well, I guess I better go help mother."

"Yes. It's only fair."

She departed in dignity, halting only once to turn and glance back at them.

"Do you have to leave today?" Debbie asked, once they were genuinely alone.

"I do. I told Joe I would."

She came a little bit closer, the first time to his knowledge that she had done so. "We shall be man and wife," she said suddenly. "Isn't it strange?"

He nodded slowly. It *was* strange. They were carrying out the roles that had been assigned to them, even if neither of them could know what those roles ultimately portended. They would have to wait and see.

"I sure do hope I die before you do. I couldn't stand it."

"No! No, you have to go on living. We don't live long in my family, we women don't."

"You're going to live a long, long time — I'll see to that. Me, I'll probably get killed in the war."

"No, and you'll probably have two or three more wives before it's all over. My uncle did. What war?"

"*I do not want any other wives*," he said slowly, pronouncing each word. "If I had wanted other wives, I would have married other wives." (He could feel his gorge rising.) "I just want Deborah and Deborah and Deborah."

She edged closer, the second time she had done so. The distance between her lips and his was somewhere approximately between seven and ten inches and conceivably less. She *had* been sweating; he could see three tiny little drops not very far from where one of the curls had escaped their confinement and was lapping at her forehead that otherwise was stainless. He dare not think about her waist and whether he could encompass the whole of it within his own two hands alone. Instead he reached out to support himself on the column that supported the building on this side.

"Well." he said. "I'm going to kiss you this time for sure."

She came closer. The fear that sometimes he had found upon her face had gone away.

"Someone had to be the first to ride a horse," she said.

They kissed, awkwardly at first, and then came back for more. She was a living creature in her own autonomous right with secrets and desires that belonged to her alone — he recognized that in the way in which she was willing to take on half the responsibility for the kiss. Carefully he placed one crude hand on her delicate back, left it there until he could have counted to about five, and then took it back again.

"I do love you, William."

"Nobody could drive that nail just by firing a bullet at it. I was the only one."

"And I'm going to be a good wife, too."

"I figured you would. And I'm going to have us a brick business, too, even if it takes a hundred years. I promise."

"Take more than any hundred," said Jesse from the loft, "the way y'all are carrying on."

He departed at a little before nine, with thunder in the east. The mare was willing, the evening cool, the stars outstanding, and the man himself floating in a dream. Two miles beyond the river he caught and passed a lone traveler — Blephy   limping homeward with a watermelon. William said nothing at first but then, blaming it on his mood or perhaps the weather, actually turned and waved.

TWENTY

He woke a little earlier, Jesse, than he had wanted, but then got up anyway and went outside. The day was dreary and overcast, the way he liked, and the sun so thin and feeble that one could nearly have believed it were February once again. His routine called upon him to feed the animals in the order of their impatience, a system that when violated had results that could be heard for miles around.

He arrogated three eggs from three of the hens and broke them open and gulped them down. Next he drew off about half a liter from that gimpy cow whose milk was usually the sweetest. Today, however, he was disappointed — the fluid had separated and looked like chalk suspended in water. Finally, his last chore of the morning, he brushed his teeth and brushed them well, using for that purpose a splayed willow twig.

He ran to the levee and was about to pass through it when, jumping back in great surprise, he found that once again the commissioners had plugged up the passage that he and his friends had reamed out with such great effort this past November. He was also startled to see that a goat had leapt from the levee onto the roof of one of the Negro shacks where it was grazing eagerly on the tin cans and other debris. Here in the shadow of the levee all things were cut off from the sun, a contingency that had left this entire part of the state in a semi-darkness closely akin to outright night. The crows were numerous, the sun still lingering, and the breeze nudging at the weeds in such a way as to make Jesse feel that he was wading through a lake that reached up to his knees.

Half a mile further he came to a knoll that permitted him to see for a considerable distance into the direction in which he was traveling. He could definitely see the far-away city of Montgomery, recognizing it from the smoke, the steeples, and the black onyx statue, higher than the clouds, representing one of Alabama's most admired governors. He could see further than that and what he saw looked to him like those living and extinct volcanoes that marched along the border with Tennessee.

He had all kinds of time — he was young and nothing needed to be done that couldn't be done when came the time to do it. Summer and winter he liked to lie on this particular hill and, clutching at the grass, gaze down into the heavens spread out below him like a newspaper on the ground. And should his courage fail him, he could always turn and lie face-down.

After a certain time he arose and pressed forward, pushing his way between the uncomprehending cattle. He jumped a creek and then, finding that he had leapt further and with less effort than usual, turned and jumped back again. The stream was full of mosses and stones in which the trouts had made their nests; indeed, bending near, he could see any number of new-born troutlings trying out their fins. Normally he wouldn't intercede; this time, however, one of the larger minnows was behaving in such a way as to cause Jesse to plunge his hand in amongst them and... Too late.

He arrived at the edge of the woods and after waiting there for a few moments, drew back into the trees. It was a defeated sun that Jesse saw running off weakly into the west; shielding his eyes, he tried to follow its flight, but only to spin around in great surprise when suddenly the girl came up behind and touched him on the shoulder.

"Boy howdy!" he said. "I thought you was your father coming to kill me!"

They laughed. She looked good to him.

"He probably *would* kill you," she said. "If he knew you were here."

"Well don't tell him, OK?"

They laughed. She had worn a red sweater in honor of the weather and her cheeks were of the same bright hue. As to her hair, she had arranged it in a way that he had not seen before.

"I'm fixing to kiss you," he said threateningly, pointing his finger at her. "And you can't stop me neither."

Horrified, she turned and tried to run to the right, all quite in vain. And yet when he did kiss her, and did refuse to call an early halt to it, at that time it did seem to him that she was kissing back. He felt a little wave of fear that soon passed over however.

"Boy howdy," he said, giving her time to breathe again. "Well, looks like Debbie's going to marry that fellow. And if she can do it, there ain't no reason on earth why we can't do it, too. Want to?"

She had taken a little flower, had broken it off, and now was sallying about in front of him holding the thing in her mouth. This was what worried him: was it honorable to wed someone who looked to be about twelve years old?

"Maybe," she said finally. "But first I have to find somebody I want to marry."

"Damn you!"

She ran, he chased. He caught her down by the pecan tree where the ground was still littered with last year's shells. He knew that women often pretended to be weaker than they were but marveled anyway at just how weak she was. Having put her on the ground, he declined to rest his weight on her, contenting himself rather with kissing her on the ear and several other different locations along the neck. It didn't seem to annoy her, not to any considerable extent.

"You're so brave," she said, touching him on the scar and then tracing it from length to length. "I guess this is where the bullet went in. And this here, that's where it came out."

"Correct."

"But what about here"

"That's where it went in again."

"Oh Lord. People just didn't realize how brave you are."

"They know now, I reckon." And then: "I'll kill *anybody anytime.* If I have to. That's just the way I am."

"Would you kill me?"

"Shore! You get yourself another boyfriend and I'll kill you for shore. Him, too."

She sighed with pleasure and then suddenly blinked, closing off his view of the sky. (For he had been watching it in her eye.)

TWENTY-ONE

Two days went by during which William accomplished any number of things. But when Wednesday came and soon thereafter went and the machine began to give off too much smoke, Joe Butler turned his attention to the gourds that had filled the garden to overflowing and were encroaching upon his hut. He was pulling them out by the roots and taking them down to the river when Mr. William came riding up.

"You got those cedars all cut up like I told you?" the man asked. (He had not yet dismounted.) "I'm going to need 'em for the house."

"Yas, suh! House?"

"And that older boy of yours — he knows how to stack brick don't he?" (He dismounted now.)

Joe groaned. Already there was so much to be done and now here again something new was being thrown at him.

"I'm going to put it right up there on that rising, Joe, so she can see the sun come up. And I tell you this, there's not going to be any two-by-fours in *my* house, no sir. She wants four-by-fours, four-by-sixes."

"I 'spec so, yas suh, four-by-fours. Who?"

"And the toilet, Joe, it's going to be *inside the house.*"

"'That how she wants it, yas suh."

"We're going to make our own brick, too."

"Is? I declare."

"But first I got to build a kiln." (He remounted.)

"There he go," said Joe, speaking just loud enough for the other person to hear. "Can't wait till *tomorrow*, he got to do it *now*!" And added then: "Yas, suh."

He drove toward town, William did, but half-way there had to stop and punish the mare. Like all lower animals, horses lean toward self-indulgence and need a certain sort of person to save them from inclinations of the kind. Next, someone had disfigured the countryside by casting off an empty snuff can. Again William stopped, scooped it up and then pushed the horse at a gallop to the edge of town where already the oyster bar proprietor was in process of closing for the night. He believed, William did, that a business should keep *regular* hours and that it were a moral mistake to abridge them in any way. He stopped, the third time he had done so within a journey of just five hundred yards.

"Having trouble, Simon? Trouble at home?"

"Why no, Bill. What made you think so?"

"Well! I see you're closing up already." He pulled out his watch and looked at it.

He arrived at the bank just as the man was locking his desk and preparing to exit the place. It was the most famous desk in town, known to contain all sorts of deeds and warranties and the like. William went to him straightway, saying:

"Need $800."

"That horse of yours," the banker said, "looks like he's about ready to faint."

"And I'll pay up by March."

"You don't have to pay that much for a horse, Bill. Hell, I got one you can have for fifty." (He was having trouble with the desk, so much so that William was able to get a brief glance at what looked to him like a .45 caliber revolver nestled among the warranties and deeds.)

"And if I don't pay you back, you can kill me."

"Say what?"

"I'll stand out in the middle of that field of mine — I'll have me a big house out there by then — and you can shoot me. Nobody will blame you."

"Oh for God's sake Bill." Taking off his glasses, he began to knead the bridge of his nose, a thing so narrow and poorly attached that William thought it might actually come away in his hand. "*Collateral* is what I need. And you don't have any."

"I do."

"Yes, you do. But you've used it all up already."

William looked at him evenly and then slowly and without vanity extended his right hand and allowed the man to look at it for a long time. It was smaller than your average sort of hand, but so swollen by work and blisters and layers of callow that it appeared older by far than the remainder of the man.

"Jesus. And what's this here, Bill?" the banker asked, shifting over into his stronger glasses and bringing the hand closer to his eye.

"Railroad spike. Long time ago."

"Jesus. And there! What, you been messing around with dynamite?"

Outside the horse had fallen onto its side but was making good progress in getting back to its hoofs again. Pushing his mind into the future, William could foresee the time when he would own larger and more enduring horses than this one and possessed of better blood — dozens of them. And when he was young, once he had seen a fancy saddle made of painted leathers and bestowed with a silver horn.

From the bank he went direct to the warehouse and finding it shut continued on to the man's home, where the family had gathered for prayers and supper.

"How are you, William?" the man asked, getting off his knees and coming forward. He was wearing an apron and bib, both quite soiled, as were also his fingers and beard.

"I'm ready to buy that bellows. The one in Troy."

"Oh?" (He had to bend somewhat in order to view William through the hundreds of little holes that comprised the screen. Apparently he had accepted that old story as to how a tad of cotton attached to the screen would ward away the flies.)

"That's a pretty high-priced hickey, William. Cost you a hundred and fifty-two dollars and some change, near about."

William took out the money and after giving the man occasion to gaze upon it, returned it to his vest.

"Yep," said the man, "looks like that ought to do it. Tell you what — I'll get it for you this coming Monday."

"No, sir. Need it Friday."

"Bill, Bill, Bill. Sometimes I try to remember how it used to be. Before *you* got here. You don't remember those days do you Bill?"

"And I need to borrow your nigger, too. I'll pay you next summer."

"You've already got one Bill! I've seen him."

"Need two."

"Bill, Bill."

He drove straightway home, surprised to find the garden full of empty places. Gone were the turnips and gone the corn while the one remaining row of cabbage had turned to gunk from too much sun. Someone would have to answer for this. But first he wanted to step off the boundaries of his new property and reconfirm they had not been altered in his absence.

He wanted his wife to wake at dawn and see the sun nudging up behind the levee. Desired the house to stay in view of the river and the slave quarters now slowly crumbling back to dust. She should see the brick mill (where he would already have been working for the past two or three hours), and witness smoke climbing to join the clouds. Accordingly he marched eighty-five feet in that direction, sizing the parlor and two bedrooms against the lay of the land and then marking the spot with a twelve- cent piece, the shiniest thing he had. The inside bathroom came almost as an afterthought, whereupon he marched fifteen feet further and marked it with a copper cent destined to be rediscovered eleven years later by his eldest son.

He wanted his sons all in one room, a cordon between his wife and the outside world. (He knew, of course, that the outside world would come all the way up to his door someday and take away his land and house and everything.) Wanted a big barn and wanted it like a hotel, with individual chambers to accommodate the personalities that would reside in it someday. He went to it now and stepped off almost a hundred yards before he came to himself and began backtracking, erasing more than half the building. He knew a tinsmith in town and knew, too, the sort of weathervane he would ask the man to build. Nor had he forgotten about Joe Butler's house, which was to lie at a certain distance from his own while yet providing space enough for the man's current and former wives and offspring.

"Fetch me two or three of those rocks," said he to Joe, who had just now come up and was standing behind him. "I don't have any more coins."

"Yas, suh. You ain't gunna put that old house *here*, is you?"

"*Your* house, Joe. I've already done mine."

The ground was mostly sand and yet if a person went down a few inches, soon he came to Alabama clay. Joe probed with his finger and, finding matter, grinned.

"How many children you got, Joe?"

"Got nine. Used to have ten. How many *you* got, William?"

William ignored it. He had just been called "William" by a Negro, who had also the temerity to point to his lack of children. William looked at him sharply but then, slowly, relented and ended up by picking up a pebble and throwing it at him.

"You can't do that, Joe, when we got company — call me 'William.'"

"Yas, suh. I ain't seen much company out here."

He laughed, and soon after William joined with him.

TWENTY-TWO

He awoke at just after four in the morning and after doing what needed to be done, rode out to meet his store-bought bellows. The train had sixteen coaches and fifty-two cars, a heterogeneous arrangement in which the individual wagons listed perilously as they strove to adhere to the hickory tracks. William urged his horse from one end of the train to the other and then turned and came back and called for the engineer who, however, couldn't interpret him above the noise. He was surprised, William was, by a well-dressed woman who reached out suddenly from one of the coaches and patted his horse on the nose.

He might as well have remained in town, and when finally the train did come to berth and the refrigerator cars had all been opened and the leaden seals scattered in fragments along the tracks, and after a dozen boys had gathered up the metal and run away, at that time William was able to talk to the driver.

"You bring my bellows?"

"So you're the one."

"Where is it?"

"They can fire me if they want to, I don't care. They can take my pension, my wife, uniform, I *won't never haul anything like that again.*"

"Where is it?"

"Where is it? Where is *this* — that's what I want to know."

Not answering, William looked back at him evenly.

"I come here, lose two wheels. Y'all still got wooden tracks out here for Pete's sakes! And that trestle — I wouldn't let a goddamn squirrel set foot on that thing!"

William left him and went back to look into the cars.

"Hell, I wouldn't let a *lizard*..." the man called after him.

The first car was empty, although he thought he saw a bale of straw in the corner. Came next a wagon crowded with cows and a tired-looking man with a pointed stick.

"I'm looking for my bellows," William said.

"Fellows? They ain't here."

He moved on, passing a drunk person and then a blind Negro with a banjo and begging jar. It was William's obligation to contribute something, provided the man was any good.

"Or would you prefer a swig of whisky?" he asked.

"Yas, suh!"

William retrieved the coin and returned it to his pocket. Already the heat was affecting the refrigerator cars and he was by no means certain that the fruits and vegetables would arrive in wholesome condition at the next town. Came next a load of newsprint and scrap iron and then, finally, the car in which his oversize bellows had been broken down into two parts with the membrane folded up on top. He climbed aboard and ran his hand over the implement's wooden surface, polished and smooth as a musical instrument's.

It needed the rest of the day to transport the pieces home and settle them on level ground just next to Joe Butler's shack. By this time it was dark and they were both too tired to attempt their first batch of brick.

"We'll do it tomorrow," said William.

"Yas, suh. We got to cut those pines 'morrow."

"We'll do the pines on Thursday."

"Yas, suh. We ain't got no clay."

"Build a kiln, too."

"We got to work for Mr. Johnnie on Thursday."

"I haven't forgot."

"Don't know 'bout... What you say."

"Kiln?"

"Don't have none of them, no, suh."

William waved him off to bed. He had not eaten in two days — he realized it when he caught the faint and far-away scent of scorched chicken emanating from the Negro settlement. At the same time he was assailed by the smell of honeysuckle bearing down upon him from all sides, leaving him in a weakened state. It would kill him someday — honeysuckle, roses, magnolia, and the rest of those things. Nearer at hand he could hear a hog grunting in the woods, a whippoorwill calling every few seconds from some new unexpected location, and then the almost imperceptible sound of a flight of crows seething past just overhead. Moving to the edge of his property he thought that he could hear children calling far and near, all of them highly devoted to squeezing the last drop of pleasure from the terminating day. And of course there were *always* crickets, crickets in the grass and crickets in the woods, and one cricket in particular who had selected a place in William's hair.

He did love it so. Wasn't it necessary to live *some* place in order to live at all? And if it were, wasn't it good that it had turned out to be *this* place, *these* crickets and hogs, *those* fields and woods and Joe? And if he had not deserved to come forth in the time of the prophets, or even of the war, oughtn't he be grateful for having been inserted into life at *this* time, instead of in the days that he could foresee when he pushed his mind forward?

He had not slept in eighty hours; even so he could still keep on his feet by advancing slowly from tree to tree, each time testing the ground in front of him. Sheltering his eyes, he examined his sawmill from two different angles, a devilish contraption that had altered the ancient ratio between effort and result. It might be evil, probably it was, though not so evil surely as failing to repay his debts. And saying so, went to gather his boots and carrying hod. He was determined to excavate at least some clay before he slept and was prepared if necessary to work by lantern light, or fireflies, or proceed by touch alone.

TWENTY-THREE

She used to stay upstairs in hot weather and crochet doilies and related things. After so many years she had a collection of them, along with books of verse and specimens of sewing. On the wall she had all sorts of ribbons and medals that Jesse no longer wanted, and in her chest of drawers some forty-three letters in tiny script authored by William Pefley. And then from time to time on these hot days she might lift her head and gaze out over the acres that her family possessed — *that* was when Jesse usually came and knocked three times politely at her half-opened door. He hardly ever set foot in the house itself and she viewed it as a compliment that he would do so today.

"Getting married!" he said, and then jumped back and spun around and pointed at her in a kind of scandalized amazement. The girl kept on sewing.

"Yes, sir! Now Debbie, are you really going to let that fellow take you away from here? *Far, far away*, she's gone and she won't come back. Who's going to look after the hens and them, that's what comes to my mind. Mary won't do it."

Debbie snapped off the thread, tied it, and kept on sewing. She had a way of brushing the hair off her forehead even though she and everyone else knew that sooner or later it always fell back down again.

"Yes siree. Babies! Y'all going to have babies coming out your ears." And then: "You ain't never had any babies before. Scared?"

"Don't you want to have babies someday?"

150

"Me? Ha! Oh I reckon."

"Well when, Jesse? You're going to be twenty-two years old pretty soon."

"Twenty-what-did-you-say? A man's got no business with babies, Deb, not less he's got him a *wife*. You see any wives in here?" (He looked around for them.)

"What about Clara Phipps?"

"Cla...? Hee! Old Clara, yes siree. She won't even come over here unless I'm gone!"

That was true.

"Well. There's Lulu."

"Great God A'mighty!" He threw himself on the bed and laughed on it.

"Well, there's..."

"There ain't nobody. See?"

"There's Ruth."

"She's thirty goddamn years old, Debbie! And she's done ruint two husbands already. Maybe more, for all I know."

That's true.

"Well, you'll find somebody."

"Where will I find her, Debbie? Find her standing out in a field somewhere?"

"Oh, Jess."

"Sure, I could meet her on Sundays. 'Now you people just run on along to Church and I'll go meet my girl.'" (They did often meet on Sundays, Jess and his actual girl.)

"I worry about you Jess."

"You need to be worrying about May 22nd. What you going to do, Debbie, when that fellow comes after you, crawling across the bed real fast? Expecting you to know about things."

She bent nearer over her work. Seeing that he had found his target, he left the bed and seated himself across from her.

"It's real easy to make a mistake in a case like that — that's what they tell me."

"Mistake?"

"Shoot yeah! You'd be surprised all the things that can happen." He took up his right hand, extended his fingers, and then counted off in silence the five major things that could happen. Finished with it, he continued over to the other hand. That was when Mary came in and, seeing him playing with his fingers, went back out again. The cat meantime had taken up in Debbie's lap. Immediately the girl began stroking the animal and measuring its ear between her thumb and forefinger, as if trying to come to an understanding of its thin meaning.

"You got to be careful, Deb. That fellow's liable to put you to working in the fields."

"Oh he will not."

"He'll have you working *all day long.* He will."

"She got a letter this morning," said Mary, who had returned, accompanied this time by a glass of ice tea.

"I ain't surprised. Me, I never get letters."

"But she won't let me see it."

"Except one stinking little birthday card 'bout five years ago."

"She's ashamed of it."

"Oh I am not neither."

"Why, if she weren't ashamed, why she'd let us see it."

Deborah looked at each of them in turn, doing it twice. Finally, slowly, she rose and went to her chest of drawers. The letter had been torn open in a sloppy sort of way — until it occurred to him that it might be due to haste. Returning to her chair, the older girl removed the letter and after examining the first page, and first page only, returned it to the drawer. The second sheet she handed over to her brother. Drawing apart from the others, the boy now read through it slowly, stroking his chin.

"Hey, look at this picture."

"It's a brick."

"What, did *he* draw that? He's a worse fool than I thought."

"It's a *brick*! He makes bricks, good ones. And I'm going to make 'em, too."

Mary snatched away the paper and gaped at it. "That ain't no brick! Anyway, it's got something on it."

"It's his trademark."

"Oh. He's got him a trademark now. He ain't got a decent pair of shoes but he does got him a trademark."

Deborah grabbed back the paper and folded it rapidly. "No wonder you don't get any letters, if you don't know how to appreciate them."

The boy started to reply but then, thinking that she might be right, turned morose suddenly and looked down at the floor. "Well now, just a minute there; I'm not the only one, Deborah. Lots of people don't get any letters."

Mary had gone, which is to say had gone to her sister's bureau where she was trying out the perfume and the combs. Soon she was posing in the mirror with a ribbon held to various parts of her coiffeur. "I wouldn't let anybody marry me," she said in dreamy voice, "unless he was just *desperate*."

"Yep. He'd have to be."

The children's mother drifted by and seeing them congregated there, came inside. "Are they teasing you, Debbie? I won't have that in this house."

"Show her the brick."

"Oh. And there's Mary over there, too! And all this time I thought she was dusting in the parlor."

The girl sighed but then finally did come to her feet and go away.

"And can that be *Jesse* over there?"

"Yup. Looks like him."

The mother pointed him to the door. "Were they teasing you?" she asked, once she was alone with her daughter.

"They think they are. But it doesn't work."

"Well that's good. What brick?"

"Mother?"

"Yes?"

"What if...?"

"No, that won't happen. You could always come home if you had to. But you won't have to."

"But what if...?"

"No, no, no. He's just a boy! Well no, he's a man. But he doesn't know any more about the world than you do."

"He doesn't even have any good shoes."

"He will, he will. Now listen here, that child's going to have all the shoes in the world. I know about these things and if it was me, I wouldn't worry about anything. And I *sure* wouldn't worry about the future. All you have to do is look at him."

"Yes."

"Your father had some of that. Of course now, he's a good deal older than he used to be."

Deborah agreed, and agreeing, put the cat on the floor. "I wonder what he's doing now."

"Well let's think about that: 'what is he doing now, what is he doing now?'"

They thought, both of them, both of them concentrating seriously, slicing through space and time to where William...

TWENTY-FOUR

... was carrying a hod of clay.

He had worked all night, interrupting himself only once for a half-hour's rest in Joe Butler's shed. Nothing outraged him more than these bodily infirmities that forced him to leave off what he was doing just as he was getting into the stride of things. Why? If they truly desired an improved world, God and the prophets, why must there be such a thing as sleep? It was a mystery.

He came awake next morning at just after ten, but failed to leave the bed. In the dreams that followed he remembered the story of one of his father's cousins who had perished when he was only four. And what possibly could he have accomplished, that boy, to be granted relief at such an age as that? It made William mad, mad that he hadn't received the same benefice and mad, too, that the story had not gone on to give the particulars of the case. And where was he now, that boy — shrieking in Hell or playing childhood games in Paradise?

He rose finally at about eleven-thirty in the morning and, blushing at the lateness of the hour, went to check on his garden, his machines, and the calf that he had bought last week in Troy. The garden was gone, the calf had broken free, and the sawmill boiler was throwing out torrents of thick black smoke that lifted only a short distance before falling back and settling on the ground.

A Negro boy stood at the controls while another was feeding the furnace with tree branches and other debris. These were Joe's children, reckoning from the looks of them, even if William had never seen either of them before this moment. He was not accustomed to other people taking the initiative and yet, when he came to the window and looked inside, he found some two gross or more of well-shaped bricks stacked up in good order in the heat. There was nothing to complain about.

"That's a pretty good fire you got," he said to the boy, who seemed to understand what he was doing. "How long they been cooking?"

The boy looked to the sun and then pointed to the position it had occupied when the cooking had begun, a distance of about three hours.

"That ought to be enough, three hours."

"Yas, suh. No, sir, needs more." He pointed again, this time indicating a position in the afternoon.

"What's your name?"

"Calls me Grady, yas, suh. Sometime they calls me Doc."

William waited for the rest.

"Some folks calls me Tyrone."

The other boy meantime had gotten on his hands and knees and was inserting the branches of wood one by one in a scrupulous effort to keep the chamber filled with fire. William looked on for another few minutes and then, finding nothing to say about it, strode across to where the boys' father was slicing a massy cypress log that was almost too dense and water-logged for the blade. William witnessed it, saying nothing. The machine was his and it was no great matter to him if others could operate it better than could he.

Thousands of bricks and tons of mortar — he needed all of that and more. Needed kegs of nails and sticks of lumber and sixty plates of glass both large and small. Climbing to the top of the knoll, he again marched off the dimensions of his new home, widening it here and lengthening it there and stocking it mentally with a better grade of furniture than he would have been willing to settle for only a few days earlier. For his wife he wanted a dresser with a beveled mirror and numerous little drawers and hiding places for her diaries and pearls. And although he could not name *all* of her possessions, he did know about the combs, the cameo that had been given to her ancestor by Napoleon Bonaparte, and the long and narrow purse of glass beads that formed a perfect home for gold and silver coins, provided only that she had any. Sketching in the sand, he designed a chair and dresser and then, using his finger, outlined the picture of a baby child that was out of all proportion to its size. He wanted toilet facilities *inside his house*, and far away ceilings to fend away the Alabama heat. But when came time for winter, that was when he wanted four distinct fireplaces representing each of his four sons, and chimneys of stone to serve as memorials long after the house itself was gone.

TWENTY-FIVE

They married the last day of August, according to the Alabama calendar of that year. Rain had been predicted, high water and an early death for crickets; in fact the weather was proving mild and genial and the crickets, instead of vanishing, were showing up in the largest numbers since 1884. Riding forward slowly on his most stately horse, William took note of everything. He passed a farm he would have liked to own and then, soon after, crossed a river full of astounded-looking fish who came running up from far and near to sniff his horse's feet.

He was dressed in his best clothes and had rented the finest saddle in the county, a compound affair of red and yellow leather. His wallet also was of leather and held sixty-five dollars in paper and three in coin. And, of course, he was aware at all times of the watch that had come down to him from his fathers and that in recent days had begun to give the time again — a sign that boded favorably for his marriage as he believed. It is true that his shoes were nearly worn out, a deficiency he had sought to remedy with the materials available to him.

Toward noon he encountered a funeral procession of some dozen persons carrying aloft the tokens and other rubbish of the Catholic sect. In this instance William pulled off along the highway and removed his hat but declined to dismount. He had no personal complaint against these people and it saddened him beyond words when he pushed his mind forward for a momentary glimpse of their unutterable fate. Suddenly William stopped, blushed, and then got down quickly off his mare. He hadn't seen the flag and hadn't realize until now that the man had served in the war.

Twenty miles from the settlement he stopped and spoke to a farm woman who fetched him a jar of water direct from her well. She also brought two red roses for his lapel.

"Getting married, I said to myself. That's what I said when I seen you riding by in that great big suit of clothes and everything."

"Yes, ma'am."

"Well you're a fine-looking fellow, all strong and pretty-looking. How about *her* — is she any good?"

William looked back at her evenly. "She is, yes ma'am. I'm just sorry she's marrying a person like me."

The woman laughed and spat and then took a swig out of the gourd she was carrying. "I used to have me a husband once. Long time ago. And he was *lots* better than me. Better than you, too."

"Yes, ma'am. I guess he's in paradise now."

"Well. I didn't say he was *perfect*, you understand."

"In paradise, and looking down at us right now."

She glanced to heaven and then began to move back in the direction of her house, a tumble-down affair with grass growing on the roof. William had been checking the skies for the weather and when next he looked to the woman she had reached the top of the hill and was going down the other side.

"Looks like rain," he called.

Faint was her reply, and far too far away to hear.

He passed the night among interwoven magnolias sharing eighteen great white blooms. Nineteen would have been excessive and made the air too sweet. It did not, however, rain, and when toward dawn he arose and prayed and spent the night's last minutes giving testimony to the stars, and plucked a cricket from his rose, and fed and admonished the horse, and got back into his clothes and mounted and then pushed off.... Summer was over and the last of August finally getting under way.

He had not expected to be greeted by these five little girls waiting in the roadway with ribbons in their hair. Having brought no presents, he gave each of them a copper penny and smiled upon them as brightly as it was within his nature to do. Four persons (Deborah not among them) stood waiting on the porch. Had it been *his* house and family, the porch would have been six times larger than it was, with fretwork and wooden furniture and a parrot in a cage. William smiled and lifted his hat and rode on toward them. Meantime the dowry mule had been combed and oiled and tethered to the gazebo where it stood watching interestedly. But mostly William's gaze traveled to the upstairs room. It was there, in that room, that his wife was being folded into a complicated system of apparel calculated to extend a woman's innocence and test a man's patience for a last five minutes or so, depending upon his ingenuity and fingers. As realistic as he was in these and all other matters, he could not easily account for his heart, which was near to exploding.

The people had been good enough to fetch a preacher of William's own persuasion. Two other men, Baptists he believed, represented Deborah. He shook with all three of them but then ended up falling into an embrace with his fellow churchman, who wore a red beard. He had been wrong to think that Deborah's mother was upstairs wrapping her daughter — here she was, dressed in green, her hand outstretched to shake with him.

"Why Mr. Pefley! You certainly did choose a good morning to be out riding."

"Oh for God's sakes Gladys!"

William held up his hand for silence. "Mama and daddy can't come," he announced. "But they wouldn't mind if I got married."

Mary had come out, had gone back in, and now was on the porch again. Three times she strolled about the groom to view his clothes and bearing.

Her father had a newspaper under one arm and was holding a lighted pipe in his teeth.

"Got three bass yesterday," he said. "And Jesse got a four-pounder."

William looked for Jesse, finding him standing off at a distance. They waved, each to each, and nodded slightly. Of all that group, he was the one William trusted most, but also the one most likely to go to Hell — it was a mystery.

They went in. Right away William noticed Deborah's brothers, all of them (save Jesse) apparently drunk. He disliked the way they had appareled themselves in a mixture of suits and ties and work clothes, a palpable insult that would *not* be forgotten by the groom. He passed by, William, refusing even so much as to acknowledge them. Three gifts, one wrapped in Christmas paper, had been set out in such a way as to make them look like more. Paying no further attention to these, he stood to one side with his hands behind his back. There were twelve or thirteen people in the two adjoining rooms, all but one of them allied with Deborah and her family. William sauntered to the man in the red beard and then, finding they had nothing to say to each other, continued on to the wedding cake. It appeared to him that the bottom stage of that cake was being asked to bear too much weight — which is to say until he strolled around to the other side and saw the scaffolding that held it up. Mary meantime had gone away and gotten into a different set of clothes but now was back again and playing at the piano. All conversation came to an end as the piano grew louder and more and more tragic until at last the girl also began to sing. Suddenly William pulled out his watch and looked at it. He was supposed to have been married several minutes ago; instead the three ministers were still turning through their Bibles trying to agree upon a verse. It surprised him when he went to check on the weather to find Joe Butler and the tallest of his six sons waiting in the yard with a gift of some sort wrapped in brown paper. William acknowledged them kindly and permitted them to pass the item through the window. For they had come by train (he later learned), and were anxious to get back home.

Sooner or later, his wife would come downstairs. Running his mind forward, he tried to remember what she looked like. Had she changed over the past several weeks, or had he perhaps been mistaken about her from the start? He saw two women whispering and smiling to one another in the adjoining room, as if they had information that might have made him change his mind. William, however, looked back evenly at them.

The music came to a stop at 10:44. From among the crowd an elderly man with a disfigurement on his nose came forth and offered William a receipt and a document (gilt running around the edges) that needed to be signed. He looked for, and found, the signature of his wife who, judging by her script, was just as nervous as he.

"You can pay me later," the man said gently.

"How much?"

"And Pastor Breem — it was so good of him to come all this way."

"How far?"

Jesse came up. "Well aren't you even going to open your presents? They's a box of shotgun shells in there — I know because I gave 'em to you!"

William thanked him and shook hands.

"I'm thinking I might get married myself. Someday."

Up until this point no one had disturbed the punch, not until Blephy suddenly emerged from the foyer and helped himself to a goblet of the stuff together with another wedge of cake.

"About three dollars usually," the magistrate said. "'Course now, it's up to you."

His mother-in-law floated past. "Why Mr. Pefley," she said.

"I'm waiting to see your face when she comes down those stairs," Jesse said, calling to him across the floor. "You ain't never seen anything like this!"

The magistrate had gone away, leaving William with nothing to do but return his billfold from whence he had taken it. The ring itself was in a pocket of its own where it could by no means get confused with other things. Again William took out his watch and then, finding that it had petered out on him again, rapped it sharply three times across the back of the chair. And now he would never know how late he was at getting married.

In fact it was 10:56 when the girl appeared at the top of the staircase, sending the crowd into moans and sighs of satisfaction and delight. Right away William took off his hat. He would have liked to go forward and guide her down the steps, except that Jesse was standing in the way while examining his face. She was dressed in white moccasins, white veils, and a white cape that fell to the ground and followed after her — he had never seen anything like it. The music was louder and more official now, Mary making no further attempts to sing to it. His bride appeared not to have noticed him among the crowd. Or, having noticed, preferred to pay no heed. Saddened by that he moved into the light that came from the window, arriving there just as she stepped down to his own level. In order to retrieve the ring and show it to her he had to put on his hat again, but by this time she had already drifted past him toward the parlor. His role was to follow after, he believed, but he was slow to get past Jesse and into the room itself. Finally he found a place for himself in the corner where a cage of blackbirds used to be kept. The portraits were gone, most of them, as also the canned fruits and vegetables.

It came as a relief when at last the minister in the red beard began to read aloud from Ezra. He preferred old prophets to young, William did, especially when recited by a man who looked like a prophet himself. Hearing those familiar old words, William's heart began to settle and his mind grow calm. He had expected to hear the full chapter and was brought up short when, suddenly, the man called a halt to it. Even now William was not absolutely certain about the order to be followed, and whether there might not have been a last-minute change in the identity of the groom. He looked to Jesse lounging in the doorway — the fellow had not been allowed in the parlor as a child and no longer sought it as a man. Behind him stood the enormous cake in the foyer (now listing dangerously to one side), and behind that Deborah's worst brother flapping his arms like wings.

He was called to the front of the room but Deborah still didn't look at him. Standing there, he smiled graciously, knowing that these smiles of his were unlike those of others. And in short he wasn't sure that smiles belonged upon a serious man. The ring was there — he could feel it against the middle knuckle of the hand that hung down on that side. He was to be married now, if time endured, and very soon new generations of men would come pouring from him and from her, people of integrity to turn the world around. She was very near. Looking into her face from that distance he could divine the fund of molten gold in which her heart was wont to float. And gave to her the ring he held, and from his lapel a rose.

TWENTY-SIX

He walked out of that place a changed man. Wandering down to the barn as if in a dream, he fed and consoled his horse and then, realizing that he had left his wife behind, turned and ran back to the house. *They* had joined together, Deborah and he, but not so his new mule and horse who continued to stare at one another with open distaste. He spoke to them severely, but then finally had to use his quirt and all the strength that he and Jesse could muster to connect them to the carriage that would take them home.

Home? He had some acres, two worn-out machines, a few Negroes, and a house that promised to be enormous when it was done. Had sixty-five dollars in paper and two in coin. It was true that he was rich in debts, that he had a certain kind of face and could see several hours into the future with perfect clarity. Had a watch that weighed two pounds and a pair of boots that had served a long time and begged to be retired.

Surrounded by relatives and friends, he and his wife sat looking straight forward in the buggy. The journey promised to be problematic — (it was clear that they loathed each other, the horse and mule) — but not anywhere near as problematic as the night that soon must follow hard upon.

"You think you're nervous *now*," Jesse said, grinning at them. "Just wait till night."

"Reckon I'll have to use the quirt," William said sadly, referring to the mule.

"Yup, that ought to do it," Jesse replied, referring to the wife.

The girl's father walked around to her side of the carriage, spoke, and then came to his. "Cotton's up; you might want to think about that."

"I thought about it. Believe I can do better with my bricks."

"People will always be needing cotton."

"I expect. They're going to want bricks, too."

"Daddy, they need bricks more than *anything*," said William's new wife. Hearing those words, he turned and looked at her for the first time in twenty minutes. Everything he saw met with his approval, a strange and unique experience for him. Her hair, contained as it was within a veil of very fine mesh, was as tidy and as good as anything he had ever seen. And then, too, he had always had a special respect for her profile (because it was noble and good). Oh yes, she would of course die someday and someday rot in the ground, but not for a long, long time. Suddenly his mind flashed forward to the home toward which he was directing her, a ten-room mansion of which, however, one room only was fully prepared.

"Well I suppose you'll just want to turn around and come right back here, once you see where I'm taking you." (He was oblivious to the people circulating around them.) "Will you?"

She answered, but so softly that he couldn't hear.

"Will you?"

"I really don't care where you take me," she said, whispering calmly and with deliberation.

He nodded. Those were serious words and he needed a moment to understand what they implied. He whipped up the team and drove forward for about six paces, causing the people to chase after them for that short distance.

"But what if... What if life is *hard* for us, and so forth."

"I don't care. I want it to be hard."

And now he *was* amazed.

By driving into the west, they were able to prolong the daylight hours. He found his mind slipping back and forth between his bride on the one hand and on the other the several jobs of work that awaited him at journey's end. And then, too, his first loans would soon be due.

"Well," he said without looking at her. "We ought to be all right for a year or two."

She waited for the rest of the story.

"My father was always poor. Reckon we'll be poor, too."

She snickered gaily and then reached over — and it was the first time in their married life that she had done so — and squeezed his arm. "No, we're going to be rich I think."

"The bricks, you mean?"

This time she laughed out loud. "No! Because of *you*."

There was some truth in what she said. He could imagine himself poor and himself rich; what he could *not* imagine was the possibility of ending up like other men.

"Well," he said. "If the bricks don't do it then the cotton will. Going up, cotton is."

"Yes, and I know how to pick cotton, too. Daddy used to have cotton, and Mary and me, we used to…"

The man turned pale. Reining in the team, he pulled the buggy off to one side and sat for a time, saying nothing. When finally he did speak, he did it very slowly, enunciating each word. "I hope I don't live to see that, Deborah, the day when you have to work outside in the field. I had rather be *dead* and *buried* and gone to *Hell*. It just can't be. Never, never. We shouldn't even be talking about it."

"Oh. Yes, let's not talk about it."

"Buried and rotten and with a knife in my heart."

"No, no. Oh look at those clouds!"

He glanced to the clouds, which made no impression on him. "Rather have my two arms drop off than to see you out there in that field."

"Well I just won't go out there then." And then: "We sure did pick a pretty day for our wedding!"

"Rather be in Hell. Just sit there for thousands of years."

"Bill! Please, I want to show you something."

He slowed somewhat, allowing her to probe about in the white lace purse she carried. He had changed his mind about the rain, which had run off toward Georgia seemingly. He caught up with and passed an elderly Negro in opaque glasses paddling forward with a gnarled staff. Came next a handsome farm that could have been handsomer, had only someone troubled to arrange the pile of firewood in a more attractive manner. Itself the sun had just begun to weaken and was giving off that faint sulfuric aroma that typified that moment in the day. Plenty of stars tonight, he judged. He did not however expect to be guided by them on this bright night. The road was clear.

"We have this," she said, showing him a bundle of American currency in which right away he spotted a fifty dollar bill.

He reined in. "My gracious."

"It's two thousand dollars, Bill. And a little more."

"This is *your* money, Deborah, not mine."

"Mine?"

"Absolutely."

"Well then, I'm giving it to you."

And did so.

At 6:46 the sun shut down briefly but then soon came back on again and continued to burn more or less steadily for the next twenty-seven minutes. He took it as a sign, William did, and began to keep his eye out for a place in which to pass the night. An abandoned grist mill came into view but when he went forward to review it, found it full of cobwebs and two inhospitable raccoons. He was tempted to stop at his favorite farm in these parts, a large property with mown fields and dark purple lake. The cattle here were serene and the two-story white house had probably a dozen rooms in it, of which some were likely vacant.

"I'm thinking I'll ask for a room," he said, pointing to the place.

"No, Bill, please. They don't even know who we are."

He parked at a distance from the building but then changed his mind and drove directly up to the front porch where the man himself was drifting slowly back and forth in an iron swing suspended from the rafters.

"Looking for a place to spend the night," William said.

"That right? That's probably what I'd be doing, too — if I was in your shoes."

"We can pay."

"But I'm not. In your shoes, I mean."

William looked off across the field. The man was set up very enviably here, but not as enviably as William when William came to be as old as him.

"Don't have a spare room do you?"

"Well, let me see." He sat up, filled his pipe, and then began counting off the spare rooms on his fingers. "There's Nana's room. She's dead now don't you see. And then there's the south room. But you wouldn't like it. No furniture. Roof leaks." He grinned.

"Can you recommend a place?"

"Oh shoot yeah! You name it, I'll recommend it."

It needed all of his resources not to wish this man in Hell.

The stars, just he had predicted, were plentiful and bright. In the distance he could see the lights of Montgomery pulsing evilly in the night and behind that, much further still, the brilliant glow of orange-colored ooze pouring out over the brim of one of Alabama's most eminent volcanoes. They could have gone on traveling for hours, except that it seemed to him inappropriate on their wedding night. Meantime he was learning a great deal about the woman, especially her tendency to remain cheerful in spite of what was going on around her.

"Well," he said finally, drawing to a halt. "I reckon we're lost."

"Well, no wonder. It's the roads — running off in different directions all the time. You want some cake?"

"I have come this way a dozen times. And now I'm lost."

"Yes, but that's a *good* sign. If it starts badly, it's bound to turn out wonderful before it's over."

"All my life the moon has been directly overhead. Look at it now."

"Oh, moon! That will just have to take care of itself. Here." She reached the piece of cake to him and then waited, knife in hand, to see if he would require another.

"Well. We could go back I reckon."

"No. Jesse's there."

"Or, we could just keep going."

"Yes, let's see where this road goes. I'm curious."

They went on. The team had not been foddered since morning and signs of insubordination were beginning to show up in their behavior. He was not however interested in punishing them at this time and in view of his wife. Up front a lone traveler was pushing forward into the night with a pole and lantern, but William was prevented from consulting with him when, suddenly, the fellow turned from the highway and went crashing off through a field of sorghum. Glancing to the stars, William now realized for the first time that significant numbers of bats were hovering just overhead. He grabbed for his wallet, desiring to make certain that his two thousand and some odd dollars had not fallen off onto the highway when he wasn't aware.

It was well past ten o'clock in the evening before another house came into sight. He estimated that it lay about a thousand rods from the highway, but after he had driven that distance and further, and as the lane continued to narrow until at last the wagon overlapped it on both sides... He could not turn back now, not if he wanted to remain the sort of uncompromising person that he was. And if at first he had discerned two separate lanterns glowing in the woods, now there were none.

"We could just wait right here," she said. "And pretty soon it'll be morning."

William, his anger rising against the mule, said nothing. He *would* continue to the house and *would* speak to the people, and if it entailed a great deal of trouble to do so, that had no importance whatsoever

"Bill?"

A small animal dashed across in front of them. The moon had turned its dark side to them (or had hid perhaps behind a star), and all that he could see was one wan light that might at any moment disappear. He believed that he was in Coffee County still, and never mind that the landforms in this district seemed unfamiliar to him. And then, too, the cicadas and tree frogs were oddly silent just now, though he knew not for certain whether that were a propitious thing or not.

"I can't see, Bill."

Other developments followed, especially when the buggy ran suddenly down an incline and came to an abrupt stop in a creek bed.

"Thank you dear, but not just now," he said, declining the cake that was being offered him.

A minute passed. It was not true that the crickets were altogether silent; he could hear a fair number of them calling from the meadow on the other side. Suddenly he flailed violently with his quirt, hoping to bring down one or more of the bats. The moon meantime had come back again, leaving William and his wife to marvel at its magnified reflection in the stream. Stretched too thin, holes now began to show up in the texture of that otherwise bright image.

"Well, I better talk to these people," said William, pointing to the faraway house, "and ask if we can stay the night."

"All right."

"You stay here."

"No Bill, I'm coming, too."

"I'll be back pretty quick."

He got out, adjusted his hat, and then began to march downstream at a moderate but steady rate of speed.

TWENTY-SEVEN

She sat quietly, looking into the woods. Those small noises and movements, they were caused by the breeze, she believed, or birds searching for things to eat in the dark black night. Ten minutes of it, with her nerves growing somewhat more at ease, she climbed down from the buggy and went and stood at the head of the mare. She would have liked to victual both animals, had only she been given the formula that William used. Meantime she continued running her hand over the mare's black velvet muzzle, a soft terrain with about a dozen widely-separated bristles growing in it. Searching deep within the horse's eye, she saw there not just moon and stars, but many other things as well.

TWENTY-EIGHT

He found a place where the water could be forded but had waded only a short distance before he saw that either he must turn back or allow himself to get wet all the way up to his waist. His shoes and belt were of leather (which was not even to mention his wallet), and would need several days to dry. At first he was shocked by the temperature of the water, but grew accustomed to it soon enough. Snakes, crawfish, eels — they wouldn't pester a person at this hour. Even so he was relieved to come to dry land where, confident of his footing, he could travel so much more efficaciously, and fast. Here he paused and, turning in the direction of his wife, called out in the secret message code they had developed for contingencies like this. Her reply was weak and faint and needed a time to reach him.

"Caw! Caw!"

He went on. There *was* a house up ahead, and two lights shining from different windows. A large dog came bounding toward him, but instead of attacking, continued on toward the river in order to pick up the scent at its point of origin. William passed a tin shed abandoned many years ago, now rusted down to almost nothing. Just as bad were the lightning rods and weather vanes on the gables, all of them broken off or pointing away uselessly in various directions.

He strode to the door (which held a pane of stained glass), and knocked three times politely. The dog had meantime come back and was using his nose to compare the scent of William's shoes against the tracks they had left behind. Inside someone was coming slowly down the stairs, as William could plainly see by pressing his nose against the glass. "Caw!" he heard, although this time the noise was almost out of range. Suddenly, finding a connection between the man and his tracks, the dog retreated to the edge of the porch and began to bay very loudly. William had left his revolver with his wife.

Courteous by nature, William pretended for a long time to be unconscious of the face peeping out at him from between the curtains. He knocked again. It was a small face, and pale, and might almost have been a child's but for the cigarette and thick glasses. Suddenly he grabbed for his wallet, William, finding it intact. He was not greatly bothered by the dog, not even when the creature somehow managed to get his tooth snagged in William's shoelace. He would have liked, William, to have a meal and dry underwear; instead...

He knocked again. A second face had come to the window, this one a Negro's. Disposing of his patience, he turned and confronted the people.

"I am *William Pefley*," he said, "and I am out here *knocking on your door!*"

Right away the faces disappeared. He had seen enough of them to know that both were women and both were frightened, and that the room behind them was large and comfortable-looking and decorated mostly in shades of brown and gold. He waited for someone in authority to make an appearance and when none did so, he went back and...

Knocked upon the door.

"What you want!" (It was the Negress speaking.)

"I am *William Pefley*, and that is my *wife*!" (He pointed in the direction of the parked carriage.)

"You better git on out of here! We don't need no williams. Git!"

He could feel a headache coming on. He gazed down at the floor, pressing at his temples. Finally:

"I can pay."

"We don't need none of yo money! Git, git!"

Came then a second voice, this one sweeter:

"Pay?"

"Yes, ma'am."

"How much?"

"Ma'am, I've got *two thousand dollars* right here in this pocket. Two thousand."

"It's so dark out there. And you probably haven't eaten either."

"I have not."

"Well that's no good."

He and the dog went back quickly to the carriage, rescued the girl and carried her across the water in their arms. It was only the second or third time that her face had been this near to his.

"Gosh, you carry me as if I didn't weigh *anything*!"

Never in his years had he held a woman like this. "When we reach the other side," (he wanted to say), "we'll be one person." Instead he said nothing. "I won't drop you," he said.

It was no surprise to him that animals had a natural liking for his wife; it *did* surprise (and anger) him when this individual dog tried, first, to separate them and then force William back across the creek. At once he gathered up a stick and was about to use it when he was prevented by the rueful expression on Deborah's face. He had forgotten to set her down and when at last he did so, she took him sweetly by the hand, only the fourth time she had done so.

Several lights had come on inside the house; moreover, William believed that he could see someone of authority waiting just inside the door. His wallet was where it should be and this time he had brought his weapon with him as well.

"*William Pefley*," he said, once he reached the door. Slowly, too slowly as it seemed to William, the man consented at last to shake with him. He was dressed in a nightcap with a tassel of some description that interfered with his line of vision.

"Looking to rent a room," William said. "I can pay."

"So I've been made to understand. We *do* have a room. But I don't really know who you are, do I? Don't know your family, don't know where you're from."

"Coffee County — that's where we're from."

"This is Coffee County."

"This is where I'm from."

"Well, that's all right then. Your family now..."

"Christians."

"I see."

"And this is my wife. Her daddy was with A. P. Hill."

They were taken behind the house and thence to a defunct corn mill with a waterwheel that was still intact. Even in pale moonlight William could see that the structure had been built in the traditional way, with massy timbers joined and notched. Someday the whole world would look that way. They entered by aid of a rope that forced open the door.

"You'll want a lantern I imagine."

"We will."

"Kerosene is six cents now. I don't know, I just don't — what's happening to the country."

William turned and looked at him evenly. "Burn in Hell, that's what they've got to look forward to, people like that. We'll want some supper, too."

He had to tread carefully because of the perfect dim. Here, where the sound of the river ascended through the flooring there was enough moonlight to set the spider webs to glowing. By no means would he allow his wife into these precincts, not until he had swept and secured the chamber that destiny had assigned to them.

"I'll fetch the carriage."

"Yes, do. And I'll fix things in here," Deborah said.

"No. I'll do it."

"Oh. Then *I'll* get the carriage."

"No, dear. It's way over yonder and you'll get wet."

"Then I'll help Mrs. ——" (she mentioned the woman's name) "with supper."

"No, dear. She's being paid."

The bride looked about for some job to do. "Couldn't I sweep the floor?"

"No broom."

By 11:07 the carriage had been brought forward and the cake carried inside. The money and gun William kept on his own person. But when he came outside and found his wife feeding the horse and mule on unmixed oats...

"No, dear," he said, taking the bag. "They won't know what to think if somebody else feeds them."

What followed surprised him even more. Slowly, gently, patiently, she pried open his fingers one by one and returned the bag to her own possession.

"I'll do it."

He stood back. She was too generous with the oats, especially for the mule who deserved rather to be punished for his recent attitude. It was while he was standing there that the squire himself emerged from the house and came to join him.

"She's young and all dressed up," the man said, speaking confidentially, "and she ain't afraid to work neither. Me, it took me *twenty years* to get my wife to do anything. She *is* your wife, right?"

William turned and began to fumble for the papers that showed they were married. Suddenly the man took the pipe out of his mouth and pointed to the team.

"I see you've got yourself a mare and you've got yourself a hinny, and you've got 'em hitched up together like that. Don't believe I've ever seen that before. Good Lord!" He laughed.

William, whose expert knowledge pertained rather to bricks and timber than horses and hinnies, said nothing. In fact his mind had begun to separate into two parts, one part for the present moment and the other looking ahead to what might be happening in about an hour from now.

They were served with slaw and fried chicken and a miscellany of warmed-over biscuits with marmalade. It was near to midnight now and they were alone. Below them the million-year-old brook continued to push past, even as for all the other brides and grooms dating back to prophetic times. William ate sparingly, his mind still divided.

"Wish I had a setup like this," he said, nodding down at the defunct waterwheel. "I'd hook my saw to it. Wouldn't have to worry about steam."

"Oh, steam! We can get along just fine without that."

He started to speak, but changed his mind when he saw that he had nothing to say. "Looks like rain tomorrow," he said. We could use it."

"I know! It's so dry this year."

William agreed. "That's why we need it."

"It's either raining too much, or not enough."

"This year it's not enough."

"No."

Both people now pushed back their chairs and began working in tandem to clear away the dishes. A few bright stars could be seen through the tattered roof. Came then the far-away call of owls mixed with the noise of the coyotes and wild dogs who held that part of the county. He stepped outside to listen, where soon he was joined by his wife.

"It's those wolves again," she said.

"No dear, dogs is what they are." And then, after thinking about it: "They're pretty much the same really, wolves and dogs. Except that wolves are more fond of evil."

"Oh. But they can't bother us here. Can they?"

"Lord no, not as long as I…" He drew out his gun and let her gaze upon it. In the distance, too far to hear, a jagged bolt of lightning made a sudden appearance, lingered briefly, and then slowly disintegrated — a transitory staircase to heaven as it pleased him to believe.

For some minutes they stood studying the doings of the night. He had already kissed her six times before they were married and one time since, making a total of seven up until this point. Now, taking her into his arms, he kissed her again whereupon she right away went limp and her hat fell off.

He could have used a drink of spirits; instead he put her to bed and, working slowly with his carpenter's hands, removed all her clothing, every bit, each item disclosing some new marvel to his eyes. Never had he seen anything like it. And if at first he thought she might be sleeping, he had to reconsider that when she smiled at him and opened both eyes brightly. They were of *one* mind now.

TWENTY-NINE

He drove home quickly, hoping to beat the rain. His experience in marital matters had increased significantly in just one night, a truth visible to the black man waiting at the gate.

"You cut those pines?" William asked.

"I been fixing to, yas suh." Helping the woman to alight from the carriage, he was unwilling to speak about business at this time. Six sons he had and each son (but one) had two names. The one left over had three. It was the tallest of them who now came forward and offered to take the woman's cake and luggage into the unfinished house. Immediately the groom led her to the northernmost corner of the structure and pointed to the work that had been done.

"Most people use two-by-fours," he said. Me, I use four-by-fours, four-by-sixes."

She marveled.

"I did this," he said, pointing to how the bricks interlaced and overlapped and formed, as it were, a lattice between the earth and bottom floor. "Hard to find anybody in this day and age to do this kind of work."

"Can't *nobody* do it," Joe Butler said.

She marveled, even going so far as to kneel and touch the mortar with her gloved finger. That was when Joe, able to stay silent no longer, said:

"How come you bring back that ole *hinny*, Mr. Bill? We don't want him around here. And look, they done got him all covered in *oil*!"

"I believe Mrs. Pefley wants to go inside now."

Using the wheelbarrow, the six men quickly put together a temporary staircase to let her ascend into the house. She gave heed to the floor joists, the gaps between them, and the earth beneath. One room only had been floored and papered and stocked with furniture, and even here a great deal still needed to be done. She glanced to the bed, a heavy appliance, dark and deep, which sat about twenty-four inches above the floor and needed a little staircase of its own.

He gave the woman an hour and fifteen minutes of privacy while he inspected his calves and bricks and the little bit of timber that Joe had felled and hauled and stacked in the heedless fashion of the members of his kind. On the other hand, he was extremely pleased to see that the hydrologist really had carried out his promise, putting him in possession of a hand pump that reached (he later learned) more than a hundred feet through shale and substrate and thence into the high quality waters that also supplied most of the rest of the county. Keeping a neutral expression on his face (the Negroes were grinning) he brought up a fistful of the rose-tinted stuff and sipped at it astutely, finding the aroma acceptable as also imbued with a certain undeniable mischievous quality as well. Years had gone by, eons, whilst this treasure had effaced itself, remaining well out of view of prospective land buyers and the like.

Strolling down to the river, he surprised an enormous sturgeon lolling in the wash. Already the trees had shrugged off most of their leaves, exposing opossums who had been tardy moving to other quarters. Far away a hawk had died or gone to sleep in mid air and now was falling ever so slowly to earth — William waited till the thing had disappeared behind the horizon before turning and heading home to his wife.

"Reckon I'll go downtown," he said.

"Yes, do. I'll wait here."

"Want you to meet some people."

"Bill, I'm still in my wedding clothes."

"Need to go by the bank, too."

They walked the distance quickly, the woman doing as well as she could in her Montgomery shoes. He never wished to call attention to himself, but had no objection to calling it to his wife. Gazing straight forward, he was obscurely aware of people coming out onto their porches. She had the smallest waist in the county, his wife did, and on this day was dressed more conspicuously than anyone.

"William?"

He stopped, turned and bowed to the mayor's wife, who had actually left her porch and had come down halfway to meet them.

"Is this your new wife? My goodness."

"Yes ma'am."

"Well gracious! And so pretty!"

He waved it away. Deborah, blushing meantime, continued to look down at the sidewalk. She *was* pretty, would never be prettier, and had only a little time for her beauty to be seen. "Yes, ma'am," he said. "But I reckon she'll have to die just like everybody else. Die and rot, just like you and me."

"William! I'm not going to talk to you anymore. God!"

They continued on. He was half-hoping the surveyor and the preacher might happen to see them, though it were a sin to hope so. Two Negro boys slowed as they approached and then moved off the sidewalk. They passed the oyster man, who seemed thunderstruck by the woman in her parasol and wedding dress. Up ahead the bank now came into view and in front of it a small knot of men who, judging from them, had been telling stories and joking obscenely. These, too, fell silent as husband and wife walked by. All his life William had wanted it this way — to be a person of substance, have wife, and occupy a position among his fellow men.

He entered the building, went straight back to the opened vault and pulled his wife in with him. Of the boxes that he had leased, one was for deeds and papers and the other for memorabilia along with a box of shotgun shells and two sacks of coin. Together they looked through these possessions, the woman giving special heed to some dozen photographs rendered largely illegible through the processes of time. The third drawer, holding nothing, had been reserved by him as a hedge against the future. They stood, husband and wife, looking into its contents. Suddenly he took the two thousand dollars from his vest and began to sort the stuff according to size. The bills were upside-down, some of them, while others had wrinkles in them.

"You're twenty-three years old," he said understandingly. "But when you get to be twenty-eight, why then I expect this box to be full of money."

She looked again into the void.

"Completely full. But if it's not, well then I'll just go out into the field and get hit by lightning."

"Oh, Bill."

"And by the time you're thirty, we ought to have thirty cows, too. At least that many."

"Thirty! We'll have to get a bigger box."

"And that land across the river? It's good land, Debbie, real good — I'm expecting us to have our share of it."

She clapped hands. The banker, meantime, had perceived them loitering in the vault and, holding his hand far out in advance, came to join them.

"Oh my goodness, I've heard about this — you're Mrs. Pefley. I knew it. Knew it soon as I saw you!"

They shook all around. He owed this man several hundreds of dollars, William did, and he saw no reason, William did not, to prohibit him from staring at his wife.

"She's a beautiful, beautiful woman, Bill, my goodness yes. I knew she would be. Lots of children!" (He glanced at her belly.) "We need 'em, we sure do."

Her belly was the smallest in the county. Suddenly he reached out, gathered up a pile of William's twenty-dollar bills, and began to smooth out the wrinkles. Long were his fingers and green, and no one knew how to organize bills of currency better than he.

From the bank William went direct to the grocery store and after giving the shoppers time enough to view his bride, continued on to the courthouse. He had hardly ever seen so many people crowding the hall, farmers for the most part, many of them having come to pay their taxes. The assessor's office was staffed by an old woman dressed in jewelry and a set of glasses that hung by a chain. He waited until her attention settled upon him at last.

"Afternoon, Martha. This here's my wife."

She looked to the clock, surprised to find that it was, as he had said, afternoon.

"They's a property over by Lonegran's store," he attested. "'Bout half an acre. Already been sold I reckon."

She had expected to be asked a question. Hearing none, she continued to struggle with a plat book that must have weighed twenty pounds. That was when she caught sight of Deborah for the first time. They waited as she came up for a nearer look, did look, and then stood back to see her from a different angle.

Halfway to the livery they encountered the Methodist minister hurrying home with a bottle of milk in a sack and a loaf of bread under his arm. Quietly the two men circumambulated each other, the minister finally saying: "Charming, charming. But tell me this Bill — did the 'prophets' lead you to her? No really, she *is* charming — all you have to do is look at her." He stepped back three paces to judge her from afar. "Yes, graceful, I would say, yes. Graceful rather than... Yes."

Apart from horses, the livery itself was vacant. William led his wife down to where two geldings stood leaning up against each other inside a cozy cell. Having allowed them a good long look at his wife, he turned and came back, moving slowly past the stalls. Outside the sun had run down near to the horizon and thrust its lower quadrant into the earth itself; seeing it there and knowing that night was nigh, knowing further that he was part of a two-person family now and that his bed was wide, he took his bride by the waist and led her on to the restaurant, where he had scarcely ever been wont to go before.

They fell silent, the cook, the blind man, the newspaper vendor and the shoeshine boy. Right away William conducted his woman to a place near the rear but then changed his mind and came back to a table with gingham napkins and a matching cover. He was grateful for the silence and solemnity, and for the waiter with his fine manners and attitude. Of course it was William's natural habit to deal coldly with these people, as indeed with most other people as well.

They ate in dignity, the first time in their married life they had supped on a restaurant meal. Outside the day had turned to night so suddenly that it seemed either that the weather was making an error or that God was ceding to the urgings of the bats and night-adoring crickets. They were having a glass of wine, were William and his wife, the second such glass since they were married. She drank first, drinking but little, and then pushed the cup to him.

"Well," he said. "After you been here a while, you might get to like it."

"Bill! I like it now."

(He was extremely pleased.) "We're just a bunch of poor people of course. Ignorant. However, that dudn't mean we don't have some godly people hereabouts." (He proceeded to name three of them.)

"Yes, I knew it would be nice. And it is."

"Real peaceful, too. He's shot three people just since May."

"Who, Bill?"

"Sheriff. That's how come it's so peaceful." He pushed back the wine. "Now Deborah, this is my plan and I want to see if you agree with it. First, we need to finish the house and..."

She agreed.

"...then we need to have children. I want to get started on that right away. And I want to clear about thirty acres 'tween us and old man Callaway, put some cows on it. He promised he'd buy some brick from me and if he does, why then we're going to need a bigger kiln. If we had two kilns, Deb, shoot, we could make some *money*." Suddenly he pulled a diagram from his coat pocket, unscrolled it on the table and held it flat with cup, bottle, and pocket knife. Together they poured over the diagram. Another minute of it and the woman had left off looking at the paper and had turned her attention instead upon her husband's face.

"Bill?"

"I'd burn coal, if I had me a better boiler."

"I think you should do what you think best."

"In that case we better stay with pine."

She agreed. There was a rigidity in her husband's face, particularly about the mouth. On the other hand, if she moved slightly to one side, there was a significant amount of innocence in the eyes. She was fascinated by this and everything, including even the two blue veins that stood out on the back of his hand as he made a note in the margin of the diagram. Suddenly he drew yet another folded paper from his vest and began reading it with an expression of worry on his face.

"What's wrong?" she asked.

Bill said nothing. The waiter had returned and then, seeing them occupied, had gone away again. Outside a great white venomous moth, big as a large man's hand, had attached itself to the screen and fallen to sleep there. Debbie sipped at the wine and then pushed it back again.

"Bill?"

"I don't know about that older boy of Joe's. He might be all right." Suddenly he drew out his watch, looked at it, lay it on the table and then from his shirt pocket extracted a letter of many pages that was almost too fat for its envelope. Debbie focused on the stamp, a rare item, bright red, bearing the picture of one of the presidents or someone of that kind. "They want me to go back, work at the store."

"Is that what you want?"

"That will have to be your decision, Debbie. I won't do it."

"I'm glad."

"Of course now if he made me a *partner*..."

"He should. Really."

Suddenly her husband brought out a list of materials for the hog house he expected to build. He had a pretty good handwriting (for a man), but she had trouble with the superadded curlicues that burdened the message itself. From her location, the words were upside down.

They walked home slowly in the gloom. It was such a black and heavy sky that only the most resolute stars could stand against it. The toads, on the other hand, were profuse, and had joined together in an unlovely song too rich by much in consonants. William was aware of all sorts of little currents and miniature tornadoes on every side, the work of the wind in the powdery night.

"And do thee love me truly?" he half-consciously wanted to ask. Instead he said: "Careful here. It's dark." (They were holding each other in their individual ways — she in her way and he with his arm about her exceptional waist.)

"Truly I do," she might almost have been saying. "O look," she actually did say. "Joe has lit the lantern for us. See it glowing in the woods?"

THIRTY

The boy came in summer, arriving as a child, William went in to look at it and after finding that matters were more or less as they should be, congratulated the doctor and shook hands with his wife. It was the first of his sons and he was of course pleased with it, even if it seemed to him that by this time he ought to possess twice as many. The same held true for his house, which was only three-fourths finished by now. Truth was, he called for all four sons to come at once, and a finished house with all sorts of dark and heavy furniture in it made to last three hundred years.

He did take consolation in his bricks, artifacts of yellow (fossils in them) that chimed together sweetly when they touched. He liked to lay them down in parallel walls and fill the space with mortar. Took pleasure as well in his own personal trademark — two candles in the sun.

He composed his bricks out of his own clay, together with unreserved helpings of the public sand that lay about in all directions. He had sawed his timber, too, and had joined these variegated elements — clay, timber, sand, bolts and nails — had fitted them all together by aid of his own Negroes.

"We need more land," said he to his wife, who had come outside to gather some of this year's scuppernongs. He could not help but notice, William could not, that she was using for that purpose the very pair of scissors that two days earlier had separated her from the child.

"Because I don't know how long that vein of clay will hold out. Where's the boy?"

She was wearing a sunbonnet of such depth that he could not with any
real confidence identify the person at the bottom of it. She had suffered tre-
mendously from the baby and appeared to have lost all interest in speaking.

"Plenty of land over there," he said, pointing to the mostly unexplored
territory beyond the river. (In fact he hoped in time to possess both sides
of that stream and set up his own personal ferry to be operated by one or
another of his sons. [He'd never of course be able to control the river itself,
nor veto the boats and ships and migrations of the fish.] That land also had
a great many walnut trees.)

"If we had just a thousand dollars, I believe we could get a start on
things. Pshaw, eight hundred would be enough."

She turned and looked at him. "We don't have any money?"

"No, dear; I've invested all of yours. And besides, we need furniture."

"Oh. Couldn't we get the furniture later?"

"I don't see how."

The child that had been sleeping in the vines now suddenly came awake
and began to look about in great surprise. William lifted the thing gingerly
and gave it to his wife. From where he stood he could see in one unified
glance both his calf, his garden, his child, his heap of uncooked bricks, and
both the bamboo grove that filled to overflowing the south-easternmost
part of his tiny demesne. These things had been bestowed upon him for a
certain duration and either he would improve and amplify them and make
his mark in life, or else go down without complaint to the torment that
awaited at the center of the world. It is true that he had replaced the boiler
of his steam-powered saw, using for that purpose above a hundred dollars
from his deteriorating funds. But these days when he wanted to slice water-
logged cypresses apart, his machine had the strength for it. They grinned,
he and Joe, seeing how the logs "fell apart," as it were, like a well-done roast
collapsing into layers beneath a knife.

"It don't stop for *nofing*," said Joe. "It just keep on *goin' and goin' and
goin'!*"

Some of those beams were sixteen inches square. He regretted it, did William, that he had not incorporated them into his own house; instead, he turned his attention to the golden-hued bricks piled up almost to the tin roof over the cooling shed. Retrieving the child, he held him up to the kiln and encouraged him to spy in through the little window, made from mica, where the process of vitrification was taking place in front of his face. These mellow bricks were the best in the county and contained all manner of antique sea shells that dated back to Bible times. They watched the process until the child wearied of it, whereupon William carried him to the chicken coop and set him comfortably among the hens.

He was beginning to understand that the boy would need more age on him before he could contribute in any way to the work that needed to be done. As to the child's character, if he had any, and his underlying integrity, it was not possible to make a determination at this time. Looking deep into those black eyes, there did seem to be a kind of goodness there, as if the boy had chosen to take on his mother's traits.

"He's going to be a good-sized boy," said William, "when he gets to be a man."

His wife said nothing. Sitting at the extreme end of the little cement bench that William had set up in the garden, she had drawn up into herself and appeared to be suffering from the cold. In fact it was the middle of summer and more than ninety degrees of mercury in the tube. William watched worriedly as she eased herself to the ground and began to work desultorily among the flowers.

"I reckon he'll be an architect, or something like that. Believe he's going to be a Christian, too."

From far away came the sound of the eleven-o'clock whistle, a promise and a forecast of the train that soon would follow hard upon. The day was full of crows, the most sardonic of all fowls, and William could see some fifteen or twenty of them riding past gleefully on the breeze. The woman meantime had taken up a fist full of weeds but seemed not to know what to do with it.

"And a doctor — I do hope one of my boys will be a doctor. He'll do it, if I tell him to. And preacher — we need as least one of those. Maybe that'll be the next one, around May don't you think, or June."

She groaned.

"And surveyor — county shore could use one."

It was his custom to work steadily until the sun began to fail and then, as darkness closed in, to retreat slowly toward the house. He fed the dogs and oiled his boots, each task bringing him nearer to the kitchen door. It was not until 8:49 that the last little tiny spark of light went down behind the horizon, whereupon he rose up quickly, went inside, and locked the doors.

He dined that night on a rillettes of pork, his head still full of boys and bricks and other things. His wife meantime had drawn off into some other part of the house, leaving her food mostly untouched. It now began to dawn upon him that she might be sick, a suspicion that confirmed itself when he returned to the kitchen and found the sink full of unwashed dishes. It was not like her to abandon her work this way. Nor like the child to go so long without complaining.

He found her sitting by the window in the northeast room.

"You're tired," he said. "And the garden is too big. Can't expect you to tend it all by yourself."

She turned and spoke. "That little vase Aunt Lena gave me? There's $200 in there Bill."

He pressed the back of his hand to her forehead. She was full of fever and had little beads of perspiration between her lips and chin and in the region about her nose. Uncertain as to what he ought do, he went out onto the porch, lit the lantern, and signaled Joe Butler to shut down the kiln. He judged that the child might be dead already, owing to the silence that came from the crib.

"I'm going for the doctor," he told her once he had returned. "Going right now."

"All right."

(He knew, of course, that he could not leave her. Knew, too, that doctor Krump generally spent the evening hours in a state of abject drunkenness.)

"Where's the child?"

She pointed. Knowing that the boy was dead, he hated to go into the room, hated to draw back the covers, hated everything about it up until the moment he found the child sleeping in his own sweat while hugging to himself a clothen chicken made of straw. William tested the boy's temperature with his hand, appalled at the warmth. He turned and ran back to the woman.

"I'll send Joe for the doctor."

"Joe? He won't go when it's dark."

That was true.

"*Is* it dark, Bill?"

"Looks like it." He really did not know what to do, a new experience for him. His first impulse was to carry her into a different room where perhaps conditions were healthier, his second to go and do the dishes himself, his third to fall on his knees and pray out loud to the same God Who always herebefore had shown such favor to him. Instead he ran to the bathroom and after igniting the carbide lamp, sorted hurriedly through the rather good collection of medications he had accumulated over the past three years.

He wasted several minutes with the literature that accompanied the little blue jar of *Pedodyne Foot-Bath Comfort* manufactured by Kay Laboratories, a treatment that had proved ineffective even when used for indicated conditions. Next he opened the flat tin box that held some dozen of *Rawleigh's Carthatic Pills*, a treatment for torpid liver mainly, although sometimes employed for other illnesses as well. Pink and hairy, remarkably heavy for their size and weight, the pills were as big as pecans in the shell.

He took two, placing them for momentary storage in his tobacco pouch. He still possessed almost a half-bottle of *Wine of Cardui*, a milk-colored solution recommended by Doctor McElree in his *HOME TREATMENT OF FEMALE DISEASES*. But whereas the boy also was sick and yet no female, William passed over this and went to an as-yet unopened jar of *Thedford's Black Draught*, which he viewed as by far the most likely of his medicines. He preferred old pharmaceuticals to new, and dark ones to light.

He poured a glass of calomel to the depth of about two inches and then crushed the pills and dispersed them in the solution. The *Wine of Cardui*, which he deemed appropriate for his wife but not the child, he decanted into a coffee cup. Finally he took a vial of astyptodyne and carried everything into the room where the woman had fallen off into an unsteady sleep.

"Drink," said he, causing her to take it down in two prolonged swallows. The fluid had filaments in it that looked like mucus, vitamins he assumed. But when it came to the *Black Draught*, which he knew from experience to be a grainy sort of stuff (full of sand as it were), he let her sip at it until it was about three-fourths gone and then took up the corner of the bed sheet and blotted her mouth and chin.

"William?"

"Yes?"

"I want my mother to see the baby. Do you promise?"

His mind formed a vision of the child sleeping in a coffin full of flowers. He managed to break one of the tablets precisely down the middle and dissolve it in calomel. The combination was powerful and gave off a chemical heat.

"For the boy," he said, holding the drink where she could see it. She smiled sadly.

By midnight he had dosed both of them to the degree that he thought best and then, as a preventive measure, threw two cups of the same material down his own still-healthy gullet. He did not like to step outside the house at this hour and therefore made no effort to medicate the animals. If it were an epidemic, he prayed for it to pass by quickly, but if a punishment to be visited upon him alone, then he begged to know wherein he had offended.

Night, too, was going through a crisis — the clouds were in turmoil and a green and yellow light was leaking around the edges of the sky. Taking his lantern with him, he went a few steps in the direction of the hen house but then shortly turned and hurried back again. In Joe's house the family had come together in the proscenium where some dozen people of different heights could be seen in profile each time the lightning struck. There was still some glow coming from the brick works, and occasional wraiths of smoke lifting skyward. Sixteen crows (mixed with ravens) stood athwart the windmill, stymieing the propeller with their weight. Suddenly just then from the village he heard the unmistakable noise of the sheriff's weapon — three great explosions separated by short pauses.

William possessed two Bibles, one of them thicker and more primitive than the other and bound in heavier boards. Opening to Ezekiel he read silently for a short time and then carried the volume in to his wife. The light was poor; even so he was aware of the woman watching contentedly as he turned slowly through the pages. She was interested in everything he did and didn't worry very greatly about herself — he had needed a year and more to apprise himself of this strange nature of the woman. Finally he began to read out loud in his Alabama accent, the aptest for this particular writer. Having gone through twenty verses, he stopped and gave himself time to sort out the meaning.

The world, devoted to sin, hung by a thread. And when he turned his mind to the people in town, those that were good and those bad, he was shaken by the advantage (advantage in numbers) held by the latter. Dying, his wife would go instantaneously to heaven and possibly his son as well, all of which suggested that he really ought not hold them to earth any longer than they wanted.

"Is it worse now, dear, or better?"

She smiled. William patted her three times on the back of her hand and then went to look at the child. The building was so large, with space enough for a numerous family, that he had to travel through four rooms before coming to the long, narrow cell designed to accommodate infants during their first few weeks. He was nearly out of fuel, William was, but by tilting the lamp to one side he was able to get a good enough view of the boy to see that he had his thumb in his mouth and was drawing on it. Again William tested the child's temperature, finding that it remained very high.

"Are you better now," he asked, "or worse?"

A long time went by without an answer. Coming nearer, William gazed at the child's fingers, things so inconceivably tiny that, really, it might be better if he *were* taken to paradise. He considered himself an able man, William did, and yet even with his normal fingers the world was almost more than he could manage. And thinking so, he opened the book and began to read out loud in a condemnatory voice that caused the child's eyes to come open and fix upon his own.

He himself still remained healthy though he expected the disease to set upon him at any moment. Finally, at just after two in the morning, he went to the attic and then stepped out onto the roof in the place where two gables came together. From this position he could see any number of bright white shiny stars, all of them cut from the same cloth as the far-away lightning that continued over Pike County. Meantime to the north a volume of magma was working its way down the slope of one of the larger volcanoes, a viscous stuff as red as paint. The night was alive with stars and with a commotion that had broken out in the chicken house where once again the hens were contesting for the softer nests.

"She's dying, I reckon," he said, pointing his face to the sky. "The boy's already dead, near about." (He believed that if he remained long enough in the full open air, perhaps he'd be infected, too.) And then, speaking as earnestly as he knew how: "I've done bad. But I didn't know it was bad when I did it." And then finally: "I still don't."

Not true. It was a sin and he knew it, this everlasting desire of his to be dead and to die and be done with it, and then climb at last to heaven through the interstices overhead.

THIRTY-ONE

Thunder and lightning still disturbed the night. Moving from place to place within the barn, Jesse was able to follow the storm as it worked its way from side to side of Pike County before then turning in a more eastwardly direction. But when he looked to the west and tried to imagine what was happening over in *Coffee* County where his sister and that William fellow lived...

He smoked at leisure, a black cigar, fourteen inches long, that he had assembled out of the materials available to him. (He had two kinds of tobacco, a black one and a green, both of them stored in the same sort of Mason jars that held his beer. His pipe, when he wasn't using it, he also kept inside a bottle.) Suddenly, that instant, a bolt of lightning dropped out of the sky before bifurcating noisily at a distance of about an eighth of a mile above the surface of the ground — for one brief moment it looked like a very thin and uniquely tall man with jagged legs but no arms or hands.

The members of his family had gone to bed, save only Mary whose silhouette could be seen dancing romantically with an imaginary man in her upstairs window. Down below meantime the cows, long asleep, were listing dangerously, placing in peril the smaller animals that shared their cells. In addition to their company he had a cat, a mule, a crowd of besotted hens dreaming behind blue eyelids and, from time to time, a rat, whose appearances were so brief that Jessie had never yet obtained a good look at him. Had also a bed of straw and two pillows of hay.

He waited until nine and then rose up and went below and pushed his way through the livestock to the outside world. There was still no rain, although he continued to look for it from moment to moment. He strode hurriedly down the sandy road, traveling on tiptoes as he approached a row of Negro shacks. There were dogs on nearly every porch, men sleeping in hammocks, whole families that had come out-of-doors to watch the lightning — they all fell silent as Jesse moved noiselessly past. An hour ago the thunder had been larger by far than the combined voices of the cicadas and tree frogs, but now the proportion was so far reversed that it was more like the other way around. He knew better than to look for them, knowing as he did the uselessness of tracking to its source the sound of insects on such black nights as this. Instead he turned his attention to the moon. Or rather to that fragment of it, a five-sided object, still left over from the storm.

By 9:27 he had come to a halt before a tumble-down shack in the shade of the levee where a leashed goat was feeding upon the trash that had cumulated on the roof during the preceding years. Jesse spoke to the creature and then, getting no reply, ran around to the other side where he blundered into a very large Negro sitting behind the building in an upholstered chair. A boat paddle leaned against the house while on the porch sat three watermelons arranged on top of each other in pyramidal form. The boy yawned, took out his knife, and then began to pare his nails in the little bit of moonlight that still existed.

"Evening, Blue," he said, squinting at his nails.

"Yas, suh." The old man's voice was hoarse, hoarse and vague, so hoarse indeed and vague that no one could have understood it who didn't know in advance what he was sure to say.

"Kinda late, ain't it — for you to be sitting out here in that big ole chair?" (He pointed to the chair, a once-luxurious piece that had sat for years in the vestibule at the county attorney's office.)

"Yas, suh. Got me a trot line down to the river."

Jess jumped back. "Trot line!"

"Yas, suh."

"I don't understand that, Blue. It's fixing to rain pretty soon."

"Yas, suh. That's the best time."

He might be right. Thinking about it, Jesse went and peeped into the metal tub (both handles missing) that he had just now discerned for the first time. He jumped back again when he saw the fish that it contained. And although a white man would not want the eels, he would have been proud enough of the other things. Jesse gathered up the largest of the catfish and held it to the light.

"Garsh, Blue," he said, "this-un ought to run ten pounds!"

"'Spec so." And then in a much quieter voice, speaking confidentially and bending forward in the chair: "She's waitin'. Down at the tracks."

He climbed the levee and sampled the night. Really, he saw no reason why it shouldn't always be like this — colloidal and blue, dark but translucent, tenuous as fluid, 9:42 in Alabama. He saw two bats warring with a nightingale and then, down among the shacks, a plumed cock pacing nervously up and down someone's gable. (For dawn, supposing it came, would come in the East, bringing streaks of violet and gold encrusted with brand-new stars.) It was still a long time before that however and the rooster had perforce a significant delay looking him in the face. Jesse whistled to him softly, causing the bird to pause only very briefly in his rounds. Other birds were on other roofs, while further he could see a flight of sparrows wheeling ever so slowly about the spires and steeples of Montgomery in the distance.

Berries grew along the ridge of the levee, though it was difficult to harvest them in the blackness of the night. The path, on the other hand, was evident, the result of the Negroes who trod this way to church each week. Jesse took care not to step upon lost children likewise difficult to discern. He did see a lizard, frozen by indecision, caught in the middle of the trail. Lifting him by the tail, Jessie introduced himself with the usual phrases. A comet blazed brightly in the creature's eye, but then quickly fell away.

He knew that up ahead there was a tunnel in the levee, knew it because he had put it there. Having arrived at the staircase, he climbed down with precaution lest the steps, carved out of sand, disintegrate beneath him. A shack stood some yards away and it was here she had tethered her horse. At this time the rain began to fall.

"I didn't know if you was coming."

"I did though."

They ran into each other's arms. He could see that it was she from the smell of pine needles and firewood and the powerful medicines she was made to take. Her body was not much larger than a sheaf of weeds bound by cords and he was afraid from moment to moment that he might lose her within his arms. After a minute they separated and then stood admiring the rain, which could by no means affect them where they stood.

"We ought to go somewhere — you want to?"

"No! It's raining."

"Yeah, but..."

"Besides, I have to go home."

"Tarnation! You just got here!" Suddenly he brought her around and began tickling her among the ribs where she couldn't endure it. In the noise that followed, the horse brayed twice and an elderly man — neither of them had seen him before this time — rose up from his chair on the front porch of the shack and went inside. Even then the boy did not immediately leave off what he was doing.

"Stop it! Just stop right now!" (She was crying and laughing at the same time. He had seen this in her before, this sort of behavior.)

"Shore," he said, "I'll stop. But if I do, why then you got to go to my place."

"Your place? You don't even have a place!"

"Shore. Got a barn."

She laughed cheerfully. One would have thought she was pretty, at times like these.

"Got a barn, got a book. Shoot I got everything a man needs in there."

"Oh you do not. You're crazy, is what it is. Everybody knows it, too. What book?"

"Yep. But nobody messes with me. You ever notice that?"

"Well sure not! They're scared."

"They *should* be scared! Hell, I'm scared myself, and I'm not even going to do anything to me."

"I'm not scared."

"Well then you're the one what's crazy." Again, he tickled, again she tried to stop him, failing again. Meantime two persons had come back out onto the porch of the shack. The dog, however, they left inside.

"Come see my barn, you want to?" Jesse asked her.

"No!"

The horse was old but discreet, loyal to a degree and able to travel noiselessly on sand. Steering the thing by language instead of reins, Jesse pointed out the route and spent the rest of his time with the girl. Seated behind him as she was, he made no criticism when she took him by the waist and chest, holding tightly. Halfway home he turned himself around and rode backwards through the rain, face to face with the girl for the rest of the journey.

"Somebody's going to see us."

"I don't care."

"Yes, but then you're crazy aren't you. Crazy, crazy, crazy."

They kissed.

"And I'm getting all wet, too."

"You don't care."

They kissed.

"I don't even think you have a barn."

He had wormed his arm around her waist. No doubt remained in his own mind certainly but that they formed a strange-looking creature now, man, woman, and horse.

They parked well away from the barn and ran through the drizzle. The building had some warmth to it, owing to the animals and the bales of hay that in some places were piled to the ceiling itself. His lantern was stowed under the roof and he needed a moment to lower it by means of the thread and pulley.

"Aint got much fuel," he said, testing the lantern, weighing it, and then lighting it anyway. The girl meantime continued to marvel at the animals. It surprised him that she opted for the cattle, but then changed her mind at the last moment and instead went and scratched the mule on its nose.

"You *do* live here!"

"Yup. Real peaceful. Most times."

The cattle, still snoring, were teetering back and forth on their feet. She chose therefore to visit the pig next, a depressed creature who lay in a heap at the further end of his long narrow chamber. At some point in the course of time the animal's ears had come under attack and hung in shredded condition over the eyes. Jesse stood back, interested to see what the girl's response might be.

"Just look at that! Those pore, pore ears!"

"I see what you mean. Guess I'll have to take 'em off."

"You better not! No, I'm not kidding." She stared at him hotly with bulging eyes. "He's got ticks on him, too!"

He had to pull her to the stairs, had to place her shoe, a cast-off relic that once had belonged to a man, had to set it down firmly on the first rung of the stairs and had then to prod at her once or twice to encourage her to the loft. Again he stood back, giving her time to appreciate his private quarters.

"Gosh," she said. "What's *that*?"

"Bed."

"And... ?" (She pointed to the pillows.)

"Pillows."

She smiled brightly, smiling both *at* him and *with* him, as it seemed to him.

"And look, he's got him a book up here." She went to check it and then, seeing that it was not a Bible, put on a baffled look. Jesse, meantime, had stretched out on the bed and was looking up at her with his hands behind his head.

"Well, time to take off your clothes, I reckon."

"I knew you was going to say that. You're the worst thing I ever heard of! I aint but *fifteen years old*, and you want me to... You're going to Hell, Jess, there aint much doubt about that anymore."

"All right, just take off *some* of 'em. And when you get to be sixteen, why then you can take 'em *all* off, shoot."

"No!" And then: "Why can't I wait till I'm eighteen, and take 'em off *then*?"

"Eighteen? I'll be old and dead long before that day comes around." Suddenly he grabbed for her, missing by an inch. She was fast, he gave credit for that. Next thing he knew, she was halfway down the stairs and then, after the thing following that, could be heard feeding grain to the chickens out of a shallow tin pan. He groaned and rolled but then finally gathered himself up and went to join her.

THIRTY-TWO

In the days that followed, the health of the mother and child recovered. They used to come out and sit in the garden during the best hours of the day.

"Looking poorly," William said, sharpening the blade of his scythe with part of a grinding stone. "Better take some medicine."

"No, Bill, please."

He went to get it. The Black Draught was exhausted and in its place he had resorted to a quarter-bottle of Croton Oil that had been shelved along with the lubricants required by his machines. He poured out half an inch of the stuff and mixed it thoroughly with buttermilk. He was surprised when he got back to find that she had arisen under her own power and was trundling off hurriedly toward the bamboo grove.

The baby, contemptuous of sickness, lay spewing and humming in the intertwined arms of the scuppernong vine. Already the child was familiar with Alabama and its ways, so much so indeed that it must have seemed to him that the environment here was composed predominantly of wasps and honeysuckle and that warm days would never end. William dosed him carefully and wiped away the buttermilk.

In the afternoon William got into his best clothes and after suiting up the child as best he could, drove slowly to town on the back of his gentlest mare. Hushed to silence by the world, which now showed itself to be so much larger than he had thought, the baby said nothing. They moved past the oyster man standing proudly behind his samples — three large invertebrates open to the sun. William had intended to file past him without speaking; instead, the man spoke in such a way as to require a decent answer.

"Howdy, Bill."

Bill lifted his hat. "Afternoon."

"I *thought* I saw something in those saddle bags of yourn. See? There it goes again — squirming."

Keeping a sociable expression on his face, William opened the flap and let the child peep out. "My son," he said.

"Ah ha. But they told me he *died*, Bill."

"No, sir. Well, I'll be moving along now." Again he lifted his hat, this time more imperceptibly than before, and then strove to realign his horse with the path.

"The woman now, I *know* she's dead. I was real sorry to hear about that, too."

"Not dead," said William.

"Not?'

The horse was having trouble with the direction and the boy meantime had turned in such a way as that one leg was sticking out. Saying nothing, William parked the animal, came down, and then went and adjusted the child. It was as if their mutual appreciation for each other was growing by the moment — he for his part because the baby almost never cried, and the child on the other part because his father was reliable. They looked at each other. The oyster man meantime had come out from behind his counter and was judging the boy at close range, even going so far as to test his belly once or twice with his unclean thumb.

As William entered, the town seemed to be in a more or less normal state of affairs. He lifted his hat to the glazier's wife and then nodded to the banker, the baker, and the bone meal man. He had forgotten about the train, which came to harbor here each day at this time, cutting the town in twain; he would have to drive a quarter mile out of his way to get around it. But first, the sound of small boys as they clustered around the refrigerator cars waiting for the seals to be broken, as if the lead that fell among the tracks was already as good as the bullets and toy soldiers it would furnish. Two blocks further he found the tinsmith and iron monger working together on a project of some sort. Came next the levee. Forcing his mare up the incline, he stayed for a moment on the summit gazing off to where his brother-in-law dwelt in the far northeast. There, among three hundred and fifty acres of beans and corn, it was all clear skies, blue nights, bright stars, and naught but peace and happiness.

The pastor of his church lived alone in a cabin that William admired very nearly as much as he respected the man — a home of two rooms designed to endure for five hundred years. Admitted into the library, he found himself glancing frequently at the floor, an oaken domain so tightly put together that not even a knife blade, howeverso thin, could have been wedged between the adjoining planks. Fifty men could have been crowded into that middle-sized chamber without the slightest prejudice to the underlying joists. The pastor had a writing desk, a stain-glass lamp, and a fountain pen with capacity enough for a pint of ink. Also interesting tools of various kinds were sitting about on top of the bookshelves and windowsills, a set of precision screwdrivers, a leather-punching device and other kindred instruments of various sorts.

"Been wanting to see you, Bill. Glad you came around."

(The walls, too, were thick. No word exchanged in the privacy of that room could escape to the outside world.) William nodded and took off his hat.

"I was terribly upset, Bill, to hear about your wife."

"She's going to have a baby."

"But..."

"Not this one." (He pointed to the child who had made himself comfortable in the minister's rose-patterned chair. "Another one."

"But I though she'd died!"

"Near about." His eye turned to the stained glass window in which some half-dozen bald-headed prophets in robes of green and gold were conferring worriedly. Another such window, this one an illustration of a certain famous parable, had been etched in five different dyes applied directly to the glass itself. "But I gave her some medicine."

"Ah!"

(And finally, the man had a library, fifty volumes of the most portentous-looking volumes that William had yet seen. These also lay over against the wall that fronted the fireplace, reaching almost to the painted ceiling. Any man who had dipped into that number of books was the man for William. They looked at each other evenly.)

"Charles Turl," said William at last, speaking very slowly, "they claim he's got six hundred acres now."

"Five hundred eighty I believe. Father left it to him."

"You know what kind of man he is?"

"I do, yes."

"Me, I got nine acres."

"Ah."

"I worked fourteen hours yesterday. Like to of died. Day before, too."

"Ah, William, William. Come let's sit over here at the table."

William sat and waited until the man could return from the kitchen with a wedge of cornbread and a glass of clabber for the each of them. They sat facing one another over the narrow table, both gazing down sadly at their own hands. Outside the sun had fallen beneath the level of the stain glass windows, denying the prophets their former glow. Bill spoke first:

"All my life..."

"I know that, Bill."

"All my life. If I know what's right, I'll do it. And if I don't know, why then I won't do it."

"Yes."

"He killed that nigger. And his wife — comes to town all black and blue."

"He *will be punished*, Bill, we know that."

"I used to think so, don't think so anymore."

"Careful, Bill. Judge not."

"Wonder why that is — that God loves people like that."

"Well I reckon He can love who He wants to love, don't you imagine? What are you going to do — tell him he's got to love *you*? He don't. Now look here, you got a job to do — you got to be perfect so's other people can... So they can be what *they* have to be."

William nodded slowly. Neither man could bear to look at the other.

"And so he gets to go to heaven."

"We don't know that."

"And I got to go to hell."

The man pushed back slightly and changed position. "In our church," he said finally, "there's two schools of thought. Some say that we're all going to go to heaven, all of us, except we got to spend a little bit of time in hell don't you see. To make up for our foolishness and whatnot. Sins."

Bill waited.

"And then there's them as believe we're all going to Hell, William, as sure as anything. Except some of us get to spend a little bit of time in heaven before we have to go there."

William nodded slowly. This latter school accorded with his own intuitions, even if he had never heard it told out loud before. "Well," he said, "I expect that's right. I never heard anybody say it though."

"Oh, no. No, no, they couldn't stand it, Bill, most people, if we talked about it. No, this is just for you, Bill, and me."

"I see." He started to rise. The man pushed him down again.

"You haven't given that child a name yet, have you Bill?"

The baby sat in his place, a full participant in the conversation, as it appeared. (He didn't know, not yet, about the fate that lies in store for human beings, or the fewness of the years.) Leaving them, the minister disappeared into his back room but then immediately came back with two Bibles and laid them on the table. William, who preferred ancient names to those that were merely old, turned through the pages slowly. He liked to try out the words in his mouth whereas the minister, a more educated sort of person, had begun to write down a list of people who had been famous in their day for some of the characteristics obviously possessed by William's boy.

"There was a fellow called Dan, but I don't know *anyone* named *Zurishaddai,*" he said, peering at William over the top of his glasses.

William nodded. "Simeon's boy."

"Ancient name, Bill, real ancient."

William nodded. Both men now were in the book of Numbers, both reviewing the same names, and both experiencing a similar sadness that they had not themselves lived in those days instead of these. William's fore-finger continued to bump up against all sorts of likely names, too many indeed to winnow down to just the proper one.

"Maybe we ought to wait," William said. "Name all of 'em at the same time."

"'All of 'em'? You've only got the one."

William nodded, stood, and then began to make preparations to leave, requiring the other man to make haste with the christening bowl. Meantime the child had soiled himself, having given no hint of it in his behavior or facial expression. William was disappointed. It called forth the first in a long line of disciplinary actions that he was duty bound to carry out against such conduct as this.

They drove home quickly, the man squinting forward through the gloaming while the boy kept a backward-looking vigil from the saddle bags.

THIRTY-THREE

In the fullness of time his wife grew better and when she came outside these days, she stayed longer and got more done. Her second boy was developing quickly now and growing more complicated all the time. (She had contracted this pregnancy, she believed, while still swollen with the first one. Now, insofar as she was able to judge by touch alone, the fetus had put on ears and a nose, which accounted for the peculiar sensation she experienced in that area each time the infant smiled.) This was to be her favorite, she suspected it already. And now in August she liked to sit among her vegetables and sing to them and to the boy, sometimes continuing to hum even when her husband approached.

"You all right?" he asked, startled by the noise.

"Just singing."

He came forward, throwing his shadow over her. "We had as many peas as we got gladiolas, we'd be in good shape."

Debbie said nothing. She had naturally expected the shadow to move away after a certain time; instead she found herself weeding with more alacrity and with closer attention. The world was more serious than she knew — she knew it — and time shorter, and many decisions there were that still needed to be made. In all these matters she relied upon her husband who had never failed her.

From far away there came the afternoon whistle, the sound of timber being cut, the making of bricks, and the noise of wagons passing before the house. She hardly noted the figure of Molly Bright, a tall and willowy

Negress in a yellow bandanna who had been stirring for the past half hour in an iron yard pot frothing over with ammonia and clothes. She would have estimated, Deborah would have, that they now had fifteen Negroes domiciled upon their land, a number that included the children but ignored the three or four women who came and went, usually staying very briefly. Of the children, two were white — her own and a twelve-year-old albino whose contempt for the Negroes was growing more pronounced with every day.

She rose with difficulty, and then went to retrieve a little pointed spade designed for weeding around certain kinds of flowers. Concerning the new barn, it was being made primarily from brick, a tedious process that put pressure upon the masons and kiln alike. At the same time three rooms were being added to the house — 1) a "reading room," (he called it), with stain glass windows, 2) a creamery and confectionery (attached to the main structure by a passageway), and 3) a second-story sleeping porch with space for three beds. With these in progress, she could not help revealing some little pride when people came from town to see her husband's newest projects.

She took comfort in her things. She had a staircase, twenty inches tall, leading to her bed. Had an enameled box bearing the picture of an ostrich and inside it her smallest and most valuable of things — pearl earrings, a nugget of ore that might be gold, a broach that had been gifted to her ancestor by Napoleon Bonaparte, and a few thin kerchiefs incorporating examples of her grandmother's embroidery. William's letters, held together in pastel ribbons, lay in the bureau's bottom drawer. She had other letters besides, some of them going back to a time when the county was as yet experimenting with its own first crude postage stamps. She owned a vial of perfume that was too valuable to open. (Prior to the death of the distiller, only one sole gallon had ever been run off.) And, of course, she had her gloves and scarves and under things, a whole drawer full.

Roving mentally to different points about the home and land, she took pride in her plum trees and the jams and jellies they supplied. But if the weather prove inimical to these, they still had a muscadine vine, a nutmeg and two pear trees, persimmons and scuppernongs, and the very old and ancient fig that had been rooted in this spot for a hundred years and more and had influenced the orientation of the house. Grainy, full of seeds and meat, the figs themselves grew in clusters in which each individual fruit was lemon-size.

She went indoors, taking with her an oversized fig ripened to the breaking point. Her kitchen was especially well-equipped and she was able to recount by rote almost everything she owned. A firkin hung from the trammel, and beneath it two butter boxes painted with historical scenes. Her tools, laid out side by side, might have been a surgeon's — a pie crimper, custard dipper, wafer iron. She took comfort from the Betty lamp that sat on the second shelf, and her collection of ladles and spatulas, her butter scoop and apple parer. Her knives were clean, lengthy and thin, and bore evidence of their employment by three generations of women. Her churn, on the other hand, was new, even if the pestle had snapped off at some period and been imperfectly repaired. She had a flour mill and two cook stoves. And although she possessed the keenest cleaver for miles around, her fingers still were ten. (Two cook stoves, yes, but one was set aside for pastries chiefly.)

Moving in imagination to the sewing room, she hurried to see if her bodkins all were there. She had a sleeve board (eighteen inches long, well-mounted), two darning gourds of unlike sizes, and a fluting and goffering iron that had come down to her from her people. Here in this room, much work still needed to be done.

She slipped into the parlor and scrutinized the clock. There was no doubt but that it contributed more than anything else to the solemnity that she and her husband expected in a home of their own, especially at noon when the chimes seemed either to be foretelling the rest of the day or else looking back regretfully upon what actually had passed. Here, exactly in the center of the room, William had installed a nine plate stove, heavily ornamented and with a flue that ran directly up and through the ceiling. The mantel piece held their pewter, family photographs, a stereoscope (they had only a few inserts to go with it), and a paraffin lamp with a tiny wick cap that looked like gold but in fact was merely brass. She delighted in the chandelier which, however, they seldom used, owing to the difficulty of burning in tandem eight matching candles of commensurate length.

Still dreaming, she went outside, took the bicycle from under the porch and gave herself and the unborn child a ride of about twenty feet. Any further than that and her husband might see her.

And then finally, last of all, she imagined that she had gone to the barn to visit their joint possession, the mule called Maude who had come to them at the end of May to take the place of the hinny.

"And if we had us some *working* people out here, instead of just a bunch a..." (He was still there, his shadow, too.) "We'd be all right."

She smiled and waited and after a moment or two had passed, her husband withdrew at last, followed shortly by his shadow.

THIRTY-FOUR

He rose on the seventh day and after a small breakfast of curds and partridge eggs, took down the double-barrel shotgun that had come to him after his brother's death. From the window two thin spirals of smoke could be seen ascending skyward through the branches of the pines; they said to him that the timber-cutting and the brick-making were going forward satisfactorily and needed no interference from him.

Autumn was coming in and the world, which only recently had been expressing itself in primary colors, was now changing over ever so slowly to weightier and more mature hues betokening wisdom and the sadness of things — brown, russet, umber, and the rest. "Ah, me," said William speaking inside himself. (He had passed through the unfinished barn and had come out onto the deer path that carried through broad fields before converging at last with the far-away river where random blinks of light would be riding on the current. Here, in the edge of the woods, he had placed brand new skeps, five in number, for his ghymick bees.) "Ah, me, they're getting sleepy," said he, stopping to watch as the insects came staggering home one by one with their disappointing loads, oftentimes missing the little door altogether and then having to explore for it by touch alone. And yet he could remember a time when they traveled in battalions, as it were, each man of them transporting almost his own weight.

He could foresee five solid months of fasting and cold weather, a time of slow growth for the trees and too much idleness for people who enjoyed that sort of thing. Ah, me. Ahead the Negro shacks came into view along with a few actual Negroes themselves seated upon their porches or standing to no visible purpose in their yards. Two dogs with dirt on their noses squirmed out from beneath one of the houses and then, identifying William, whimpered and squirmed back in. Dogs, hens, the cow, they had turned into Negroes, too, all by dint of living here. William waved to them in friendly fashion, realizing too late that to them it must have seemed as if he were threatening with his gun. To atone for it he took the pipe out of his mouth and spoke, speaking warmly across the unfenced yard where bottles and other trash lay at hazard. He observed the rim of a wheel three-fourths buried in the sand and an old-fashioned grindstone (the treadle missing) worn down to a radius not much greater than a coin's. A child was urinating off the porch.

"Howdy," he said. "How you folks making out over here?"

"Yas, suh, Mr. William, doing good, yas suh. Un umm!"

"Is that *you* over yonder, Sambo?" he asked, pointing the stem of his pipe.

"Sambo dead."

William looked again. In truth this new person was a far thinner sort of individual than the one who used to be so good at stacking lumber. William kept moving. The last of the shacks was in the poorest condition of all, indeed William did not see how it could endure the winter to come. Truth was, he did not understand these people. Give him a hammer and the little bits of discarded lumber that he himself would gladly have supplied and these houses would soon be livable again and strong. He was especially baffled by the panel of disintegrating cardboard that covered one certain window in lieu of shutters or glass. And if he would have abominated white people who behaved like this, here he was generous and understanding to a fault. It was a doomed and dying race, bypassed by history, and would soon be gone. "They're not to blame," said he, talking to himself alone. It was then that the dogs, who also wanted to go hunting, again slithered out from beneath the shack and ran to join him. They possessed, these animals, all the earmarks of their social station. One, indeed, had no ear at all.

They entered and then moved slowly through a field of weeds that looked like wheat, William harkening to the numerous little temporary paths that wended in and out before then running off on trajectories of their own. He chose what seemed to him the most-traveled of those trails, but only to have it peter out on him before he had proceeded a hundred yards. Each path, each track, each intersection told of some transaction that had occurred under the sun — boy chasing deer, woman carrying water jug on head, man and wife meeting on the trail, people fetching flowers or broomcorn weeds. In a place like this it would not have surprised him to blunder upon one of the prophets standing up to his chin in weeds. Or even his own dark angel, come to fetch his soul away.

Instead, contrary to the urgings of the dogs, he selected the left-hand trail that meandered in and out, tending generally in the direction that seemed to William best. He would not wish to return home without at least a bird or two, lest it appear to people that these expeditions of his were but for pleasure. And saying so he stopped, broke open the gun and fed one heavy shell into each of the barrels. He was not like those who fire about at random, nor would he venture a shot unless he could slay a thing cleanly. The very last he wanted was for one of God's creatures to suffer from wounds inflicted needlessly by William, no.

He had never cared for modern life, William never had, and although it were a sin to blame one's own mother for it, it did seem to him that the world could just as well have gone along without him. Denied life, he could have been spared seventy years of labor, of disappointing children, a wife who would have to die someday, and finally the ineluctable Hell itself with its heat and torments, its buckets full of eyes and moiling rats. Meantime the smiling sun, made happy by such prospects, burned with impatience for it. William stared back at the thing evenly for the space of about five seconds, until forced to look away. He was small and he knew it, and ignorant, and he knew that, too, and had been brought forth onto the table of the world in order to give amusement to those too great and too far-away to be concerned with unimportant persons.

All day thick deposits of clouds had been cumulating in the sky, one on top the other. In Pike County it would be raining vehemently now, but not here, not where it most was needed. Instead, a mere drizzle began, a grey nuisance that got beneath his collar and disturbed the combustion in his pipe. The dogs meantime were running off and racing back, grinning continuously in the field. William was a witness to it when the thin one stopped, poised, and opening wide his mouth, lunged face-first into the drizzle.

They came to where a single willow had grown up in the middle of what once had been an indigo field. Here he secured the gun (removing both shells), and then drew out a short brown paper bag with half a pound of boiled peanuts in it. Soft and soggy but full of good smells, the nuts had been festering in brine for full two days. His habit was to open the things one at a time and chew slowly, extracting the nutrients down to the last little bit. Having gone through about 40% of them in this way, he called the dogs and held out half a dozen nuts which, however, they refused with detestation. It was meat they respected, meat only, and preferably when mixed with entrails and feathers.

Past the river and over the hills he could hear a crowd of wolves speaking to one another over wide distances. Bill listened keenly, intrigued by their keening. Six black crows had followed him all the way from home; now, staying carefully out of range, they disported themselves in plain open view, choosing for that purpose an area of the sky where it was impossible not to see what they were doing. William went for his gun and reloaded slowly. It happened sometimes that crows would lose account of things and drift back into range.

He went on. A few rods further and he frightened a rabbit who went loping off to the right. But Bill's desire was for quail and neither he nor the

dogs made any effort to impede the animal's escape. Suddenly he realized
what it was that he enjoyed about this weather — that the gnats were gone
and for the first time in months he could look out upon the world without
myriads of pestilential little creatures loitering in his face. Also, from where
he stood he could analyze at leisure the wall of timber that lay just across
the river — long-leaf pines and plenty of hardwoods. The woods were deep
and trees like that continued, he supposed, all the way to Burney Creek.

He desired to possess the world in its entirety and have a sufficient
number of men under his instructions to set it right again. He squirmed
with schemes and plans; his hands ached, he could feel a headache coming
on. He envied generals, respected sheriffs, and admired all those who carry
out on the ground the hard things that have to be done. And his very own
son — William smiled to think about him; only six months old and already
accustomed to taking punishment without complaining.

He moved steadfastly down along the woods. Ahead a gang of mules
watched gravely as he approached the broken-down shed that sheltered
them from the rain. They seemed almost ready to speak, but then as always
opted against it at the last instant. Sometimes he got inklings, William did,
of the thoughts and viewpoints of horses, but never of these, never mules,
and never mind that both species shared the same configuration, very generally speaking. Forty yards further he turned to see if they were still watching his movements. And they were.

His tobacco had broken through the membrane of his pouch and had
leaked out into the pocket itself; working with one hand only, he now gathered the crumbs between his thumb and finger and refilled the pipe that
meanwhile had gone cold on him. It was in the middle of this process that
the dogs grew suddenly nervous and began dashing in and out, yelling at
the sky and far-away hills. William stopped, planted himself and lifted the
gun. He had five seconds, perhaps less, before the partridges would either
leap up and run off into the wind or else remain where they were in a high-

risk effort to hoax both man and dogs. William's plan was to fire the right barrel first, which aligned with his primary eye.

They lifted and flew, two score of quail producing a huge throbbing noise that startled William in spite of his preparation. Finding his target, he fired, but then had to wait a time before the bird realized the seriousness of what had taken place. That was when the smaller of the two dogs, appalled by the noise, turned suddenly and ran back in great haste toward the Negro cabins. Suddenly, as if to prove that William was not the only one abroad today, another hunter retorted at that moment with gunfire from some other field.

The brick maker spent the next hour trolling slowly in the same locality, hoping to frighten up a second covey in the area between the river and the proscribed land owned by a certain farmer with whom William was not on perfect terms. He moved in dignity, his gun at attention, pipe burning lowly, protected by a rumpled hat. To see him there was to apprehend in advance the gentleman and social pillar that he was scheduled to become. He could not know that he was being watched by at least three sets of eyes — an elderly Negro and his wife regarding him grudgingly from their cabin half a mile away and, less grudgingly, a grinning wolf who had come up to the edge of the forest to slake his life-long fascination with the activities of men.

"There he go," the old man said, "messin' around *all day long* in that field. Look at him."

"Um umm!" said his wife. "Raining, too."

"Why?" thought the wolf, "*why?*" And: "What next?"

He marched, William did, down to the river and pondered how to cross it. The water was high, coffee-colored, and running forward hurriedly at perhaps three times its ordinary rate. The fish (those that had not been swept away), were doing well to hold their positions in a current like this. William tossed in a pine cone and then marked how it bobbed up and down, sometimes almost vanishing from sight as it tumbled head over heels on its long voyage to the Gulf of Mexico. Truth was, he had never visited the opposite shore nor examined at close range what looked to him like one of the best growths of hardwood and long leaf pine that he had ever seen.

It would have been preposterous at this time of year to strip down to nothing and undertake to swim across, abandoning his gun, enduring the cold, striving to hold his clothes above the waves. Holding his clothes above the waves, enduring the cold, abandoning his gun, William stripped down to nothing and swam across. He was somewhere between 36 and 39 years old at this period and was pleased that his strength and durability had held up pretty well over the last years, better than he had expected really, and that his courage remained at good levels insofar as he could compare it to that of other men. He expected to reach the other shore at a place where two trees had tumbled into the stream comprising a staircase, as it were, to dry and level land. Meantime his one remaining hound had turned back and was trundling slowly homeward, much depressed.

For only the second time in his life William was consciously trespassing on someone else's land. He had expected dense forests, oaks and pines for the next thousand miles; instead, pulling himself to the top of the bank, he found himself looking down upon a long and level plain containing haystacks, cattle, and a bright red two-story house with a buggy in the yard and a suggestion of smoke rising from the chimney. He counted the barns, both of them oozing over with bright yellow hay. If there were any defects in this extraordinary scene he couldn't detect them. Two bulls he saw, pied and square, indignant animals facing off at each other across a well- built wall of rocks and bricks. He appreciated everything he saw but especially the windmill with its spoon-like blades designed to catch the breeze and hold it there. Old fashioned bee skeps — he counted some twenty of these set at equal distance along the space that ran between the smoke house and root cellar. They added to the farm's natural defenses.

Studying the view spread out before him, William suffered. He owned no pond himself and his trees tended to be rather more slender and farther apart than these. And in short he lived on the less prosperous side of the river, too close to town, too far from Enterprise and Opp. "My God," said he, "we work *thirty hours a day*, Joe and me." This other man, the one with two barns, how hard, pray, did *that* one work, what? Obviously he needed more boys if he expected ever to eventuate in an estate like what he saw in front of him.

Thinking deeply, he made his way back to shore. The river itself, previously so hasty, seemed almost to have ground down to a stop, wherefore William expected easy swimming all the way across.

Easy swimming? Not really, not when he realized he had just that moment been hit on the ankle by a water moccasin or mayhap rattlesnake.

THIRTY-FIVE

And so this then was to be the method of his death — he had always won-
dered about that. Brief glimpse of the snake himself, a four-foot moccasin
swimming off with a satisfied air. Were it better to drown, or ought he drag
himself to shore in hopes that his remains might someday be found and
delivered back to Deborah and the others? This much he knew for certain, that he could never allow himself to be discovered without clothes.
Accordingly he swam as hurriedly as he could to the opposite bank, pulled
himself from the water, dressed, and then stumbled for possibly a hundred
yards further before the agony hit him in full force.

"Great God!" he said, speaking inside himself. For years he had been
rehearsing for the flames of hell, never once imagining that he must beforetimes also be afflicted with this. That was when his foot began to swell
beyond the capability of his shoe to contain it.

He wanted to die right now, immediately, shrugging off all memory
and ambition and coming into God's presence in such misery as that he
might be forgiven the many iniquities he had carried out, if not in action,
in his mind at least. "Good gracious alive!" he said. "Boy howdy, that hurts!
Whew. Don't believe I've ever felt anything like this." And then: "Where's
that knife? Maybe I could cut them laces and get that old shoe off afore its
too late."

He found the knife and cut the laces, exposing him to the sight of a pale
white foot that, in comparison with his lower leg and ankle, looked like a

child's, the most grotesque thing he'd ever seen. But had not long to wait before the foot was as huge as the rest of him.

He wanted to die while facing the sun, but then changed his mind and positioned himself in line with his house and barn. He was in debt for more than a thousand dollars, and meanwhile his enterprises had only just lately begun to bring money into the house. Pushing his mind into the near future, he foresaw how his wife would now be returning to Naftel, the widow of a man who had wasted his life. Next, he envisioned her as the bride of another man, a smirking sort of person glad to have the acres and businesses and sons that William had prepared for him. Further still, he saw himself roasting in the hell of unending flames more awful still than what he was undergoing now. That was when he *heard* (rather than felt) the flesh tearing apart on his lower leg, where the tissue already had expanded about as far as it could.

He did *not* use the shotgun on himself, nor make any effort to retrieve it. He liked to imagine that when the sun went altogether down, the pain might relent somewhat — an irrational hope as he admitted to himself in moments of clarity. Came now the more likeable of the two dogs, a black and white hound who whimpered once or twice in ostensible sympathy before then heading off through the twilight to his own snug place beneath one of the Negro shacks. It left William with just enough light to insert the knife into one of the deeper of the seams that had opened up, slice open the leg and try to push the poison out. Of tourniquets, it was too late for that.

He dreamt that he was traveling down a long narrow path that led from the sandy wastes of southernmost Alabama. Moon was high, whippoorwills calling, willows forming a corridor through the night. It came to him that when morning came, he should find himself in a more admirable sort of place, a region of well-built homes, fat cattle, and a better breed of humanity than any he had known. Here, working against a backdrop like that, a place of 4 x 4s where rust and mildew had been banished and men preferred to take a beating than use bad language, or give short change, or disgrace a woman, that would be the place for him. Paradise was over yonder and earth was over here, and a person's duty was to draw them nearer — this was *still* a big part of his philosophy and never mind that just now he was dying out in the middle of Jonas Wilkerson's (a friend of his) 200 acre field.

He woke on Monday or, possibly, Tuesday, to find his left leg and nearby leaves encased in dried blood rendered a purplish color by dint of the eight (or thirty-two) hours that had gone by. The swelling was almost as bad as in the beginning and yet he *was* able to bend his knee a few degrees, an unexpected boon that made him wonder if perhaps he was fated to go on living for another few years after all. He could imagine himself crawling homeward, surprising his son who had done nothing — the boy was less than two years old — had done nothing to save him. Also wanted to surprise the smirking visitor who had come hastening forward to marry his widow. Thinking of it, he could feel himself turning into a more harsh sort of person, an unwanted result of the poison he had absorbed. Even in a wheelchair or on crutches, he would know how to repay his transgressors. Meantime, although his left leg still did hurt him of course, the pain seemed to be lessening in proportion as the limb itself went on rotting. If he stood now, perhaps the thing would drop away, leaving him a good deal lighter and, in some ways, a more agile man.

Perhaps it was Wednesday. Far away he could hear the eight o'clock whistle calling Negroes to the cotton mill, and further still, a rumbling noise coming from the state's northeastern volcano fields. And saying so, he stood and, moving forward at a rate of about twenty feet each time, went for his shotgun that remained more or less where he had left it. His pocket had six shells in it, four of them dry. According to his memory, the moccasin had been swimming to shore in this precise vicinity, and he had long ago decided that he would track the thing down and kill it, though he need 10,000 years.

THIRTY-SIX

He rose early — (Deborah's father we're talking about) — and breakfasted happily on sprats, coffee, and two servings of flatcake with strawberries on them. Having done as well as he could with these, he then shaved, took off his glasses, and got back into bed. He was older than he used to be and the minnie ball lodged in his lung was almost as much a source of irritation now as on the day it had been granted him. God's great hand, the one that could reach into the world and come out on the other side, why had not that hand entered into *him* and drawn the bullet out?

There had been a time when he could go on sleeping among the sound of roosters shrieking, cattle intoning, hogs grunting, dishes clashing, and his wife walking back and forth. But not now, and never again, not since he had come to the age of 60 and passed unnoticed into extreme old age.

Groaning, he stood and moved unsteadily toward the wash stand, stopping only once in order to come back and get into his socks. The pitcher was full of cold water (sediment in it) that came from his own well. Squinting into the mirror, he lathered slowly in the semi-light and had almost finished shaving before he recollected that he had already discharged that duty some thirty minutes before.

He wandered at large throughout the house, informing himself on the whereabouts of the people. Mary, of course, had locked her door and no doubt was sitting at her vanity trying on different sorts of cosmetics and perfume.

"Mary? You plan on staying in your room *all day long*?"

"What?"

"You heard me."

"What time is it?"

"You fed the chickens?"

"What?"

Jesse's room, on the other hand, was open but had no person in it. The old man stepped inside and, holding his hands behind his back, spent a moment viewing the boy's collection of framed and mounted sea shells that hung along the wall. He remembered the day, the man did, when they had chased up and down the beach together, pouncing on the things each time the ocean delivered one to shore.

Debbie's room likewise was vacated, the girl herself having run away, abandoning them on her marriage day. Stepping inside, it mollified him somewhat to see that in addition to the lampshade, the wallpaper and rug, she had at least been good enough to leave behind *some* of the furniture that had come down to them through the family. She had also bequeathed the best view the house afforded, a southeasterly prospect of hills and fields, a narrow stream as jagged as lightning, and seventeen chewing cattle standing well apart from each other. This was the scene when, that moment, Deborah and the William fellow came riding over the hill in a two-horse carriage.

He hurried downstairs and ran for the kitchen.

"They're coming!" he said. "Debbie and them."

"I told you two weeks ago they was coming!" his wife retorted. She was working on something in the sink, a rabbit he had to suppose, judging by the little tads and bits of fur. Except for that, her pots and kettles were all absolutely clean and arranged along the board in order of usefulness.

"They got a baby with 'em."

The woman stopped, covered the rabbit with a towel, and then proceeded slowly to wash and dry her hands.

"That'll be your grandbaby, Hubert! And that woman coming up the walk? That's your daughter."

It was coming back to him. He stood, plucking at his chin. The door at that time held a pane of frosted glass and in the late morning light the visitors looked more like ghosts than like any descendants of his. They stood, he on his side and they on theirs, viewing one another with difficulty through the skewing glass. He thought he recognized Molly as well, and Jasmine, who not so long ago had been an employee of *his*.

"Daddy!" cried the girl, once he had opened for them. They embraced at length, both drawing back in time to let the babies, the one in her arms, the one in her belly, and the one in her womb, to let them have their meed of room. Over her shoulder the old man could also see the children's father, who had never learned to smile and wasn't smiling now. Suddenly the daughter's mother came running up and after taking the boy-baby into her arms, held him to the light. He wore, the child did, a little suit of work clothes adapted to his size.

"Why he looks just like..."

"No he don't."

"... your uncle Tully."

"Oh, he do not. Tul never looked *anything* like that."

"Looks just like me," the grandfather said, growing visibly nostalgic. "Boy howdy, I was a rascal in those days!"

"We're going to have more of 'em, too," said William flatly, looking off across the fields. It was chilly in the doorway and the young family was beginning to look forward eagerly to being invited inside.

They congregated in the parlor where right away the old man set to stoking up the stove. With the exception of Jesse and one other person whom William had never seen before, Deborah's brothers were missing, Entered now Mary looking languorous and bored and waiting, as it seemed, for the solemn William to kiss her hand. She would be copulating within six months — it was the unexpressed assumption of everyone there.

"Look at the baby!" someone called to her.

"I don't think I'm going to have children," she said in a martyred voice. "It wouldn't be fair to the child."

"That's for shore," her father said. "Didn't work out real good for your parents, neither."

"Well," William sold. "Sold eighty ton of brick last week."

"And besides, I don't expect to live that long."

"Eighty!"

Came finally the household cat, who proceeded to march about the room with tail held high. Her glory was in her rectum, which she wanted exposed at all time.

"Jesse's been acting real sorry last couple months," the grandfather said suddenly, a propos of nothing. "He didn't get much of a crop this year and then, next thing, he lost his best cow. And that trash girl that died — what was her name?"

"Rain, rain, rain. We like to of floated away."

Spoke now the child for the first time in its life. The people listened scrupulously, as if in the possibility that some remembered piece of wisdom might emerge from his month-old lips. It was his father's habit to set the boy up in his own chair where he was expected to dispose himself like an adult.

"Well," William said, rising. "Reckon I'd better see to the horses."

"Oh, you don't have to bother yourself about that Bill, I'll go out there later on and..."

William left the parlor, which anyway was too crowded for him, and walked quickly down the hall. His limp was all too obvious and on his left foot he wore a custom-built "shoe" that no one had wanted to mention. Good smells came from the kitchen where a tall Negress, Molly's replacement, stood grumbling over the stove with a fork, a wand, and a long-handle spoon. Outside the day was bright but chill, the trees hushed and still, and the mercury falling precipitously. He predicted a long bad night.

The barn was tall, dark, well-timbered, and full of stalls tailored to the individuals that occupied them. Satisfied with their accommodations, his geldings were foddering happily when he came in. He spent a moment, William did, stroking the pastern of the more dutiful of his two animals. Across the way some dozen hogs were watching raptly, their perforated snouts sticking through the gaps.

"We brought the boy," William said loudly, believing that Jesse could hear him. But no answer came to him from the darkness up above.

"Hogs looking good. Except that white one there. Believe I'd slaughter her if she was mine."

A single straw dropped from the loft and came to ground amongst the hens; otherwise no sound could be heard from overhead. Shielding his eyes, William looked upward into the motes and sunbeams, finding at last what looked like Jesse's face, an ovaline blur with black holes for eyes and his other features.

"We're fixing to have some eggnog," William went on. "Want some?" And then: "Your daddy wants you to come inside."

No reply came down to him from overhead.

He expropriated, William did, six eggs from a like number of hens and then turned and hastened to the house. There was no question about the coming night — that it would be cold, colder than cold, and windy, too, those strong winds very likely bringing yet further cold and wind. Already he had made a number of trips to the coal bin, returning each time with enough fuel to keep the house warm for a period of about forty-five minutes, depending upon the actual temperature. November was finished and the days, such as they were, were being issued in an abbreviated form that curtailed light and warmth while exaggerating everything else. Thinking of it, William was seized by a sense of urgency as he ran for the house. Someday, he knew, winters worse than for a thousand years would come to Alabama and refuse to go away. Suddenly Mary brushed past, herding before her the family's dogs and two small goats.

They gathered about the table that William remembered so well. But instead of the rich and varied meal that he had come to associate with this place, the meal tonight consisted chiefly of collards and ham, black-eyed peas, cornbread, buttermilk, and jam. Darkness had come in quickly and with great pressure, putting an awful strain upon the blue-tinted windows scintillating now with starlight and candle glints. (The moon was large but low, very low indeed, indeed it was resting squarely upon the horizon which also looked low tonight.) "Pass the butter," the old man said, holding out his hand for it, the same hand that not so long ago he had used for slaying foreign soldiers.

William passed it along to him. A product of their own cattle, the butter came in a five-pound cake stamped on top with pale yellow bees and sunflower blossoms. With the chill worming its way into the house beneath the doors and around the edges of the window panes, the family began unconsciously to huddle more closely over the food, which gave off a tiny warmth of its own. Bursts of steam, almost invisible, lifted from the black liquor in which the peas were drenching. They could hear the wind of course, though no one chose to discuss it. "Milk," the old man said, holding out his glass for it.

He looked upon this house and food, William did, as but one more evidence of heaven's undeserved graciousness. And someday, he knew, darkness would come rolling into Alabama and never go away. Meanwhile across from him his good wife was attempting to feed herself in the small intervals of caring for the boy. They looked at each other. Until recently the boy had been gourmandizing almost exclusively on milk and William was pleased to see him now reaching out for more substantial fare of the kind that he would need in days to come for putting in a good day's work. "Wont you take some more ham William?" the child's grandmother asked, rising from her place to carve it.

He could not refuse. Suddenly, recollecting that he had not removed his hat, he apologized and set it in his lap. His manners had improved since he had wed into this family and he knew better than to crush with his thumb the season's last fly, a great dying beast now trundling ever so slowly across the rills and elevations of the heirloom tablecloth. He never burped, William, not anymore, not unless he were outside or alone in the barn.

"It's him," the old man said sadly, nodding toward Blephy who had sidled up to the house and was pressing at the glass.

"He's got his own place!" Mary said. "Let him go to it."

Suddenly they heard the mule yelling loudly from the barn, a warning about worse weather yet to come. It was cold outside and cold, too, in the barometer which hung on the wall just next to the historical engraving of General Wolfe at Quebec. There, next to the companion portrait of Montcalm expiring calmly among his men, six of Jesse's golden medals were mounted in a frame. Rising painfully, the old man remained for a moment in a state of confusion before then directing himself at last toward the barometer. "Bad," he said, pointing to it. "Going to be cold, real cold. And when we wake up tomorrow, the river's liable to be frozen hard — that's what I'm thinking."

They gathered in the old people's room, the largest chamber in the house. The fireplace had been designed for coal and although rather small, it still gave off a better grade of heat than could be had from wood. They watched silently as the grandfather poked around in it, nudging the individual coals into position. It was a new experience of course for the baby, who was seeing this strange but insubstantial phenomenon — fire — for the first time. Great was his enthusiasm; life promised to be more interesting than he had supposed. Suddenly he fell asleep.

Came now the winds, a high-powered force that bent the branches, scattered Blephy far, and threw scads of leaves back and forth across the yard. With the child nine-tenths hidden beneath one of the camphor-smelling quilts, Debbie took advantage of the moment to wrap herself in a shawl. William had started to speak but changed his mind when the three women, who looked tonight like witches, turned their gleaming eyes on him.

"It's nine-thirty, near about," the old man said, referring to his watch. (He was forever going back and forth between his time pieces, his barometer, his pipe and calipers and his half-dozen pocket knives.) "It'll be frozen by now I reckon. River I mean."

They shivered violently. The human body could endure only so much before a person's circulation failed and the blood came to a stop in its viaducts. Suddenly Mary got up and went to check on the kids waiting hopefully on the porch. It was cold and they knew it, and their value as livestock, the only that they had, was at its lowest point in the year.

"Daddy?"

"No. They have to stay out there."

William smoked. This untoward weather, it was the start of the world's next phase. Meantime at home he doubted there was very much brick-purchasing going on. He wanted bricks to sell, trees to cut, peas in bloom, more children, larger bills of money, fewer debts. Thinking of it, he held out his glass for the eggnog being brought around. There was no doubt but that someone had put a drop of brandy in the drink. Not however so large a drop that he must turn it down.

"Piano," the old man said, pointing to it.

They went to it dutifully, the two daughters, and took up next to each other on the bench. From this point of view they looked less than ever like witches to William.

"Sing."

They did. Long time since last they had cooperated on a piece of music and meantime the older girl had developed a darker voice by virtue of her child and marriage. Hearing them and the weather outside, William continued 1) to fill his pipe, 2) watch the fire, 3) listen to a train running through the night, 4) think his thoughts and, 5) drink his drop. A minute of this and he was in peril of being mesmerized by the warmth and the agate lamp glowing greenly in the hall.

"We could of took that hill," the old man said lowly, once the music had stopped. "They was *scared*, too, them boys was." He drank. "They come down here, tell us what to do. Wisht we could of kilt *every danged one of 'em!*"

"That's alright, Papa. You killed a lot more of them than they did."

"Ever blessed one of 'em! Babies, chickens, everything they got. Kill 'em all!"

"We will, Papa, we will. Just have to bide our time, that's all."

Meantime the dogs had promoted themselves from porch to hall and then, advancing one paw at a time, to the most comfortable room in the house. By 9:48 they lay in a pile at a distance of about twenty-three inches from the fire. The old man poked at them randomly with his stick, producing a few weak moans and nothing else. One dog, who lay nearest to William, had a face that recalled to him his great aunt on his father's side, dead these many years. Suddenly, that moment, the baby came awake — (he was lost in the corner of a large lacquered chair upholstered in dark leather) — came awake and looked around with great surprise.

"Seventeen degrees," the child's grandmother said, returning from her third visit to the barometer. "Those pore ole cows."

"And pore Jesse, too!" Mary said.

They fell silent. It was a sad story, that of Jesse and his unending spite for not having been allowed into the parlor when he was young.

They made up a pallet for Mary on the floor and then from the guest room brought in the second-best bed for Deborah and her husband. The house, made of rough-sawn boards, gave off explosive noises under the contracting pressures of the cold. In the barn the mule continued to cry out from moment to moment, albeit more weakly and with decreasing frequency. Meantime a train had gotten bogged down just a few miles outside of town and was calling plaintively at this hour, disturbing people's sleep.

"Now when you get under the covers" — the old man felt it necessary to give these last-minute instructions — "lie real still. And pretty soon the sheets will get warm."

The baby had fallen off to sleep again and they were able, William and Deborah, to settle him in such as way as that he wouldn't drown in the depths of the feather mattress. Already, three times, Mary had moved her pallet from one place to another, striving to get *away* from the dogs while yet remaining *near* to the heat. Itself, the fire had turned out successfully, depositing a wealthy bed of orange coals that pulsed and shifted and looked like blushing faces. Having put the child to bed, William then focused his attention upon his wife and the two further babies lodged inside her at disparate stages of development. "Sleep," he said, "and I'll watch the fire."

"Me, too," Mary said, "I'm watching the fire, too."

"We still have some eggnog."

A dog rose, turned disconsolately in a circle, and then collapsed back into the pile. William finished his drink, knocked out his pipe, and then joined his wife and children beneath two heavy quilts invested with the smell of mildew, turpentine, and camphor. The lamp continued to throw awful shadows on the wall, including that of two hulking men who appeared to be stabbing each other repeatedly. But neither the lamp nor coals had force enough to illuminate the furthermost corners where in semi-darkness the family portraits lurked.

William's bed had six souls in it, taking account of the dog who had joined them and the two small persons that remained as yet unborn. Outside, in fields and valley and miles above the town, *this* was the night that winter had reserved for Alabama. "Ah, me," said William, thinking of the effect it would have upon his brick-making and other operations. He turned then to check on his son lying next to him in shirt and overalls, surprised to see that the boy had come awake and was watching the shadow-drama unfolding on the wall.

He woke, did William, about four hours before dawn. Mary had lied, insofar as she had promised to keep watch on the fire, and he had no alternative but to rise and find the tongs and add some dozen chunks of coal to the depleted grate. The fire had burned down altogether and the embers (those that were not extinct), were producing but very scant heat. Finally, taking the poker, he stirred about in the stuff, causing a few blue embroidered flames to spurt up hopefully in search of something to feed upon. Certainly the dogs and kids were cheering for him, as also the escaped parrot of last summer who had chosen to return at just this time.

THIRTY-SEVEN

The third child, pressing upon the second, arrived in summer with July and August following hard upon. These days when the family gathered in the arbor there were six of them, if one included the most recent member synthesizing just then inside the woman's bowels. They used to bring chairs out of doors and sit in the shade of the scuppernong vine. Anyone passing by at just that time would have seen them there.

Three times a day he went to look in upon his bricks. He had thousands in different stages of cooling, each brick worth 4/10 a cent of profit for his Negroes and he. It was true that his vein of clay was changing over from yellow to rose and thence to an ocher-colored material that yielded the most durable product of all. Lifting a brick in each hand, he would strike them together critically, judging the timbre by its chime. Or, he might go and stand for a time next to Joe Butler's boy, a tall and silent individual dressed in goggles who drove the kiln as if it were a locomotive.

"Good heat," said William. "Looking good."

"Woya no bodo ram!"

(He had expected in advance that he would not be able to interpret the boy's language.)

"Dr. Jordon's going to want some of these. Putting up a big fine house over on Pine Street."

"Mara. Jobo no lohador."

He moved, William, from the kiln to the steam-powered saw, where stood Joe himself bending over the cradle. The man had worked his way through a great many large trees that day, slicing the trunks into clean white pages of various size. William hailed to him, showing by means of his facial expression how much he approved the man's work.

"Looking good, Joe."

"Yas, suh, un hmm! You sho is right."

"Come on down here Joe, we need to talk."

The man grew nervous. William waited patiently as he turned off the power, swept away the shavings, threw some oil into both bearings, and then slowly and reluctantly came down to earth. He was growing grey about the temples, the Negro was, and no longer was the thirty- or forty-year-old man William had always assumed. Together they strolled to the garden, a ruined site cluttered with last year's exploded gourds. A few shocked chickens were feeding at random among the weeds.

"I wanted to pay you, Joe, for last week."

"Yas, suh." He held out his hand, a glove-like thing, wrinkled and torn, rather too large and too loose for the rest of him. Into that strangely pink colored palm William dispersed five paper bills of currency, the largest single sum he had ever yet given over to the man.

"You're getting rich, Joe."

"Yas, suh." He grinned. "Spec so."

"We're *both* getting rich." Thinking of it, his mind turned back again to the kiln, his several dozen tons of stacked brick, to the vein of ochre clay and to the thirty acres that contained it, to his mules and furniture and growing hoard of children — *these* were the authentic sources of his wealth. And yet he delighted almost as much in his *implements*, his weapons and screwdrivers, the measuring tape and other assorted things that leveraged his abilities and made him ten times the man he otherwise had been. Next, his mind opened and entered the shed that he had constructed last winter, utilizing for that purpose some of the yellowest bricks in his inventory. Here, arrayed in parallel on a blanket of chamois, he had nine awls of decreasing size, four gauges, two punches, a number of chisels, two rifflers and a rasp. Truth was, he was equally equipped to work in metal or in wood. He had a willow knife, a hatchel, a set of tin shears and, in the drawer, calipers and compass and a beetle and wedge. Moving to the cabinet, he reviewed his jack, his jointer, and moulding planes, his twibil and bevel, tongs, the soldering iron, his crucible and ladle. He had two vises, one attached to a sawhorse and the other the bench. Had a score of fishing poles — (derived from his own bamboo) — a score of them reclining at length athwart the ceiling beams. Had a farrier's box, a hoof parer, several hods, and in the corner his froe and adze, his father's auger, a croze and howel, his quern and scorper, a mallet and two mauls, cant hook, peavey, and mortising axe. He needed at all times a hammer close at hand, whet stone, a can of tobacco, brace and bits, several pounds of nails and screws and washers of all dimensions.

But his most crucial things were to be found in the house itself. He had increased their medicine cabinet enormously over the last months, so much so indeed that he had had to store some of the bottles in the icebox along with the buttermilk. He must have owned 500 pills of various kind, including a flat tin box of suppositories shaped like ammunition. He had a library of seventeen books.

He had alluded to his furniture — in fact, these bureaus and chests of drawers, the upholstered chairs and the serving board comprised the best index both to his current standing as also to the standing to which he aspired. He had a trunk full of lace work and four quilts in fair condition floating on top.

He had clothes, rough stuff most of it, along with two black suits that hung in the closet. Of the closet itself, it was huge and full of shelves, and it was here he had lain away for safekeeping (never suspecting he might have a grandson who would seize upon them someday), the two years' worth of letters exchanged between Deborah and himself. He had a rifle in there, cleaning equipment, and the shotgun that had been passed down to him from his brother and father.

He had two lots of property in town, thirty acres here, sixteen hundred and some odd dollars in bonds and bills, three mules, a barn made of brick (the only such in the entire county) and (and this was a negative entry), almost two thousand and five hundred dollars of debt. He was somewhere between 38 and 41 years in age, and this was what he possessed. Oh yes, and a bicycle, too, that he kept beneath the house. Or *had* kept there rather, until he perceived that someone had been using it.

"Yas, suh."

William looked at him, uncertain how long the man and he had been standing where they were. "Good," he said, patting him on the shoulder and passing over another dollar bill.

THIRTY-EIGHT

In September William hitched the mules, threw his wife and children into the wagon, and drove off quickly toward the preacher's house. He suspected that she was carrying their fourth child in her abdomen but was disinclined to question her about it at this time. In any case the day was bright and beautiful, the crops had been good, and the mules were pulling with real earnestness, putting their souls into it. They drew up even with the oyster man, who took off his hat when he saw the woman in her hat and suit and the three children sitting in soldier-like fashion just behind the driver. William had not wanted to stop but neither was he willing to ignore a person's attempt to initiate a discussion.

"Mr. Pefley, it does me good to see you heading off somewhere in that contraption of yourn. And look ahere, he's got his wife with him and all them boys. How many children you got now William? Altogether I mean?"

"Three head," William said.

Holding out his index finger, the man counted them off, coming to a stop when he arrived at Debbie's belly. He had been eating his own merchandise apparently and bore a large stain of serum on his bib and tucket.

"Looks more like four to me." (He grinned knowingly.)

"Well I'll say good day to you, Willard."

"Sure, you can say that. He sits there real quiet, don't he, that oldest boy. Smart, too, wearing that straw hat. He's my favorite person."

William glanced to the sun and then, remembering that he now had a functioning watch, drew it out, forced it open and read the time.

"This is the one that worries me, Bill," the oyster seller said, coming near and taking hold of the second boy by his shoulders. "Look ahere — see how he's looking at me?"

It was true and they knew it. A pall of sadness came down over the family.

"Deborah likes him the best."

"Well shore she does! That's how it is, Bill, they always like the worst one. Now you take me, my mama always liked me a *lot* more than anybody else."

"I like all of my boys," the woman said.

"Well shore you do! I'm just saying *he's* the one you like the best. But tell me if I'm wrong."

"We're thinking we might send him to colledge," Bill said. "Later on, I mean."

"Heh. Well that'll get him out of town anyway. Now if you want *my* advice, I'd..." He stopped. The third boy, far the smallest, had come down off his bench and was attempting to escape the wagon. William needed three seconds to seize him up in one hand and slap him powerfully, six times, across his diapered rump.

"Jesus, Bill!"

"Well, I'll say good afternoon to you Willard."

"Never seen anything like it! He ain't no bigger than a little puppy, Bill."

They moved forward. The mules had begun to chomp and dawdle in a way that William disapproved.

The cotton was high and the cows had distributed themselves tastefully among the farms and houses. Times like these, a man like William might almost believe that the downward tendency of things had been reversed by hard work and good weather, by the abundance of haystacks and the example of his own good wife sitting quietly with a smile of wisdom on her features and the sun in her lap.

They passed slowly through town, William lifting his hat to the sheriff who stopped and signaled back. The bank was open and people were streaming in and out. He knew just where to look, William did, to find the banker himself, a pale individual (the only man in the county without a sunburn), who knew too much, more perhaps than he wanted, about the town's affairs; to him William merely nodded, leaving his hat in place. They passed a knot of wives whispering on the corner, women in rouge and odd-looking hats who fell silent as Debra rode by. (His wife was in plain clothes, but knew how to wear them. She had a cameo that hung from a very thin chain.) A barefoot Negro boy sat at the curb puffing on a foot-long cigar made of leaf and newsprint. And then, finally, the town had a half-dozen dogs lying in various locations, the living indistinguishable from the dead.

They turned in at the lane and drove the short distance to the minister's house. In previous times the man had kept his property full of ducks and geese and flowers of all kinds; now, with age afflicting him, he was down to a single armadillo kept on a leash. William parked and, after giving a last admonishment to the mules, assisted his wife from the wagon. The oldest boy was able to come to ground by jumping from the step, the second-oldest by dangling from the rail, and the youngest wasn't able to come at all. He knocked three times, William did, and when the minister arrived offered up to him a quart jar of clover honey taken from this year's flow.

They were conducted to the library, the most solemn and at the same time most artful room in the township. Three glass panes, long and narrow, showed a procession of prophets moving forward as they assisted each other on the march. Marveling at it, the two boys were slow to go to their chairs. Such a tremendous amount of reading had taken place on that table that an area of about the size of a book had worn through the varnish and down to the grain.

"I'm glad to see you here," said the minister to the wife. "You don't talk very much and I don't feel like I've gotten to know you. When is the baby due?"

"Due last month," William said abruptly. "The reason we're here..."

"Yes?"

"... is so we can figure out some names for these here boys." He pointed to them, his finger halting in mid-air when he recognized that one was absent.

"Ah. Let me get my Bible." The minister rose in stately fashion and then came back with the thing, a large volume bound in boards with a great many bookmarks and other papers sticking out. They waited silently as he scrutinized the oldest son with care, even rising somewhat from the table in order to get another perspective on the child.

"Yes. I look at this boy and I don't see any evil in him, I just don't."

"Mr. Pefley doesn't allow it," his wife said quietly, her last comment of the day.

"Interesting. I have a colleague from Virginia with a face like that. Good man. Best in the world. Just a moment, I'll find his name."

He rose again, this time returning with two volumes of proceedings from the denomination's last colloquium. Here, too, bookmarks and other waste protruded from the pages. They watched with some anxiety as he splashed through the contents searching for his man.

"Dana," he said finally, gazing around at them peacefully.

"Hadn't never heard that one," William said.

"Best man I know." Suddenly he reached across the table and touched the boy on the nose. "Good stuff, this one." "Middling good," said William. "This here's the one what worries us."

The minister searched the second-eldest's face. He had seen a great deal during his time, had the minister, and his own face seldom registered anything that allowed a clear reading of his mind.

"I whip him near about every day," William said. "He don't care."

"No." The man bent heavily over his bound proceedings, turning the pages slowly. The book had a number of photographs in it, officers of the Church, though none of them bore the name for which the pastor ostensibly was searching. Suddenly the name came to him of itself: "*Givhan*, I *knew* it was something like that. Stubbornest man I ever knew."

"Givhan?"

"Certainly. Of course you could always call him 'Guy' on unofficial days."

Dana had arisen and, tiptoeing to the door, was spying out upon the armadillo. Young Givhan sat still meantime, picking studiously at his nose.

"Well. That takes care of two of 'em, I reckon," William said.

"And now we need to take a little wine don't you think? To celebrate?"

"I reckon not. I need to fetch that other boy in here so's we can..."

"Yes, by all means. Bring 'em all in."

William went out, angered to find that his third son had entangled himself in his own clothing and was weeping bitterly. He raised the boy in one hand and smote him once, once only, across the thigh. He was not as strong as he ought to be, this third one, and made an incongruous appearance in his work trousers and miniature boots. William carried him in and set him up in the chair that had been occupied by his brothers. He had been gone, William, not even a full minute and yet the minister had found time to pour himself a glass of red wine and consume about half of it.

"I used to know a fellow like this," he said, staring steadily at the third child. "Eyes like a blackbird — look at 'em. He can see us better than we can see him — that's what I'm thinking. No William, *this* is the one what needs to go to college."

They waited for the name. Outside the oldest boy suddenly let out a brief clear scream that died away immediately. He had put his finger through the wire and the armadillo had seized upon it — there was not a person in that room who didn't understand immediately what had occurred. To William, who continued every few moments to glance up at the stain glass windows, it seemed as if the prophets were trekking forward with greater and greater alacrity as the outside sun approached the horizon.

"Old man Wilson! We used to steal his pumpkins, Marvin and me. He never could catch us."

"'Wilson.' Sounds like somebody's *last* name. It does to me."

"No, *Marvin*, we'll call the boy Marvin. Let Wilson stay Wilson, and *he*" — he reached across the table and tapped the boy — "gets to be Marvin."

The woman demurred.

"Marvin Pefley. I reckon that'll be all right," William said.

"And now if your lovely wife wants to visit the garden, we can talk about those matters, Bill. Something's eating on you, I know it is."

"Yes, sir; I was hoping we could talk. But what about *him*?" (He pointed to his wife's abdomen.)

"Ah yes. Well how about 'Albert'? That's always good."

He turned the name over once or twice in his mind, William did, and then brushed off his hands and started to rise. His wife had arisen already, had gathered Marvin from his place and had found her way back to the wagon.

"You're worried," the man said, once they had been left alone. "Is it the children? Because you've brought them into the world and now you got to look after them?"

"No, sir."

"No. No, you're not afraid of looking after people are you? No, I was pretty sure that wasn't it." He drank, finishing the wine and then sat for a minute looking deeply into his visitor who for his part went on staring down steadfastly at the surface of the table. "Oh, I see — you figure maybe you ought not of brought 'em into the world in the first place — ha, *that's* what it is. This 'house of sorrows?'"

"No, sir."

"No, of course not. After all, somebody brought *you* into the world, and so... What is it, Bill?"

"Well. Everything's pretty good, I guess."

"The hell it is. What is it, Bill?"

"Well. My brother, you see, he's dead now and buried. I didn't know nothing about it. I found out about it when they sent me his shotgun."

"He wanted you to have it."

"He stayed home all that time you see, looking after Mama and Papa."

"Whereas *you* left home, is that right? Went out gallivanting through the world?"

"I was thinking about it yesterday — he was a lot better man than I ever was. But he didn't never have anything."

"Didn't have anything because he stayed home."

"I reckon." (He couldn't look at the preacher.)

"You're worse than him."

"Yes, sir."

"But you have lots of things. He didn't have anything."

"Just that shotgun."

"And I expect you already had a shotgun, didn't you Bill? And it was a lot better than the one he gave you, hm?"

The brick maker turned away, the expression on his face making his host fear that he might actually vomit on the floor.

"And you're still alive, Bill. You have to take that into account when you're adding up the things you have. You have things, you have life. You've got a *real* good wife."

"Yes, sir."

"And what's he got? Nothing."

"He's dead."

"Dead and in the ground. He'll be rotten pretty soon — we know that."

William was bending low, his forehead having sunk to the level of the table.

"He used to take up for you, too. Wouldn't let nobody pick on you."

"No, sir. I was always a lot older than him don't you see."

"Ah. And so he was just a young man then, real young. That's worse, Bill, much worse."

"I would of gone to the funeral, if they'd of just told me. I could of got there in two days."

"You know Jim Casey, don't you Bill?"

Bill said nothing.

"How much you suppose *he's* got? Fifty thousand dollars?"

"He's got a right smart of land, that's all I know."

"*Two hundred thousand*, Bill, that's what he's got. Cows, houses, land. Bonds, Bill, he's got 'em."

Bill, hardly listening, looked up to the ceiling and then across at the bearded and bald-headed prophets trundling forward apace.

"Bill?"

"Sir?"

"What kind of man is Jim Casey?"

"Well, I can't say. Never had any association with him."

From outside there came again the short, high, piercing sound of a child screaming.

"Yes you could, you could say if you wanted to. I'll tell you this much, he was sitting right there in that same chair" — he rose and leaned forward to touch Bill's chair with his fingertip — "sitting right there two days ago."

Bill stirred uneasily.

"And so when you come in here telling me you're a bad person... Bill, you don't know what bad is. It's worse than what you think."

"Well. Just seems like God would stop it, if He wanted to.

"He would if He could, Bill. He wants to."

"Well tarnation, why don't He just do it then!"

"Maybe He's weak, Bill — ever think about that? Maybe He needs help and He's not getting it. Your brother — what did he die from? Was it disease germs, Bill?"

Bill nodded.

"And how many disease germs are there, Bill? You can't expect Him to stop *all* of 'em, can you? Some are bound to get through."

"Well, I know there's a great many of 'em."

"Yes, and lots of other evil things, too. Millions and millions."

William thought about that. These were interesting ideas and gave a new tincture to things. All his life he had wanted to stand shoulder to shoulder with God in opposition to evil, even if it had never occurred to him how urgently his help was needed. Lifting from the chair he tried to shake with the man, finding to his embarrassment that the table was broad and they were too far apart. It would be dark within thirty minutes and he disliked to be far from home when evening came rushing in.

THIRTY-NINE

October was upon them. Came again the smell of mown fields and cider oozing from the press, of magnolias and browned pumpkins decaying forgottenly on the stem. To him (the man standing in the doorway), this season was a remembrance of what life used to be, and these people (he could see a few people moving past in their wagons), they represented the society that could have been. Gone the honeysuckle and gone the rose, nevertheless he considered himself as in some part compensated by this year's scuppernongs, the largest and bluest he had ever yet seen. He liked to open the smaller of the two blades of his pocket knife and after sniping off a lowlying bunch, take into his own mouth those grapes that appeared most in danger of splitting open from too much liquor too long retained.

He went inside and delivered a cluster of the things to his wife and Molly Bright, who sat apart from one another while suckling each a different boy. The oldest child he took out into the barn. He was able, the rascal was, to sit in a canvas sack and dig his right hand deep into the grain. Having collected a fist full of kernels, he was able then to toss enough of them out onto the ground to draw a few chickens to his ambit. It was, William noted, the first job of work the boy had accomplished and seemed to foretell of the even larger things that might be expected from him in days to come. He watched with satisfaction as once again the fellow plunged into the sack, again drew out the stuff, again threw it at them. William also approved the boy's straw hat. He would wear it, his father foretold, until it was completely worn out, and would then transfer himself over into another just like it.

Together they traveled to the smokehouse. Inside, the world was dark and cloudy and smelled powerfully of the smoked hogs and two geese that hung from the rafters. The coals had burned down and had very little heat left in them; nevertheless the boy was too prudent to test the ashes with his foot or fingertip. Instead he watched with attention as the brick maker drew out his slaughtering knife and commenced to carve out a chine of perhaps ten pounds which he wrapped up efficiently in heavy brown paper.

"It's a good ideer," he said, addressing himself confidentially to his son, "to give something to the sheriff once in a while."

The boy marveled, and learned.

"Not *all* of it, of course. Some."

Outside the dog, who loved October too, was bouncing from place to place and calling upon the boy to come and play. But Dana dared not abandon the old man while he was talking.

"Now the rest of it" — he bent down low, holding the meat in his arms — "is for us. Me and you. Your mother. Are you listening? A person could starve to death if he didn't have meat and..." (His voice grew low.) "... eggs and so forth."

The child seemed to understand and William, who almost never smiled, found himself almost smiling now. Calm, cheerful, and in general agreement with everything, the boy was like a fresh new pail into which the father could decant whatever he list.

"My bricks are the best in this county," the butcher said suddenly, talking more to himself than to the boy. (He had hefted the pork, some thirty-five pounds of it, onto the work table, and with his exceedingly sharp instrument was breaking it down expertly into chops and steaks and other conventional pieces. Truth was, he had rations enough for the entire winter and to spare. He possessed twice the chickens he needed and had fifteen pounds of butter and twenty of cheese cooling in the well. For this reason he felt himself immune likewise to the weather and/or bad people who might try to come at them from unexpected directions.)

"Fear God."

The boy nodded, pondering it.

"All right. Now go play with the dog for a while."

Applauding the man's decision, the child clapped hands and ran out into the weather.

They lay side by side that night, the husband and wife, each of them striving not to intrude into each other's dreams. By later standards the bed itself was short, but provided room enough for people who ranged between five foot eight and five two in length. And if they were having difficulty falling off to sleep, probably it was owing to the silence of the crickets, who had adjourned until next spring. The brick maker was however conscious of the following sounds: 1.) swallows shuddering in the chimney, 2.) a far-away train, 3.) unseemly music from Joe Butler's house, 4.) their first child making burbling sounds, 5.) the second boy snoring lightly, and 6.) the third one tossing in the sheets. And then, too, they hosted perhaps thirty mice at that period and were only with the greatest difficulty able to ignore the two or three of them rummaging in the flour mill.

The woman was first to go to sleep. Her dream material came mostly from post cards and engravings, landscape scenes and postal stamps. She believed that she was walking with her parents through a valley filled with flowers and then, next, that she was working against the clock to finish a set of old red velvet draperies that needed sewing. Dreamt that she was pilfering eggs from the hens. The shells of those eggs were transparent however, and one of them had a child in it. Dreamt she was drawing water from the well.

Eighteen inches away on a pillow of his own her husband imagined that his steam gin (he owned no such instrument) had broken apart and he hadn't the knowledge to fix it. Dreamt that his right hand had seized up, becoming smaller than a child's. Dreamt that he had taken down their old red velvet drapery and had passed it over to his wife to be repaired.

Otherwise the night was typical and both people assumed that it would go on in this fashion until morning came. Instead, toward three, the woman came awake and after lying quietly for a while experienced the desire to go to the kitchen and pour herself a glass of buttermilk.

The sky was chill and black with scads of stars jumping up and down. Dark also was the night, so much so indeed that each bat had partnered with a firefly to light him on his way. She could have cited other anomalies as well, had not she seen something just then that took her breath away and sent her hurrying back at once into the deepermost part of the house — a naked albino, white as the sun, running wildly down the levee at three o'clock in the morning.

She returned to bed. Her husband appeared to be devoid of dreams just then, but on the other hand she thought that she could hear her second boy moving from room to room about the house. Outside a bird had taken up in the trellis — the roses were dead — and was growing increasingly incensed at its own reflection in the window pane.

It was at this point that her fourth and last child began to drop quickly down the birth canal. "Good boy!" she thought, commending his decision to come forth *this* month, the prettiest in the year. Her intention was to deliver it herself and then clean up the mess before anyone could see it; instead, the pain forced from her two or three brief cries that broke her husband's spell of sleep. He uttered something and sat up. The child, fully emerged, had immediately shaken himself off and begun crawling at high speed up toward the head of the bed in order to look at last into his mother's face.

"What is it?" the old man asked.

"Albert," she said.

FORTY

He used to get his timber from upstream, float it down river, and haul it out with mules. But far better than any of this was when his kiln and saw mill were functioning simultaneously, spitting out money at the rate of about four and half thousand dollars a year. And if at one time he had wanted to be free of debt, he now borrowed money wherever he could. (They're wrong, those who imagine this must have been a mistake, or that it would come back to haunt him. On the contrary, he used those funds to build four- and five-room homes on the outskirts of town, a project that yielded him a great deal more in rentals than the interest on his debts.)

He built those four- and five-room homes and yet his own domicile remained unfinished. He used to stroll around the structure, critiquing it for the strength that inhered in the 4x6s and, occasionally, the 8x10s taken from the waterlogged cypresses that he chiefly preferred. He had a pile of these beams set apart for his own use, and would no more have thought of selling them than that he would have offered the personally-designed bricks that ran around the lower quadrant of the house. Five times ordinary size, the bricks weighed each better than twenty pounds and bore, each, four sills for the introduction of mortar to bind them together irrefragably into walls that looked like Roman work. It was interesting to see how the coloration of those bricks shifted from hue to hue as William excavated deeper and deeper into the vein of clay that lay parallel to the river. He liked to hobble on down there from time to time and watch the Negroes at work.

253

And then, finally, (and this is the last to be said on the subject), he had devised a personal trademark of six candles profiled in the sun. Imprinted on the recto of each several brick, it gave a scaled representation, down to the smallest candle of all, of his family's constituents. He said:

"Well. I'm thinking we have all the boys we need now."

She agreed, his wife, with undisguised relief.

"We had any more they'd be fighting all the time."

"They fight now," she started to say.

"So I reckon there's no need for us to be... Messing about anymore."

"They was fighting this morning, Dana and Givhan."

He paled. Inconceivable, it seemed to him, that family members should turn on each other as opposed to the outside world.

"Who won?"

"I reckon Dana did. He's the oldest."

It calmed him.

"And then Marvin got mad at Guy. But Guy got the better of him, I guess you could say."

William tried to get back to his newspaper. Two minutes went past. "Well. What about that little one?"

"Albert?"

"How about him?"

"Got a big old bruise on his forehead. But he's going to be all right."

"Didn't cry, did he?"

"Little bit."

William paled. It was a fine meal, the one set before him, though he couldn't altogether hide his disappointment that he'd been supplied no lemon with his tea.

"Maybe we ought to send Molly to go get some," he said. "Lemons."

Debbie paled. She had three of that fruit in the cupboard that stood not fifteen feet away. And then, just next to the moccasin skin, there was that painting on the wall of a cornucopia full of these and other things.

"Am I going to get a whipping?" Marvin asked, after raising his hand and waiting to be recognized. The old man turned and looked at him.

"You mean 'sir,' don't you?"

"Yes, sir. Am I going to get a whipping sir?"

"You should. When I was your age..."

"That's right. When Mr. Pefley was your age, he was already making contributions to the family."

That was when Guy got down off his chair, as if he actually expected to leave the table. William looked at him. Albert, dressed in work clothes, had been able to stay upright by clutching firmly to the tablecloth. Changing his tact, Guy asked this:

"May I leave the table now? Sir?"

Blephy turned to him. "Has your father finished eating?"

"I reckon not."

"Well then."

Dana, having cut himself a much too large slice of pie, now put half of it back. Through the open door he could see Molly devouring a far larger piece than any he had ever had.

The newspaper was but a weekly affair, and yet it held more news than anyone could have acquired through random conversations with neighbors or people about town. William, who rarely engaged in conversation, saw with astonishment that a 120-acre tract of land had gone for a price that he himself would gladly have given. A shoat had wandered off. William read the description and put it away in memory. As to national news and events going on in Washington, he snorted out loud at them and turned the page. But primarily it were the obituaries that gathered his attention, a story of men and women who now, most of them, would be screaming in hell. Old Patrick McFerson — he had never seemed to William as so bad a fellow.

"Let it be a lesson to you," he said suddenly to his children. (Guy had gone away.) "He redeemth not."

"No, sir."

FORTY-ONE

When after a certain time had gone by, he took up a position in the swing on his front porch. Thinking back over his life, he had decided that this was by far the best time for time itself to come to a stop. Wife, boys, kiln, fair weather. Moreover his house was almost finished. He liked to sit quietly and watch as townspeople drove slowly past, abashed by the size of the building and feeling ashamed of their own. He had no sympathy for those however who could have done as well as he, had only they had the character and stamina and at least some small talent for the management of Negroes.

"Be a wonderful world, wouldn't it Joe? If everybody was like you and me?"

"Yas, sir; sho is! They can't do it! Jus can't"

(He had planned on giving the man his usual forty dollars; instead he handed over an additional ten-dollar bill. The county had no currency of its own, wherefore he was made to use federal bills, bilious-colored artifacts bearing the portraits of union generals. His home, Joe's, now sheltered fourteen human beings, wherefore William had interested him in dismantling the structure and rebuilding it at a remove of about two hundred yards.)

"Thinking about getting into the turpentine business," William said, apropos of nothing.

"No, suh! No suh. No, suh, we don't need that, we got lots to do already. Yas, suh. Hope not."

They hushed. A carriage just now was moving past, inside it two of the city's most important women. William's house had the greatest amount of

fretwork ever seen in that locality, and never mind that he had had to go
to Enterprise to rent the lathe and treadle. He watched quietly as the wom-
en went through their inventory of expressions: admiration, disapproval,
hatred.

"Really!" one of them said.

William chose that moment to lift his hat and go to meet them.

"Oh! Hello. That's a mighty fine home you've got there William!"

"That? No, ma'am. I doubt we'll be using it for more than a year or
two."

"But..."

"Way things are going. Need a bigger place, don't you know."

In the afternoon, William went to the smoke house and took off his
pants. He must twice a day flush his left leg with an unguent that was supposed to restore the limb to more normal shape. As to the toes, which were
too large and seemed to have been glued to his foot without any regard to
orientation or anything else, he had given up on those. His mind reflected
back on days when he could hike twenty-two miles in a single day. The
good part was that he had endured the worst of things and ought to be able
to look forward to some pretty good years both for himself and the family
as well. Of course that was the moment he heard someone screaming from
the general direction of the sawmill.

Leaving his trousers behind, William ran in that direction. A south-
erner won't scream like that, said he to himself, unless the matter be far
more serious than the usual thing. Perhaps the kiln had exploded, or one
of the boys been stung by a rattlesnake — these were his expectations when
he came around the corner and perceived a white man and three Negroes
fighting, as at first it seemed, with Joe Butler.

They were not fighting, a truth that was borne in on William when he
descried what looked like a human arm lying in the area between the mill
and coal supply. No doubt someone had been tampering with the position
of the log and, losing balance, had sliced his arm off. And yet the log itself

had emerged from the ordeal in good order. William checked it over and then went to where Joe was striving to cut off the flow of blood, as if he could do so by holding aloft what remained of his arm.

"Great Lord A'mighty!" William said. He didn't know precisely how much blood a person contained, but however much, it great part of it would have escaped by now.

"Mr. William!"

"Hold on Joe!" (He pulled the man free of the contraption and then, foolishly, set off running toward town. Having covered a brief distance, he turned suddenly and came back. Two of the man's relatives were standing about marveling at the event, though neither seemed to have any better conception than did William as to what needed to be done.)

"Get Doctor Haskins!" William ordered finally. "Right now!"

The two boys set off, one on horseback and the other running at full tilt.

"Mr. William!"

"Tell you what Joe, I'm going to fix up a tourniquet right here and now and put it on that arm."

And did so, using for that purpose the same pale blue kerchief that ordinarily he used for anointing his leg. By no means could this inadequate rig staunch *all* the veins and other conduits that resided, some of them, too deep to be squeezed shut by dint of a mere blue kerchief alone.

"Feeling a little better now Joe?"

"Yas, suh, believe so." He grinned.

"Don't worry about that cedar. Came out real fine."

"Yas, suh."

"Going to make a real fine beam."

"Yas, suh. That Dana standing over there?"

Dana stepped forward. He had been good enough to fetch the detached arm and was holding it in both hands. The thing was appreciably heavier than he would have guessed.

"We're going to save this arm Joe, and Doctor Haskins is going to put it right back on where it's supposed to be."

Joe laughed, albeit somewhat bitterly. "Yas, suh. Be dead by then."

Marvin came forth, gazed with interest upon the puddle of blood that had collected, and then retreated into the crowd of Joe's people gathered around. William had meantime substituted his strong leather belt for the kerchief and was creating more pain with it than caused by the original wound.

"I know it hurts Joe."

"Sho do."

They carried the man, who seemed lighter than one would have guessed, into William's house and lay him on the sofa. Upholstered in maroon velvet, Joe's blood hardly registered on the woven scene of First Manassas. It was an untypical sight, all those Negroes crowded into a decorated parlor with portraits on the wall, stain glass lamps, mounted butterflies, and space enough for a piano. That was when Deborah rushed in with a steaming towel and a glass of milk. William's two younger children were outside playing in the sand, Guy was absent, while Dana stood frozen in the corner holding Joseph's arm. William turned to him.

"Take that thing out to the garden and bury it. Deep."

"Yes, sir."

"And roll some big heavy rocks on top. I don't want them dogs getting into it." And then: "Wait a minute; let him look at it if he has to."

He had managed, Joe, to lift himself a few inches in order to inspect what yesterday had been the best of his two arms. This was the moment he passed out and fainted dead away.

It wasn't till past two in the afternoon that Haskins arrived. Curt in manner, his apron covered in blood from some other mishap occurring at the same time on the other side of the levee, he marched straight to Joe and lifted his eyelid.

"Sawmill?"

"Yes, sir," William said.

"Well, nobody can blame you William, the kind of person you are. I'll make out the certificate and you…" His voice faded away.

"Dead?"

"Oh yes indeed! Certainly. You can't lose that kind of blood and get away with it."

(He might not have been as dead as Hoskins believed, and when he embarked upon his last and necessarily unreported dream, he imagined he was standing on the shore of the river. Birds were calling and he thought he saw other things as well. That was when he turned and, with both arms intact, walked into the stream, which covered him at last.)

FORTY-TWO

Long time had gone by since last William had stood in the middle of Joe's house and gazed about at the things to be seen. Ornamented mainly with postcards and gourds, a bucket for a toilet and next to that a carefully conserved pile of technical journals that neither of them could have understood, the place was a wonder.

"I was real sorry," he said. "What happened, I mean."

"Yas, suh."

He was facing full six members of the opposite race, not even to mention the woman (whom he had never seen before) weaning a set of twins on both breasts at once. Unnerved by that, he pulled forth a roll of bills and began to hand out fifty dollars in currency to Joe's wives and then twenty each to the sons who happened just then to be available.

"I owed him some money anyway," William lied.

Those faces had no expression in them, and the brick maker began to experience a desire to leave the place at once.

"I want you-all to stay right here in this house *just as long as you want to*," he said. "And then we'll have to see."

How bright and pleasant the sun when after five minutes in such quarters a man could put his hat back on and in good conscience leave the place. He was striding urgently toward the sawmill when at that moment a bright yellow carriage came and parked before the house. He would have preferred, William, to continue on to the sawmill; instead, he broached up to the driver and waited to see what he desired.

"Mr. Pefley?"

William nodded.

"I brought my equipment," (he pointed to it) "and I'm ready now to make a photograph of this house of yours, and your family and so forth."

"Real cordial of you," William said. "But right now I'm just too busy to..." (It amazed him that the fellow was willing to grab him by the sleeve and begin whispering in his nearer ear.)

"Sir! You've got some *neighbors* in this town, and I don't think they'd be real happy if... I guess we just don't want it to go down in history, how you got left out. 'Course now you can do whatever you want, if that's what you want to do." He shrugged sadly and began to pull away.

Deborah was in the kitchen. It needed William a good full minute to go splashing through the clothes in her closet and find the pale blue ensemble that in his estimation enhanced his wife the most. Next, he hurried to the kiln and after selecting the golden-most bricks that at the same time were in easy reach, assigned one of Joe's people to build a pyramid of them just in front of the house. He called for Dana, but found him there already. Next, he forced his way through Joe's back door and pushed the Negroes, all but one, into the out-of-doors where they stood blinking in the sun.

"Better bring Maude, too," said he to Marvin who, however, was as yet too small to deal with mules. "And where's that new one?"

"New mule?"

"Albert, I think he means."

Meanwhile the photographer had set up his tripod and had positioned on top of it a large scientific-looking camera the size of a cube of about two feet square. Capable of pointing in any direction, it teetered on its stand.

"That's the camera," someone said, touching the thing with his finger and then quickly drawing back.

"Get Molly out here, too."

"I know it's a camera!"

"She won't come."

He was losing track of things, William felt. The goats had been tethered to the fence, but refused absolutely to obey either William's or the photographer's behests. As to the hens... He would have to be satisfied, William, if just two or three of them ended up in the final picture.

"Well," William said, unaware that Blephy had come up and after putting on a cross-eyed expression, was posing facetiously with his hand in his vest, "I reckon we're ready."

"My God. No, I want to get the house, too. All of it."

They began anew. The Negroes seemed to have no trust in the operation and tended to keep their eyes on the ground. Young Albert — they had actually brought his bassinet out into the light where he lay with his thumb in his mouth. The family was not absolutely entire, not with Givhan gone to town. Even so, they left a place for him, a fourteen-inch gap between his mother and Molly Bright.

"Well. I reckon we're ready now."

"This picture will hang in the courthouse someday, Mr. Pefley."

"Well. If that's what they decide."

"Could you just move a few inches... Yes! Good."

He now removed the lid, the photographer did, and tried to still the crowd with his index finger, an unusual adjunct with more than just two joints in it. In the stillness that followed, an acorn dropped and one of the Negroes turned and walked away.

"Well, I guess it's over now," William said.

"Yes, and I think it was just laudable, the way everybody behaved. How much are we paying for this?"

The animals had mostly dispersed by now, leaving it to Dana to round them up and put them away. He was a tall young man, relatively speaking, calm and full of a sweetness that showed in this and all future photographs indeed. Again the photographer sidled up to William, saying:

"And how about you sir? They're going to want a picture of you all by yourself."

William thought.

"Standing in front of your house. So your grandbabies will know what you looked like, and so on. It's only fair."

"I reckon not."

"So they can pick you out of a crowd. When you all get to heaven, I mean."

He *was* tempted. Meantime the scene in front of him was dissolving, the boys going off in one direction, his wife another, Dana and the hogs and the rest of them all moving slowly out of sight.

FORTY-THREE

He spent three hours at his desk, fuddling over invoices and receipts and other related papers destined later on to be conserved in the county archives. Having positioned that desk just next to the bed (the two pieces of furniture actually touching at heel and footboard), he was able to surveil his wife while she slept in the curled-up arrangement that was her wont. She was not a large person and her snores, if they could be called that, were consonant with her nature.

William, meanwhile, had taken out a plat book and was reviewing the land holdings of some of the county's more important people. Having compiled a list in declining order of those holdings, it saddened him to find sixty-three individuals who possessed more land than he. Finally, turning down the wick, he gathered up last week's newspaper, scanned quickly through the personal doings of some of those same landowners and then, taking out his glasses and fitting them on, perused the animals and equipment being offered for sale.

He came to bed at a few minutes past one in the morning and after repositioning his wife, got into his nightcap. His Bible and revolver, both kept beneath the mattress, came easily to hand. He had planned to read in the Book of Amos but changed his mind when the volume opened as of itself upon the story of Lilith. "My gracious," said he, smacking his lips over the language and the wisdom hidden within it. The book had gold dust on the fore edges while the leaves were thin and tenuous almost to the point of invisibility.

He woke an hour later to find his wife grinning at him in the dark. Guy had departed the house two hours ago but now was returning by way of the east side window, a recurring misdemeanor that never escaped William's attention whether he were awake or not. For a moment he thought of going to the boys' room and addressing the lot of them, but then relented when he saw how tired he was. He was comforted by his Bible, his revolver and wife, his desk, and the hand-colored framed photograph in which Blephy had posed himself as the central character. William knew not whether he ought to laugh or go and hunt the fellow down.

His second interruption came at 4:17 AM when he arose, got into his slippers, and ventured to the garden. At night, the process of urine formation ought to be suspended he believed, allowing a person a full seven or eight hours of unimpeded rest. And yet, it *was* a lovely time of day, stars brightly shining and all the county's gamblers and whoremongers held temporarily in check by unconsciousness. Let it always be four in the morning, stars brightly shining, the world's imperfections veiled a little while longer by the modest night.

His third episode came a few moments later — he did not know he was dreaming — as he was standing out in the field with the tiny Albert in his arms. He had been trying to explain about matters, the duties that must come due, the labor, and the family's obligation to change some part of the earth into an analog of paradise.

"This whole area," he said, "it's going to be *your* problem someday. Instead of mine."

The child looked at him in alarm.

"And that cow? See the one I'm talking about?"

"Yas, suh," Joe said. "Sho do."

"Carrying twins."

"Get out! For sho?"

"I can tell."

"Hmm hm! I 'speck you're right, yas suh."

"And by the time this one..."

"A'bert."

"... by the time it gets all grown up..."

"All growed up!"

"... he'll have a *hundred* of 'em, just about."

"Ouwee! 'Speck so; yas, suh."

"And Joe?"

"Yas, suh?"

"I'm also planning..."

But it was at this point that the dream broke off and William, just as he had always known that he would, came awake. There was a commotion down at Joe's house and further, the sound of the courthouse bell tolling the time, expectable noises that could by no means prevent him from sleeping again.

He dreamt now that he could see further than usual, and that what he saw — tidy houses, plump cattle — was beyond any criticism of his. A man could walk for miles in this place and never find a barn or silo, or for that matter not even a blade of clover that was out of proportion to the scene at large. No mildew did he espy anywhere, neither rust nor decay nor anything else of that kind. Striding effortlessly from place to place (pastel-colored localities), he met with deferential dogs who asked to join his retinue of sons and Negroes and the conscientious wife stumbling hurriedly alongside. He saw, he thought, his extinct mother shelling peas and then, just before he came awake, the edge of the far-away sea itself, a green and blue presentation driving urgently to shore where it shattered into billions of shards of bright sparkling glass. That was when he awoke (most unwillingly), left the bed, got into his boots, and pumped three or four liters of well water into the washing bowl. The fluid was cool and came from deep underground. Having splashed himself about the face and eyes, he stood toweling himself in the dark. Both roosters were crowing and he could still hear a disturbance down at Joe's former house. His wife meantime had left the bed and was making eggs and coffee in the kitchen.

He spent the balance of that morning repairing his bridle at the upholsterers and collecting payment on his rental properties. The good weather had persisted and off in the distance he could hear the sawmill functioning with seeming efficiency under the management of Joe's second-eldest boy. He had a pocket watch, William, a folding knife, a good luck charm, and better than six thousand dollars distributed between the town's two leading banks. Under these conditions (and having nothing else that urgently needed doing), he walked home at a brisk pace and after checking upon his wife and the others, drew off into the smokehouse and secured the door. He had had four "episodes" during the night, concluding with his dream of paradise. Not content with that, he scrunched up in the corner (an odd-looking sight!) and lit his pipe. He still had one good dream owing to him and had decided to draw upon it now.

OTHER BOOKS PUBLISHED BY ARKTOS

OTHER BOOKS PUBLISHED BY ARKTOS

GÉNÉRATION IDENTITAIRE	*We are Generation Identity*
PAUL GOTTFRIED	*War and Democracy*
PORUS HOMI HAVEWALA	*The Saga of the Aryan Race*
RACHEL HAYWIRE	*The New Reaction*
LARS HOLGER HOLM	*Hiding in Broad Daylight*
	Homo Maximus
	The Owls of Afrasiab
ALEXANDER JACOB	*De Naturae Natura*
PETER KING	*Keeping Things Close: Essays on the Conservative Disposition*
LUDWIG KLAGES	*The Biocentric Worldview*
	Cosmogonic Reflections: Selected Aphorisms from Ludwig Klages
PIERRE KREBS	*Fighting for the Essence*
PENTTI LINKOLA	*Can Life Prevail?*
H. P. LOVECRAFT	*The Conservative*
BRIAN ANSE PATRICK	*The NRA and the Media*
	Rise of the Anti-Media
	The Ten Commandments of Propaganda
	Zombology
TITO PERDUE	*Morning Crafts*
RAIDO	*A Handbook of Traditional Living*
STEVEN J. ROSEN	*The Agni and the Ecstasy*
	The Jedi in the Lotus

OTHER BOOKS PUBLISHED BY ARKTOS

RICHARD RUDGLEY

Barbarians

Essential Substances

Wildest Dreams

ERNST VON SALOMON

It Cannot Be Stormed

The Outlaws

TROY SOUTHGATE

Tradition & Revolution

OSWALD SPENGLER

Man and Technics

TOMISLAV SUNIC

Against Democracy and Equality

ABIR TAHA

Defining Terrorism: The End of Double Standards

Nietzsche's Coming God, or the Redemption of the Divine

Verses of Light

BAL GANGADHAR TILAK

The Arctic Home in the Vedas

DOMINIQUE VENNER

The Shock of History

MARKUS WILLINGER

A Europe of Nations

Generation Identity

DAVID J. WINGFIELD (ED.)

The Initiate: Journal of Traditional Studies

RMB/1-19.

CPSIA information can be obtained
at www.ICGtesting.com
Printed in the USA
BVHW070055181118
533372BV00002B/347/P

9 781910 524343